BENEDICT KIELY

Benedict Kiely has come to be regarded as one of Ireland's most admired literary writers. Born near Dromore, in County Tyrone in 1919 his long and successful career spans the writing of novels, short stories and memoirs. He is well known as a raconteur and broadcaster on TV and radio.

His novels include *The Captain and the Whiskers, Honey Seems Bitter* and *Dogs Enjoy The Morning* among many other works.

REVIEWS

'Benedict Kiely is the Irish Balzac.' Heinrich Böll.

The Cards of the Gambler

'An astonishing book. . . . What is uniquely Kiely's, his thumbprint, is his easy mastery of the lyrical, and the feeling of felt life, felt experience, just beneath the surface of his prose.' Thomas Flanagan, author of *The Year of the French.*

Drink to the Bird

'Anecdotal, hilariously funny, and replete with verse, this memoir has the cadence of a discursive outpour and Joycean resonance. . . . It is immediately evident that here is a writer of outstanding achievement.' *Financial Times.*

'Mr Kiely is one of the last of the literary gents. . . . His learning is extensive and he is excited by popular as by high culture. If in one chapter he is recalling the effect of Irish rebel incursions on the writing of Spenser's Faerie Queene, in another he salutes the Everton centre-forward Dixie Dean as the only footballer ever to establish a hairstyle: the sleeked-back, middle-of-the-skull parting. . . . A charming and civilised book.' *Sunday Tribune.*

A Letter to Peachtree

There are so many Irish people who write short stories, and so few who are real storytellers. Ben Kiely is one, and he should be preserved in aspic or crowned high king or just bought in huge numbers.' *Sunday Independent.*

'Stylish, gabby, using language like a fallen angel, he mixes his feeling with a true storyteller's verse that looks like superb skill but is in fact something better. Call it instinct.' *Guardian.*

Nothing Happens in Carmincross

'Written with zest and grace, humour and irony in a style that is totally individual. . . . It must be read by everyone interested in Irish writing and the peculiar tragedy of the Irish situation.' Kevin Casey, *Irish Times.*

'I have been waiting for a novel as full of rage about contemporary Ireland as this one. And this is the book I have been waiting for.' Frank Delaney, *BBC World Service.*

'Nearly flawle[illegible]

'Compare him [illegible] t Gorky,
Benedict Kiely [illegible]

Also by Benedict Kiely

NOVELS

Nothing Happens in Carmincross (1985)

Proxopera (1977)

Dogs Enjoy the Morning (1968)

The Captain with the Whiskers (1960)

There Was an Ancient House (1955)

Honey Seems Bitter (1952)

Call for a Miracle (1950)

In a Harbour Green (1949)

Land Without Stars (1946)

NON-FICTION

God's Own Country (1993)

Yeats' Ireland (1989)

Ireland from the Air (1985)

Drink to the Bird (1981)

Poor Scholar: A Life of William Carleton (1947)

All the Way to Bantry Bay — and Other Irish Journeys (1978)

SHORT STORIES

A Letter to Peachtree

A Cow in the House (1978)

A Ball of Malt and Madame Butterfly (1973)

A Journey to the Seven Streams (1963)

The Cards of the Gambler

BENEDICT KIELY

WOLFHOUND PRESS

To the Memory of

M.J. MacManus

This edition published 1995 by
WOLFHOUND PRESS
68 Mountjoy Square
Dublin 1

First edition London 1953

Wolfhound Press receives financial assistance from The Arts Council/An Chomhairle Ealaíon, Dublin, Ireland.

A catalogue record for this book is available from the British Library.

ISBN 0 86327 477 3

Cover design and photography: Slick Fish, Dublin.
Printed by the Guernsey Press Co. Ltd, Guernsey, Channel Isles

CONTENTS

INTRODUCTION

My copy of *The Cards of the Gambler* tells us on the dust-wrapper that it was published in 1953, and that it cost six shillings, and that its author, Benedict Kiely, 'is a young Irish writer of great promise'. He was indeed: he had already published three novels, of which one had earned what was in those days a badge of literary distinction: it had been banned by the Censorship Board as being 'in general tendency indecent'. And a study of modern Irish fiction and a still unsurpassed account of the tales and novels of the 19th-century writer William Carleton, like Kiely himself a Tyrone man.

On the fly-leaf of my copy, the author has written, 'For Tom Flanagan. Ben Kiely'. Uncharacteristically, because he is a precisionist in this and other matters, he has not set down the date of the inscription, but I can supply it. It was in the summer of 1961, when I came to Ireland for the first time, the author of a book called *The Irish Novelists: 1800-1850*. It is a book much influenced by Kiely, and not merely in its section on Carleton. *Poor Scholar,* his study of Carleton, had opened up for me ways of relating works of fiction to the histories, the cultures, the landscapes to which they were responding. But — because Kiely is one of those rare writers to whom people are almost as important as words — I carried with me an introduction from a friend of his and mine, the American Joyce scholar, Kevin Sullivan. Readers who want to meet Sullivan can do so in Kiely's story, 'The Dogs in the Great Glen'.

Over the years, Sullivan and I quarrelled, in a manner only possible between friends, as to whether the finest of Ben's early novels was *The Cards of the Gambler* or *The Captain with the Whiskers*. I can see now, after this most recent re- reading, that Sullivan was right. *The Captain with the Whiskers* is a haunting and subtle study of evil and how it lives on after us, but *The Cards of the Gambler* is an astonishing book, whose imposingly large ambitions come very close to realising themselves. It is Dante-esque in its conception and design, engaging matters of ultimate concern with energy, ingenuity, a passion concealed by linguistic nimbleness. It reminds us that Kiely is only a half-generation or two removed from Borges and the Malcolm Lowry of *Under the Volcano.*

Somewhere at the centre of his creative being, Kiely has joined the arts of the storyteller and the novelist. They are very different, in some ways antagonistic arts, issuing from different psychic and cultural roots. Thus, William Carleton is a storyteller. His art rests within what he called *Traits and Stories of the Irish Peasantry,* loosely shaped 'stories' or 'tales', some of them based upon traditional narratives, and all of them written with Carleton hearing in his ear the pauses and emphases of the Irish-speaking storytellers of his native Tyrone. When he turned to the novel, save for isolated chapters and an occasional achievement like *Fardorougha the Miser,* he was blundering about in a form that was not native to his genius.

The storyteller's tale or fable is joined to his voice, and it comes, even when destined for the page, from an oral tradition. But the novel is in its essence literary, in a sense visual, meant for the page and welcomed by it. Kiely, coming a century after Carleton into a later, different Ireland, is somehow at home in the two forms. He is widely and variously read (to the point, he himself has said, of pedantry), and has a sophisticated knowledge of the modern novel, its strategies and resources, its designs and shapes.

The Cards of the Gambler rests, almost literally, upon the juncture of story and novel, with its beginning on a coast, ocean and mountain, unnamed but clearly Donegal, where the novel's faceless narrator has heard and now asks us to listen to, a very old folktale, older perhaps than Donegal itself but told in the accents of that county.

A gambler sets out one dawn to find a priest to baptise his son, who was born while he was away, losing his money at cards. 'Wherever he went, he had a pack of cards in his pocket. Whoever he met, he'd coax him to gamble'. But this day he meets God on the road, and, a bit later, Death. From God, at Death's urging, he gets three boons. The first, of course, is that he may always win at cards. And the second is the art of healing. But the nature of the third he keeps hidden from Death, whom he plans to trick at the end of things. For the latter part of his life, he is in a dual with Death, at seven-year intervals.

Kiely tells his story as it might have been heard, might perhaps still be heard, in Donegal, but then, as the main body of the novel, transposes it into a modern world of clubhouses and hotel lounges, railways and suburbs and airplanes, motorcars and telephones. The setting, which clearly is Ireland, unnamed but indisputable, and with a long detour into Spain and Lourdes, is created with Kiely's gifts, lyrical and precise, for the evocation of landscape and mood. And yet everything, because of the nature of his story, is kept within constantly shifting and unsettling perspectives. Everything is itself and yet drawn from, moving towards, a world beyond itself. Thus:

> 'A door opened in the corner behind him. A man came in briskly but no light came in. He stood in the middle of the room, looked flickeringly about him for a place to sit. Eyes focused to the shadows, the gambler saw a stout, red-faced man, middle age, middle height, wrapped in good brown tweeds that made his body look stouter and his face more rosy, wearing a loud check cap with the peak at a merry angle above his dark dancing eyes, carrying a huge black briefcase. A bookie? A commercial traveller? Or just one of those wonderful men who, hiding mystery behind merriment, sit all morning making valuable contacts over cigarettes and coffee in the public lounges of good hotels?'

This Death is a second cousin to the flashily dressed and beringed vulgarian in Max Beerbohm's *Seven Men*, but Kiely has contrived a special atmosphere for him, as we know from the quiet remark that no light came into the room with him. And we are told not that this is how he in fact looked, but rather that this is, simply, what the gambler saw. Death has no essential form. For the moment, he is a contact man, doing business for his 'boss' in a smart cocktail lounge. It may be of interest that almost the same moment in Ireland's literary culture produced *The Cards of the Gambler* and *The Third Policeman*, both of them books which contrive to engage the ultimate with a juggler's skill and sleights of hand. But then, Ben Kiely and Flann O'Brien were both Tyrone men, and distant cousins. The possibility arises of the modern Irish novel as a Tyrone conspiracy.

What is uniquely Kiely's though, his thumbprint, is his

easy mastery of the lyrical, and the feeling of felt life, felt experience, just beneath the surface of his prose. Here is our last glimpse of the gambler's one love, his wife's cousin, who, a gambler herself, has risked all for him:

> She remembered that conversation the night he attended the wounded soldier and then drove to the hotel in the market town; darkness over the dunes and the wide estuary, darkness over the green fields. She remembered it in the morning when he drove away from the town, past the market square crowded with tilted carts, over the bridge with the grey stone plaque to the memory of the local poet, up the long hill by the sleepy railway station. She looked down a slope of green fields to the silver river, the leaden-coloured wedge of the eel-weir, the bright red brick of the county hospital, the restless white foam where the river cried outwards from a cold, dark gorge. Her life was like that on this morning, a river escaping from rocks, a child running zigzag across a daisied field.
>
> Two miles outside the town a petrol lorry with defective brakes came, scattering screening stones, down a steep side road, ending for ever the journeys of the little green car. The woman died there on the side of the road, the green grass her death-bed, her head on the knees of the gambler.

The cards themselves, bejewelled and regal, make their glittering appearances throughout the novel. We see them first on their felt-covered table in the clubhouse, 'a green field where kings and queens and jesters in two different colours, red for blood and black for death, lie on beds of red diamonds, dark trefoil, bleeding hearts, the heads of black spears'. At the end, after the gambler has taken the cards with him to hell and almost to heaven, they settle into permanence. 'On the floor the cards were quiet. The pattern was fixed forever. The wind at last had shaped it to its own will'.

In the final paragraph, Kiely or his unnamed narrator tells us that 'no storyteller with corruption in his heart could follow the gambler into the place of wise, white light'. What is true, of course, and Kiely has the wise good sense of the tradition writer, rather than the arrogance of the post-modern. But nevertheless, to borrow one of his favourite words, and to employ a metaphor from a card game, he knows how to take every trick.

PROLOGUE

The stage is set for the telling of a story. Since this stage must be spacious enough to accommodate a wide stretch of countryside with houses, farms, men, dogs, cattle, lakes, rocks, two-wheeled carts, stacks of turf, boys robbing orchards and girls riding bicycles; since it must suggest the vastness of the neighbouring ocean and the shadowy extent of at least two thousand years, it can be constructed only in the imagination.

In the centre is a house, the sort of house that several generations of Irish exiles are supposed to have desired in their dreams. It is one storey in height, long, low, whitewashed, roofed with yellow thatch, blue smoke curling upwards from a squat stump of a chimney, and since the blue smoke comes from a fire of burning peat sods, it is pleasant to sniff when the wind blows it the way of your nose. The fields around the house are small, separated from each other by high, crude drystone walls.

There is a patch of oats still green, a triangular field of potatoes, a little oblong marked with rows of cabbages and beans, a meadow bisected by a small brook. Scattered here and there over that stretch of countryside are several similar houses resting like prim white kittens on their surrounding patches of varied green. Otherwise the country is unfertile and bare, grey rocks protruding like monstrous ribs, miles of brown, misty bogland, wind-fluttered lakes that are cold and grey even when the sky is blue and sunny. On the odd occasions when the weather is dry and warm, when the brown bogland soaks in the sun like a dusky slut of a girl absorbing caresses, those lakes look up with cold, grey contemptuous eyes at all the innocence and laughter of the warm, dry air.

To the left is the thunderous Atlantic crushing in on the land, forcing a way between long-legged peninsulas, whitening in greedy foam around a hundred islands, lonely rocks screaming with whirling sea-birds.

To the right are rigid conical mountains white with glittering shale and guarded by sombre foot-hills where no man can live.

Keep your eye on the house in the centre. The road approaching it is a white ribbon, rising and falling over brown bog, wriggling between little fields and huge rocks. A small stream bursts out of the bog and the brown water gushes across the road. There are two gateposts that never knew a gate, then chickens picking, ducks quacking, a dog barking, all the other movements and noises that belong to a small farm. There's a half-door closed against the picking chickens, and beyond the half-door the kitchen of the farmhouse, floored from the solid rock, with a table scrubbed white, a dresser rowed with plain delph and coloured delph, chairs and low stools, a basket of peat, on the hearth a fragrant red pyramid of burning peat, around the hearth ten people preparing to listen and one old man clearing his throat, spitting into the ashes, preparing to talk. Outside, the wind is blowing from the ocean to the conical mountains.

The old man is ninety years of age. He isn't tall, but he is heavily built, and when he was young he was strong and active. His face is still a healthy red from wind and sun and good circulation. His eyes are as grey as the grey lakes, but, unlike the lakes, they are deep with happiness. He's not bearded, but he has a bristling square moustache. He wears a good tweed suit and a sailor's cap with a glossy peak. His fingers knitted around the crook of a stick, he is preparing carefully to tell a story.

This story he has heard from his father, who heard it from his father, who heard it from his mother, who heard it from her uncle, who heard it from his father, who some time in the eighteenth century heard it from a travelling man whose ears had been cut off for threatening the life of a squireen. It is quite possible that the travelling man heard it from his father or his uncle or his mother or another travelling man. It has been added to, subtracted from, divided, and multiplied. It has borrowed something from this place, from that period, from that individual twist of mind or tongue. As for me, I heard it from the man you're watching, and you, if you wait, will hear it from me. When I come to tell it, I will also add, subtract, divide, and multiply. But in that place and in that house this is the way I heard the storyteller begin his story:

The gambler, like the rest of his neighbours, had a hut of a house and a small bit of land. In spite of that he was pitifully poor. Wherever he went he'd have a pack of cards in his pocket. Whoever he met he'd coax him into a gamble. He'd sit all night card-playing and lie all day asleep, and in that way his portion of land lay idle. While his neighbours were getting on in the world he was going backwards.

He was gambling one night until he lost the last penny in his possession. He came home with the dawning of day and he was broken, bruised, and sorrowful, without money or the hope of money. Coming to the house, he found the neighbour women gathered in, dancing attendance on his wife, who was lying in danger of death. A young son had been born when he was card-playing away from his home.

The women asked the gambler to get the priest to baptize the child. He thought to himself that that was the least he could do, so off with him, and it wasn't long he was going until he saw a young man drawing towards him. By the shape of the young man he knew him for a stranger. He eyed him from the top of his head to the sole of his foot, and it seemed to him from the countenance and complexion of that young man that he had never seen anyone so handsome.

'You're going for the priest to baptize your child,' says the stranger.

'I am,' says the gambler, 'but how do you know where I am going or what is my business?'

ONE

I

At four o'clock in the morning there were seven men left in the club-house. Two were business men: a draper and a grocer. One was a bookie. One was a university professor. One owned a factory. One was the club's professional golfer and the seventh was a doctor. They were all gamblers. They were all as tired as withered thistles after a long night spent gratifying their great desire.

This is the dry desire for cards, for the feel of glossy resilient pasteboard between the tips of sensitive fingers, for the chance that halts the heart, sets the half-conscious body and the satiated soul swinging in the air between the fear of loss and the hope of gain. It isn't the same thing as the desire for money. It isn't even the same thing as the wild passion for risk that sets men climbing mountains, flying in the clouds, riding around and around the shaking wall of death. It is completely different from the desire for women, because men who desire women are incomplete men who must feel and taste some warm vibrating substance to prove to themselves that they're not dead. It's also different from the craving for drink, because the drinker is trying to soothe his senses into forgetfulness or lift them up for a moment to a higher world of great ideas and accelerated words. The gambler stiffens his body, steadies his mind, opposes himself to other gamblers, and they all sit together looking for hours at a green field where kings and queens and jesters in two different colours, red for blood and black for death, lie on beds of red diamonds, dark trefoil, bleeding hearts, the heads of black spears.

At twenty minutes past four the grocer, who had fallen asleep in his chair, rolled to the floor and lay, still sleeping, like a crumpled sack.

Gamblers, when gambling, may drink and smoke without smelling the smoke or tasting the drink. The grocer was as drunk as a lord, but the drink had no power over him until the gambling ceased.

The green card table was littered with cards. The queen of hearts, the ace of spades, and the two of diamonds had slipped and fluttered down to the brown utility carpet. An empty whisky bottle, an empty siphon, and seventeen empty beer bottles stood dismally among cinders that had rolled down from the dying fire to the shiny tiles of the hearth. The air was gritty with stale smoke, the electric bulbs clouded with bad air, and the seven gamblers, six crouched on chairs and one lying on the floor, had forgotten loss and gain in sore-headed sleep.

At twenty minutes to five the morning came into the room, a thin bit of a girl squeezing through a half-opened window, unsettling heavy clay-brown curtains, her thin body naked and wet like the cold dripping scales of a mermaid, a chill breeze of a girl who knew nothing about the sun. The doctor shivered and shuddered and suddenly sat upright in his chair, his big, clumsy hands groping for his pockets with the gesture of a man awaking from sin in a house of evil fame. Had he forgotten something? Had he lost something? Or robbed a bank? Or struck a policeman? Or driven while drunk and crippled a streetful of pedestrians? The hairy groping hands rested wearily, hopelessly on his large, square knee-caps. A hammer struck upwards at the roof of his head, and with eyes that felt as if rimmed with burning rubber he saw the room: the coloured scatterment of kings, queens, and knaves, five men on chairs and the grocer on the floor, the empty bottles crunching among cold cinders, the thin, watery, repellent body of the virgin morning. 'Here,' he said, 'we go round the mulberry bush.' Three times he repeated the seven words, and then standing up and stretching sorely his stiff body, he shouted: 'On a cold and frosty morning.' But nobody heard him, nobody stirred, so he spat on the sleeping grocer, staggered across the room, opened the door, closed it behind him, wobbled from wall to wall along a tiled corridor that led to the bathroom.

Water gushed like a spring from a faulty cistern in one of the closets. Running water, damp beaded on tiled walls, in his ears the dull booming left behind by a sleepless night and the echoes of subsiding drink — it might be chill morning in the washroom of a ship that had berthed during the night while the passengers slept uneasily in little cabins. He took off his collar and tie, bathed his eyes and forehead. From the long oblong mirror behind the hand-basins a man watched him: tousled dark hair with one or two touches of grey, a square, hard brow, high big cheek-bones, a thin black streak of a moustache, dark eyes like pits under bushy black eyebrows. The man in the mirror needed a shave. He passed a shaking, dripping hand over his bristly chin; then suddenly stretching out his arm, he pointed directly at the doctor and said: 'You're broke. You're ruined. You're cleaned out. You dhreepy-looking, bleary-eyed bastard.'

Turning to dry himself in the towel, the doctor laughed good-naturedly. He spoke over his shoulder to the accuser in the mirror: 'You're a phantasm. I don't give a damn.' He was hugely satisfied with the completeness of his own ruin, for always before it had been partial ruin and the partial is thwarting.

Behind him the voice spoke from the mirror: 'You've lost everything. Even your car. You haven't the right to drive it home. It belongs to the grocer.'

'The grocer's asleep. When he comes to himself I'll be gone and so'll the car. He'll hardly claim it as a debt of honour.'

'You've lost even your honour.'

'For God's sake. That thing died in the eighteenth century.'

'Think of your wife and children.'

'Hell, I do. Don't you see the grey in my hair? I love them, but I don't live for them, as the commercial traveller from Manchester said to the girl in Swansea. My trouble is, I never think of them until it's too late. They're remorse. That's what they are. Remorse. Remorse.'

All the way back along the corridor to the room where the six men slept he kept repeating that word. It was a terrible word. Every time he pronounced it another hair turned grey. Lips parched with thirst, he sought relief from the bottles on the cindery hearth. Not a drop. Not a damned drop; and turning to leave for ever a room where he would never again be welcome, he saw the cards scattered on the small green table, the queen of hearts, the ace of spades, and the two of diamonds prostrate on the carpet, the instruments of his utter ruin and so of his supreme contentment. Gratefully he gathered them into a tidy bundle — he was always a tidy man who felt hurt when he saw the way women crumpled banknotes into chaotic handbags — and slipped them into the pocket of his overcoat. The overcoat now really belonged to the man who owned the factory, but as the factory manufactured, among other things, overcoats, there didn't seem to be much sense in leaving it behind.

He went through his pockets one after the other, searching for money, finding instead a dirty handkerchief, a chain with three keys, a tattered wallet containing a few newspaper clippings, and a snapshot of his wife. She was younger then; she was pretty. She had raced laughing across the lawn, climbed to the top of some wooden steps, sat perched like a warm, plump bird, and he had raised the camera, clicked the shutter, made the happy moment eternal. Remorse. Remorse. Remorse. And very carefully, accepting his damnation, he tore the snapshot to tiny pieces and spread them on the table in place of the cards he had pocketed.

A gaping pocket, the young professor's pocket, caught his eye, in the cloth of the professor's suit a soft little cave flowering with a coloured protruding handkerchief. Under the handkerchief there might be money. In every pocket in the room there might be money, honestly earned or captured at cards, now tucked shrewdly away in leather wallets or buried darkly and silently in soft deep pockets. He hovered over the sleeping professor. They'd never miss some of the money, perhaps never even know that some of it had been in their possession. Never in his life before had he picked a pocket, but he grimly supposed it was never too late to learn and, since he was anyway damned and had accepted his damnation, another sin could make no difference. He stooped down, his right hand twitchingly extended over the sleeping professor. The man with all his learning was young and had two days ago announced in the newspapers his engagement to a beautiful girl; and, in spite of the weariness that followed drink and gambling, he smiled in his sleep, dreaming a dream as fragile as glass, as easy to read as an open book; a dream that was a barrier as strong as a stone wall against an amateur pickpocket who remembered a pretty woman perching like a bird on the top of some wooden steps.

The grocer stirred in his sleep, snored, clawed, and clutched at the air with a hook of a hand. The man was too dishonest to sleep soundly.

If they woke up and saw me picking a pocket?

The quietness in the room was deadly with the threat of awakening eyes, staring, accusing, not understanding that their respectable accusations could make no difference to the damned.

The factory owner hunched like an animal on his hands and knees and silently vomited on the brown utility carpet.

So, still staggering a little, he fled from the room, following the morning down the long hallway to the front door. The morning was growing up, her body drying, the flesh taking to itself a first faint touch of rose-coloured heat. The seven cars were parked like dominoes at the edge of the blue gravel, roofs and bonnets beaded with dew; and beyond the blue gravel, flat green land went off towards the misty dune-fringed edge of the sea. In saucer-shaped hollows white mist was packed like soft wool. Pointed flags on greens fluttered as the morning ran past them, a runner bearing messages from fort to fort, pennants fluttering as the good news passed. Later, when the corpulent day had taken the place of the slim morning, corpulent wealthy people would walk solidly from green to green, lowering the glad flags, cunningly tapping white balls into little holes in the earth.

A curious finality gathered like a gripping hand around everything he did. Step by step across the heavy, wet, blue gravel, fitting a key that no longer in honour belonged to him into the keyhole in the door of the little green car that no longer in honour belonged to him. Because he was finally ruined he could never again walk on that gravel or sit in the driver's seat in that particular place, looking at the smooth wet grass and the little, distant fluttering flags, drinking in the sweet silence of the place and knowing, godlike, that he and the ignition key had the power to destroy that silence. With the engine smoothly running under the neat green bonnet, he sat waiting, watching the door of the club-house, giving the six sleepers their chance to awaken, to run gesticulating along the gravel, giving the greedy grocer the chance to claim the green car won over the green card table. He waited for five deliciously exciting minutes, squeezing the last ounce of thrill out of his last little gamble. But nothing happened. His luck was turning. He waited two minutes, three, four, then laughing, pressed down his foot, laughed louder as the first figure shot out through the club-house doorway, almost as if the pressing foot had released a spring somewhere within. The figure ran, arms waving, across the gravel. He waited for two seconds. The figure was the grocer, red with rage, roaring words inaudible above the sweet humming of the engine, running in pursuit as the green car glided away, stumbling and falling face forward on the gravel, kneeling and waving his two fists above his head. In the driving mirror the grocer's image, more comic than reality, waved tiny fists. Then the road dipped into a pocket of white mist and the grocer vanished and the last gamble was over.

The morning was a gracious girl running brightly across green country, peeping in at the windows of quiet little farmhouses, disturbing their shadowy bedrooms with glimmering laughter that ran to a point as white and sharp as the pointed Norse gables of the houses. The morning was a prim girl with spectacles, tight corsets, neat costume, leaving a suburban house, heels hammering along suburban footpaths, waiting for a green bus to take her to the city to a Civil Service office. The morning was a great bosomy, alluring woman shouting with laughter over the life of the crowded busy streets.

He drove through the green country, first along twisting by-roads and then down a wide highway, through primly awakening suburbs and then through crowded streets. He scarcely noticed the morning. His mouth was sour. A pain gathered like a gathering ulcer between his eyes. He was the gambler and all the gambling was for ever over, and a gambler without a game is only a damned man, and once the first thrill is ended it's no fun being damned.

II

A mile from home he ran out of petrol. The road went down a steep hill between semi-detached modern houses settled snugly in leafy gardens, over a bridge that was two hundred years older than the oldest of the houses, then up a long slope between high, grey walls. The car crossed the bridge. Far below, one of the city's little rivers twisted by gardens and cottages towards an ancient mill and a sleepy weir. For fifty yards the car ascended the slope, then stopped exhausted. He climbed out, locked it carefully, waited until he saw a green double-decker bus lumbering into view between the new houses on the other side of the old bridge; then remembered he had not money either to buy petrol or pay bus fare, and, regretting the scruples that had kept him from picking pockets, he walked wearily the last sad mile. He hummed as he walked: *Father, dear father, come home with me now, the clock in the steeple strikes two.* So father came home; no money, no petrol, not able to call his overcoat his own, his practice ruined because he had mortally offended six men on whom his connections depended. In some distant steeple a clock struck nine strokes. The morning still owned three bright hours of life.

He had always been unlucky with gardeners. Even when he had the money to pay them he never seemed to get the right men. One had spent most of his working day in the local public house, another had dug the weeds so securely into the ground that they would never again be uprooted, a third had been discovered entertaining, and being entertained by, a woman of dubious appearance in a derelict henhouse at the bottom of the kitchen garden, a fourth had turned up on one day to view the work, eaten a huge meal, gone away, and never returned. Long tendrils of neglected shrubs reached out to touch him as he walked from the garden gate to the door of the house. The lawn was like a meadow forgotten for several seasons. The rockery was grey with ragged weeds. The concrete path was chipped and cracked. And all along the road on which he lived perfectly kept gardens bore witness to the regular lives of blameless men, good providers for their offspring, attentive, and possibly even loving to their wives. That unkempt garden singled him out. He was like a man in a ragged coat disturbing the whole poise and swing and rhythm of an expensive dress-dance. He was a shouting affront to the self-control of suburbia; he and his garden, nature rank and uncontrollable, cracking the crust that ordered lives and neat gardens had made carefully over the turbulent earth.

Paint flaked dismally off the hall door swinging open on a hallway curiously empty and quiet. He tiptoed over the threshold, stood, scarcely breathing, on worn green carpet. No voices of playing children. No noise of work from the kitchen. But as he draped gently his coat and hat over the end of the banisters he heard feet moving and the murmur of voices upstairs, and one pair of feet came softly across the landing and a voice half-whispered, half-shouted: 'Is that you at last?'

It wasn't his wife but his wife's cousin, the friend of his childhood before he met his wife; the strong, dark young girl who had introduced him to the plump, pretty young girl who was to become his wife, the strong, dark spinster who lived alone in a flat in the centre of the city, divided her spare moments between love for her cousin's two children and work with a charitable organization of women who made clothes and distributed them free of charge to the semi-naked poor.

She said: 'Where in God's name have you been? But I suppose I needn't ask you.'

She stood on the topmost step of the stairs. She was tall, solidly but not heavily built, dark curling hair clustering like a halo around her strong, pleasant circular face. Her cheeks were rosy with health and good humour. A mole, brown and sprouting with one little dark hair, perched like a beauty spot close to one corner of her crimson mouth. Her body, the square shoulders, firm breasts, muscular waist, thighs strong and supple, was covered in a blue and white striped linen dress; and the sheer, glossy silk of her stockings swept curving down to soft blue shoes.

'If you know where I was, why do you ask me?'

'Don't be truculent now. There's a good little boy. Have you a sore head?'

'Why should I have a sore head?'

'If you had everything you should have, you'd have more than a sore head.'

She laughed at him and her cheeks dimpled and the brown mole moved higher on her friendly face. But, looking at her as she stood there laughing, he did not see the threadbare carpet on the stairs up which night after night, for year after year, his wife and himself had walked to bed. Instead, he saw a green shore circling a small inlet of the sea, brown and purple heathery mountains gathered around as if they were watching the water, a small stream meandering between high banks to meet the sea, a little dark-haired girl wearing a white dress and a little dark-haired boy wearing a sailor suit wandering hand in hand across the green ground. The little boy, to show his embryo manhood, leaped across the stream. The little girl, doing her best to emulate him, leaped waist-deep into the salty water, and afterwards on the sparse grass on the soft bank there was much wringing of undergarments and much bubbling laughter. No matter how often he saw his wife's cousin, he could never forget that he had once helped her to wring the water of that paradisal stream out of her drawers; and somewhere, he knew, behind the chaste, charitable mask of strong, untouched womanhood she was still the little, laughing, leaping tomboy, and she also was remembering and regretting.

He went slowly up the stairs to meet her.

She said: 'Take my congratulations, anyway.'

'Congratulations. What have I done?'

'By all appearances you can still do one part of your duty as a husband.'

'But it isn't her time yet.'

She leaned against the banister, surprised at first and a little shocked, and then again she began to laugh.

'You don't . . . you don't know which month of the year it is?'

'But nobody ever reminded me.'

'Does a husband of two babies' standing have to be reminded when the third is on the way?'

Her half-suppressed laughter shook her strong shoulders. Between them, from invisible pink cloth, drops of crystal water tinkled down to paradisal grass. She said: 'If I told this around you'd be the mockery of the city. The husband played at poker and he didn't know a thing. It's like a line from a comic song.'

But he couldn't laugh. He couldn't even retain that image

of two children happy in a green place by the sea. Life ended in ruin in a room in a club-house and life commenced, unsuspected life, in pain in a suburban bedroom. All at once he was conscious of his sore head, his ignominy, his hunger, a feeling of nausea that fought with his hunger like two primeval monsters writhing in battle in a malodorous swamp. As she looked at his pallid, quiet, unshaven face her laughter stopped, her eyes were motherly with pity.

She gripped his arm with a strong hand. 'Come in now and get it over,' she said. 'It won't be easy. The dowager duchess is here in her righteous fury. But leave her to me. I'll handle her.'

The dowager duchess was the mother of his wife and the aunt of his wife's cousin. She sat enthroned in a green wickerwork arm-chair in the corner of the room between the old mahogany wardrobe and the fireless fireplace. She didn't rise to greet him, but she laced together the fingers of her fat hands and went on talking softly, rapidly — her soft, rapid tongue could effortlessly raise blisters on a walrus — to the white-coated midwife and the woman in the bed. The white-coated midwife had goitre and popping, staring eyes. The woman in the bed had a little baby, a little white bundle; and a pretty plump face with cleft chin and eyes that kept always a smug cheerfulness, in spite of the exhaustion following childbirth, in spite of the pinching and poverty that, if it had not been for the dowager duchess, would have followed a gambling husband. In the presence of that prettiness and cheerfulness he felt almost always stung or stabbed by a keen sense of his shortcomings; but not now, not with the plump face in the bed occurring again as if caught in a distorting mirror in the plumper face of the dowager duchess, smugly cheerful eyes showing acceptance of every word that came skidding from the tongue of the fat woman in the green chair: the monstrously fat mother-in-law, ankles swelling out over the tops of her shoes, a woman who had grown in the image and likeness of a hundred vulgar jokes, a poisonous woman to provoke. She was easy to provoke.

She was saying: '. . . thanks be to the good God child you had an easy time indeed it always stood to the women of our family that they never had too much trouble not like the weak wobbly ones going nowadays with bottoms like the backs of hairbrushes which is just as well seeing that none of us ever met with much consideration from our menfolk although I'll say this much for your poor father the heavens be his bed that he was man enough not to forget when an event was likely to take place and to be somewhere at hand when it did take place not like some out gambling and gallivanting.'

She paused to fill slowly her vast bosom with the warm disinfected air of the room, then added with the finality of somebody turning a key in a lock: 'Oh, yes, indeed!'

Angry answers writhed like eels on the floor of his mind, but before he could speak the wife's cousin said decisively: 'All's well now. No trouble at all. I rang your friend at the lying-in hospital, but he didn't have to stop here for more than a few minutes. How do you think she's looking? And isn't the baby a little dote? And, oh, Auntie, your elevenses are ready in the dining-room. Nurse, please help Auntie downstairs and have a cup of tea yourself. I'll join you in a tick.'

She was a masterful woman, the wife's cousin, and her managing way made the most difficult matters of domestic diplomacy as simple as squeezing silvery water out of soft pink cloth. When she spoke commandingly the world whirled faster. The fat woman, assisted by the midwife, shuffled, red-faced and grumbling, out of the bedroom and down the stairs. He held the door open for them as they passed, but he didn't speak to his mother-in-law nor did she speak to him. Between them, more decisively than between sun and rain, all compromise, all sun-showery pretence of toleration had perished. The wife's cousin swiftly tidied the coverlet on the bed, then followed the midwife and the fat woman. He closed the door and turned towards his wife, the soft pretty face with the cleft chin, the snugly parcelled baby. His lips touched his wife's lips. He was angry not so much with himself because he'd been a blind simpleton, the husband cuckolded by himself, playing away at poker and never knowing a thing; not so much with his wife that she hadn't thought it worth while to remind him when life was on the way. But he was angry because he knew that no matter what he said or did she would never realize she'd married damnation, never say anything worse than: 'Dear, you're a bad provider. You're really a wash-out. I suppose I'll have to ask Mother to come to the rescue once again.' And mother-in-law, appealed to, would come to the rescue; her mercy and her charity sharper than nettle stings, more bitter than vinegar.

He wasn't only a wash-out. In a world of wise men mowing square lawns he was a monster, a demon. When he lightly kissed his wife's soft lips he was really a little surprised that she didn't splutter and gasp and cry out at the fetid odour of the primeval swamp, or at the crackling burning smell of sulphur and brimstone.

Instead, she said: 'Darling, where have you been?'

'Why didn't you remind me?'

'Why should I, darling? After all, you are a doctor. I waited day after day for you to say something. But you never did. You never even looked my way. Or, if you did look my way, you saw somebody or something else.'

What had he seen when he looked at her: a green field where kings and queens and jesters in two different colours, red for blood and black for death, lay on beds of red diamonds, dark trefoil, bleeding hearts, the heads of black spears; or a green shore where a little meandering stream flowed to a mountain-encircled bay, and two children happy on that shore; or merely a plump young woman perched like a bird on the top of some wooden steps; or a lost heaven far behind him and certain hell ahead? He looked now intently, great dark eyes glaring out from under bushy eyebrows, at the pretty woman and the tiny child and life commencing again to make a mockery of the hospitable, happy way in which a few hours since he had welcomed his final ruin.

The tiny child was, as children always were, red, wrinkled, and snuffling. The pretty woman looked at it, smiled, and said: 'Which of us do you think it's like, dear?' Her face was smoothly content. Her forehead had never wrinkled. Her smiling composure always worried him, for he thought that the sins of a husband should make their monstrous mark on the face of the suffering wife. She refused to suffer, or at least she refused to give him the satisfaction of realizing his own iniquity by showing any signs of suffering. She had the dowager duchess and the dowager duchess had money, and whether he failed or succeeded didn't matter a damn. That was what she meant when she smiled and called him dear and darling.

'I should have remembered,' he said humbly. 'I'm sorry. It's so humiliating for you.'

'And for you, dear. After all, other men would laugh if they heard it. Just think of the things they'd say.'

But he wasn't worried about other men. When you had nearly picked a friend's pocket, when you had fled from what other men called debts of honour, you could begin to regard yourself as a separate species, a man apart, walking alone between heaven and hell, horrors to the left and bright beatitudes to the right.

'I was worried and preoccupied. Only for that I'd have remembered.'

'I'm sure you would, darling.'

'I had a lot on my mind.'

'You have such awful luck at cards too. You never seem to win a thing. Other men actually do win once in a while. But, poor darling, you're always losing.'

He had no right to be angry. Anyway, anger, like a wave broken by a smooth rock, would be useless against the smile, the soft voice, the faultless skin. The woman in the bed was more than a match for him. She looked at the child as a mischievous little boy would look at the glittering toy successfully hidden from a frustrated searching playmate.

'No,' he said, 'my luck isn't so good.'

'I wonder you don't give it up, darling. It seems such a waste of time.'

'This time I have given it up,' he said, and in his pocket his fingers caressed the smooth surfaces of the pack of cards he had stolen from the club-house.

He had this time given it up because he had no choice. But what came next: an effort to steady himself like a man swept along in a flooded stream, feeling with his feet for the firm ground? And after the steadying effort the slow task, dragging across the years, of building up everything his passion had knocked down: credit, reputation, practice? Or simpler, much more simple, could he call it a day and make his choice between the rope, the river, and the road? Preferably the road, for the rope was rough and the river wet, and in the circle of the rope and the sinuous body of the river, hope came to an abrupt end. On the road there was life and hope and anonymity as secure as death: an unshaven, ragged walking-man going westwards through the green midlands, undertaking odd jobs at prosperous farms, accepting alms at hospitable doors, going steadily westwards to grey rocky places by the sea where the people spoke a soft ancestral language, where the earth was many years younger, more familiar with sun, wind, and rain than the earth buried under the patterned crust of the complicated city. . . .

'A penny for your thoughts, darling.'

'They're worth a mint,' he said. He stooped again to kiss her. The baby snuffled, wrinkled still more its little wrinkled face, prepared to cry. The feet of the midwife and the mother-in-law were on the stairs. So he tiptoed across the landing to the bathroom, closed the door, turned on a tap, and pretended to wash his hands. If he did take to the roads the dowager duchess had money. Everything would be fine. Nobody would miss him.

The dark, hard-faced man in the mirror looked out at him. The man in the mirror still needed a shave, so he took from the little glass-doored cabinet, brush and soap and razor, turned on the hot tap, took off coat and collar and tie. Lazily lathering his face, he chatted with the half-lathered man in the mirror: 'Come with me when I go walking. Be my shadow when the sun is shining. When the rain falls sit with me in hay-scented byres listening to the drumming of the drops on roofs of tarred corrugated iron. We'll work together in some strange farmer's meadow. We'll sleep uneasily together in some flea-bitten lodging-house in a small town where the sun shines always and the oldest inhabitants sit on barrels outside a public house.'

The razor made the first stroke. The man in the mirror smiled cynically through the blossoming lather as if he didn't believe a word he heard.

III

Shaven and clean and smelling of soap, the pain soothed away from his eyes by the cool touch of water, he tiptoed down the stairs and along the hallway to find the wife's cousin in the breakfast-room. From the bedroom came the sound of voices: the continuous monotonous whine of the dowager duchess, interrupted now and again by a soft interjection from the woman in the bed or a rattling interjection from the unlovely midwife. As he closed gently the door of the breakfast-room the child began to cry and, remembering that he had not seen the two elder children since his return, he thought: this is life, this is a parent's responsibility.

'Who's looking after the children?'

'I am,' she said. Going and coming between the kitchen and the breakfast-room, she was very obviously preparing his breakfast. Crackle of frying, plopping of the lid of a kettle, the enticing smell of rashers on a pan.

'You are. And where are they?'

'In the garage. As quiet as mice and as good as little angels. They take after their father.'

'Go on. Rub it in.'

She laughed again at him, swivelling her face around to look back at him, and he felt that he could draw lovingly the pattern of the muscles that made that graceful movement possible: her face laughing and turning towards him, her arms raised slightly, her hands tossing a coloured table-cloth over the small table by the window. He watched the cloth spread out and settle easily like a radiant wide-winged bird coming to rest.

'I don't know what we'd do without you.'

'You'd get along.'

'But I mean it.'

'Without me, you wouldn't be married at all.'

He thought that over, standing with his back to the fire-screen. 'Maybe not. Is that why you keep on being so helpful? Do you feel a responsibility? Or remorse?'

'That's one reason.'

'Are there more than one?'

'There always are, you know, more reasons than one for everything.'

'For instance?'

'I'm not giving instances. I'm frying rashers and eggs for a man who should be on bread and water. Take a peek into the garage and see if the kids are still alive.'

If his wife's mother had spoken to him in that way he'd have resented it, ignored it. But between himself and this strong virgin there was that bond, an idyllic memory; so he went out through the kitchenette, along a glass-roofed passage, peeped quietly in at the half-open door of the garage, saw the two children solemnly playing at houses, marking on the floor with empty petrol tins and blocks of wood the patterns of fairyland homes. Two small, delicately featured children with dark curling hair, a boy in a sailor suit, a girl in a blue dress. He couldn't disturb their game, couldn't break in on the little secret world they had made, not on a green shore, but on dusty grey concrete. Back in the breakfast-room he sat to eat.

'Drink a cup with me.'

'I've just had a cup,' she said. 'But to keep you company I will.'

She sat facing him across the small table.

'I think you should go and notify his reverence.'

'Your brother.'

'Yes. If you like. It saves trouble to have him do the baptism.'

'Couldn't I ring him up?'

'Oh, please yourself. But it'd look better if you called in to see him. He's always complaining that you never call to see him.'

'No, I never do.'

'He likes you, you know.'

'Really.'

'He's not a bad fellow, even if he is my brother. He's a lot more tolerant than most young clergymen.'

'Must be, if he's prepared to tolerate me.'

'That's not what I meant.' With a gesture of impatience she cracked a biscuit between her fingers. 'What sort of a bug is biting you? I remember the time when you thought you were as good as any man.'

'I remember —'

'Oh, I know some of the things that you remember. You remember that you had me once without my panties when you were too young to appreciate the situation. You were a lively boy then. You always were lively. Until recently. Look, it isn't my place to lecture you. But I know you longer than any other person in this house —'

'You certainly do.'

'I know you better too.'

'That could be.'

'And where in Christopher are drink and cards getting you?'

'They're not *getting* me anywhere. I'm there. I've arrived.'

'What exactly does that mean?'

'It means I'm a dead man. It means I'm finished in this city. It means I've no money left and I've a cartload of debts I'll never be able to pay. The car ran out of petrol on the way home and I'd to walk the rest of the way because I hadn't the money to buy petrol. I hadn't even my bus fare.'

She knit her fingers tightly together and looked fixedly at the coloured table-cloth.

'It's Africa or the road for me. It can't be Africa, because I couldn't pay my fare, and I doubt if anybody in this city would loan me the money . . . even to get rid of me.'

He stretched his arms until the joints creaked. He yawned. He was sleepy and tired. He was also enjoying the steep, giddy swoop into the abyss of humiliation.

'There's a deal to be said for the road. There's the free life and the fresh air. Would you come with me? I'm sure you'd have enough saved to buy a horse and a caravan.' He yawned again and laughed through the yawn. She raised her head and looked at him. She didn't unclasp her fingers. Her face was very white.

'I didn't know things were as bad as that.'

'They're worse.'

'Don't give me any more details. Please don't.'

Every word that told of his disgrace had been a nail driven into her flesh.

'I'd go with you in a tinker's caravan to the end of the world. You know that. That's the awful thing about you. You've always known that.'

'Not always. I found it out slowly. I wasn't certain until it was too late.'

'But it isn't possible. It wouldn't do you any good.'

'How do you know?'

'Be sensible.'

'Women are always so sensible.'

'Somebody has to be sensible.'

She flattened her hands palms downwards on the table. The blue stone of a dress ring shone from her right hand. The fingers of her left hand were strong and clean and bare.

'Look,' she said, 'it isn't my place to give you good advice. But I do feel responsible. If it hadn't been for my introducing you, you might never have met and this trouble mightn't have happened.'

'She didn't make me a gambler.'

'I'm not blaming her. I'm not blaming anyone. It's just that the two of you didn't mix —'

'Like gin and whisky.'

'Like anything you like. Then every weakness that was in you came out like a rash of pimples.'

'Thank you. Thank you.' He stood up, bowed ironically, walked across to a small sideboard, and rummaged in it, searching for something among empty clinking bottles.

'What you're looking for is here,' she said, and from the window-sill behind her she took a whisky bottle, still holding a few inches of bright yellow liquor, and drop by drop she dribbled some of it into his tea-cup.

'You think of everything.' He sat down again, soothing his eyes with the warm tips of his fingers.

'I'm preaching,' she said; 'listen to me.'

'I'm listening.'

'I wouldn't preach, only I like you.'

'You like me.'

She was silent for a while, tightening her lips until the blood fled from them. 'There is something of the demon in you. You want me to tell the whole truth. You want me to say I love you. You want to feel that everything's ruined, that we've all done the wrong thing, you and your wife, and myself who introduced you to your wife when I should have left well enough alone and married you myself.'

He laughed silently. He said nothing.

'All right, I do love you. You know it already and knowing it won't ever do you any good. Just because I love you I think you can, and must, make another start. Any money you want I can give you if you promise never again to play cards.'

He reached across the table, gripped her round, white arm so tightly with his hard, bony, dark-haired hand that she winced and looked quickly at him, momentary doubt and fear in her eyes.

'Women are wonderful,' he said. 'I declare to Christ they're wonderful.'

'Don't swear.'

'Don't be a holy Mary. My wife there up in bed, up listening to the sweet, sad voice of her father's wife telling the tale of my sins, she never tried to reform me. Why should you worry? Why should you bother? You, a good woman, pure and intact.'

Her lips again tightened and whitened. Under his gripping the muscles of her white forearm grew rigid. But he didn't even notice that her soul was in pain at his rough praise of her virginity, and he went on talking with the intent energy of a man interested mostly in himself.

'Why should you worry? Tell me that. Aren't you lucky I didn't marry you? You've missed nothing. Likely I've missed a lot. I'm the lost soul. The one groat that the sweeping woman looks for. The one straying sheep that the shepherd follows into the hot desert. Only, no wise woman would wear out her sweeping brush or no sensible shepherd would weary his feet for my sake. Except yourself. But you're wasting your time. You're even risking your own peace of mind by bothering about me.'

She said: 'You're not as bad as you think you are.' Her voice didn't tremble, but she spoke very slowly, as if she were afraid to trust to the quivering air more than one word at a time.

'I'm so bad that I won't take your offer of help. But I will borrow money from you to buy petrol to set the car moving again, and with some of that money I'll buy cigarettes and a few drinks.'

'You're honest about it, anyway.'

'Then I'll sell the car before some of my creditors seize it.'

She walked with him from the breakfast-room to the hall door. From her handbag she took green, crinkly notes and gave them to him. He counted them carefully, folded them and smoothed them, slipped them neatly into the empty pocket in his wallet. 'Some day,' he said, 'my luck may change. I may even pay you back.'

'If you ever change your mind about making a fresh start, my offer still stands.'

'You're a good girl,' he said, 'but you're a fool.' Upstairs voices murmured, but there was no movement of feet, and, secure behind the still closed door, he pulled her to him and kissed her and for a moment she yielded, but then, suddenly stung with anger, she struck him sharply on the face with her ringless left hand. He went out laughing. She closed the door behind him. She didn't speak again, she didn't reprove or upbraid. The wound was too deep for words to mend and knowing that, he went laughing away from his own ragged garden, laughing in the sunshine along the clean suburban road between the neat neighbouring gardens and the cared-for houses. He was now completely the demon, the monster, separate and apart from the pacific lives of orderly home-loving men. With one foul unjust kiss he had hammered a black crack across that memory of two children happy on an innocent green shore, had snapped the one link that held him bound to the past or the eternity that preceded the past. He was a new man beginning a mysterious journey. For the damned a beginning still has excitement, he thought, and his feet on suburban concrete were as light as the feet of the fortunate third son finding the winding road that would lead him to the crystal life-giving water in the well at the world's end.

IV

Fifty yards from the grey-walled presbytery he went looking for a drink, a warming restorative, a bright bestower of confidence, so that he could with aplomb and poise face the dark, penetrating, friendly eyes of the priest who was the brother of the wife's cousin. The bells in the steeple of the church beside the presbytery were ringing the noonday angelus. In the crowded, noisy street men bared their heads to the hot, bright sun and made the sign of the cross. Nazareth of Galilee was in the street; this is that blessed Mary, pre-elect God's virgin; memories of van Eyck's lily-bearing, round-cheeked angel and upstairs God the Father reading a book; memories of Saints Ansano and Reparata standing sour-faced sentries for the moment of salutation and incarnation as imagined by Simone Martini of Siena.

The Angel of the Lord declared unto Mary. An old woman walked down the street, dry lips in wrinkled yellow face moving in silent prayer.

And she conceived of the Holy Ghost.

And Christ was born in Bethlehem, and born above the noisy street with bells ringing from a grey steeple, and born in the minds and hearts of all men, in all places, and knowing and seeing all things, and God walked everywhere in gardens and garden suburbs, and most of all in smelly slums.

Gone is a great while, some poet said, and she dwelt young in Nazareth of Galilee.

He wasn't really a reading man. He didn't know a great deal about poetry or pictures, but he was always inordinately pleased when some happening, some stray thought or chance word — in this case a chiming bell and an old praying woman — set his mind straying among such things like a grazing animal on bare ground wandering from one scarce tuft to another. The stately sonnet about the Annunciation set something moving inside him, half-remembered fragments of verse coming to the light like broken and knotted line unwinding from a jerky reel: a verse from 'Hohenlinden', blaring like an ill-trained brass band, a line of bawdry from a song learnt at school, a big-mouthed sobbing line from a new American hit, a jingle of children's voices from an old Gaelic song. As he went, two steps at a time, up the steep stairs to the lounge bar, he was muttering aloud: 'Here we go up the coloured steep stairway that leads to the houseful of drunkards.'

The oblong, lavishly decorated room was, even at that early hour of the day, full of drunkards, not sitting morosely in corners, not sitting at all, but grouped like ring-o'-rosy children in a circle in the centre of the floor. He counted them in one quick glance: twelve middle-aged men in suits of mourning black, obviously returning from a funeral and determined to drown in drink and song the memory of death and the dead. Even as he looked and counted they joined hands and began to circle and sing, slowly and softly at first, then faster and louder and louder and faster, until the floor quivered and a white-coated attendant rushed in, waving his arms and saying something that remained unheard. Carefully avoiding a collision with the singing circle, the gambler crossed the floor, sat in a sheltered corner, saw suddenly the thirteenth man sitting beside him, looking with calm eyes at the twelve men spinning like the world spinning.

'Here,' they sang, 'we go round the mulberry bush, the mulberry bush, the mulberry bush; here we go round the mulberry bush on a cold and frosty morning'; and one of the twelve whooped like a country lad, grabbing the strong waist of a girl and whirling her in an orgiastic reel.

The white-coated attendant despairingly ceased gesturing and shouting, came across the room to the gambler, but before an order could be given or taken the thirteenth man held up his right hand, two fingers stretched and the other fingers knuckled. The attendant went, and returned bearing two large whiskies. The dance of the twelve men in mourning black ended and their singing ended, and the oblong room with crudely painted walls was silent. The attendant gave one whisky to the gambler, one to the thirteenth man, and while the gambler was still fumbling in a recalcitrant pocket the thirteenth man had paid the total reckoning.

'Allow me,' he said. 'The party's on me.'

'Thanks. Oh, thanks a lot.'

'A party for death and a party for birth,' said the thirteenth man. 'It really is a pleasure.' His voice sounded as if he really meant what he said. It was a young voice, clear-toned as a precious bell, yet with echoes and undertones of experience, maturity, vast knowledge. With the whisky halfway to his lips, the gambler said: 'A party like this must come expensive.' He turned and looked for the first time at the general benefactor, the owner of the beautiful voice.

He was, like the twelve men who had been dancing and

now were drinking, dressed in black clothes, clerical black, not mourning black; a shining white collar circling his neck; above the white collar a strong, astonishingly handsome face. His hair was golden and curling and his complexion fair, but his eyelids drooped rather with wisdom than weariness and no man could have guessed his age. He waved his white right hand in a gesture that comprehended the twelve drinking men. 'Some of them,' he said, 'don't even know I'm buying the drinks. Some do know and don't care. But I can afford it and it gives me great pleasure to set things moving.'

At that the gambler wrinkled his dark, square, forbidding forehead. Yet there was no need to be puzzled. Since the beginning of time, men sitting in taverns, inns, ale-houses, shebeens, gin palaces, gin-mills, hotels, public houses, lounge bars, have said strange things and done strangely generous things. Clerical clothes and a Roman collar were more puzzling in such a place than enigmatic words and eccentric generosity. He said: 'If you'll excuse my saying so, sir, an odd place this to find a priest.'

'Why an odd place? Don't you find priests in all sorts of places? Battlefields, risking their lives and consoling fear away from the mangled and the dying. In slums, helping the poor. In confessionals easing the tortured mind. At wakes and weddings. In the house of birth and the house of death.'

The gambler sipped his whisky and said nothing. The twelve men in mourning had stood up to re-form their circle in the centre of the floor. He was too sober and too polite to argue with a man who had just bought him a double whisky, to point out that there were places where clergymen belonged and places where they didn't belong.

'And talking of the house of birth,' said the thirteenth man, 'your child is a fine healthy child.'

'That's so.' The news had gone before him through the whispering city. This strange clergyman knew who he was and what he was.

'You're on your way now to get the priest for the baptism. The brother of your wife's cousin whom you've just kissed behind the hall door.'

With an outburst of sound like a sudden explosion the twelve men went circling into their singing dance, and, stung with surprise at the sound and the words of the stranger, the gambler leaped to his feet, then sat down as suddenly and gulped the remainder of his whisky. Perhaps the drink was unusually strong, a virulent poteen-laced concoction carried to the light for this special occasion from some secret illicit cellar. He touched his palate with the tip of his tongue. Yet it had tasted as good whisky should taste. Perhaps with the thunderous uproar of the dancers still singing about the mulberry bush, twelve men circling around an unseen bush, all men circling around the tree of life, he hadn't heard the words aright. No man had noticed him when he sealed his damnation by kissing a crack across his one pure memory. The wife's cousin would never have telephoned across the city so that the knowledge of his ignominy would go before him, warn people against him.

He said carefully: 'You know a great deal about me, your reverence. Are you certain you're not confusing me with somebody else?'

'Quite certain. You're a gambler and your gambling has been fatally unlucky.'

'Quite so. Quite so.' From dark narrow eyes, and feeling just a little irritated, he looked at the golden-headed cleric, the thirteenth man, the omniscient stranger. Some one of those six sods had followed him from the club-house, had somehow spied on his final secret sin.

'I don't seem to know you, your reverence. I don't know your name.'

For a barely perceptible moment the eyelids flickered. It was impossible to see whether underneath the eyelids the eyes were amused or curious or indifferent.

'Introductions are a little embarrassing for me. My own name is rather well known. To give it too readily looks like ostentation.'

'Oh, come on.' The gambler was coy and friendly. 'Don't be shy, your reverence. You know so much about me. In all fairness, tell me who you are.'

The sound of the singers, the hammer of their dancing feet swelled to a deafening fury. The omniscient stranger waited for a lull, and when it came he said evenly, quietly: 'I am God.'

'Fair enough,' said the gambler. Once as a young doctor visiting a poor-house hospital he had been startled by the words of a small old man sitting on a stool by a smouldering fire in a whitewashed ward, interrupting a conversation between the young doctor and a pretty nurse by suddenly shouting: 'I know. I have knowledge from beyond the grave,' then sinking backwards into silence, eyes staring at the smouldering fire. A sad little man in a rough, grey suit who thought he was the Holy Ghost. That was years ago, but the sharp memory fortified him at this surprising moment.

'Fair enough,' he said again, and the attendant carried him another double whisky.

Of course it could all be a practical joke, and carefully he scanned the faces of the twelve men again sitting, searching their faces with lingering eyes for some resemblance to a friend or an acquaintance, even to some one of the six left slumbering in the club-house, the defrauded grocer or the amorous young professor or the man whose factory manufactured, among other things, overcoats. But the twelve faces were strange alien faces, oddly old, sun-tanned, hook-nosed, oriental faces above the conventional dark cloth that western men wore when mourning the dead. Jews, he thought, but then the Jewish faces he knew in the city were fat, sleek faces, and these men had the look of refugees from some far-away place where Jews were poor or peasants or both. Whether he was dealing with a madman possessed of curious mind-reading powers or whether he was the suffering victim of a practical joke, he might as well fall into the humour of the thing. So he said, keeping every twist or movement that might prelude a smile rigorously banished from his face: 'This is an honour. A most unexpected honour.'

'Is it so unexpected? Day after day you go about wondering where I am and what I look like. Well, here I am.'

'I'm very glad to see you. But your sudden appearance here isn't really a complete solution to my wondering. I assume that the you I see is only an appearance — a spirit breathed into a tailor's dummy, even if it's the sort of dummy you'd find in an exclusive shop where clothes are made for dignified and eloquent monsignori.'

'You must take me as you find me. For your sake at

present, this place and these clothes are the most suitable.'

'For my sake? How do you know I ever wanted to find you?'

The white-coated attendant appeared with more drink. The gambler fumbled in his pocket. He said: 'Let me pay for this one. I so seldom have the pleasure.' But the attendant didn't seem to notice his gesture or hear his words. The thirteenth man, dismissing the attendant, went on musically speaking.

'I know, because I've seen you alone in your house at night reading by a dying fire, or washing your hands under a tap, and you'd hear a noise, something creaking in the wind, and your heart would stop a moment, your blood lose a little heat. You'd turn quickly, expecting and fearing to see me, and you'd see only the ordinary things — a chair, a closed door, a cat asleep, a child's toy lying on a rug —'

'There,' said the gambler, 'with all due respects to your omniscience, you're wrong. When I turn at the unexplained and startling sound I don't expect to see you.'

'What do you expect to see?'

'A burglar, a banshee, a ghost out of some tale told to me in my childhood, a man with his head under his arm, or the devil himself — ten feet high, black, smouldering, ugly as — as —'

'Sin or hell or . . . the devil.'

'Oh, I could tell you, your reverence, stories of ghosts, headless horsemen, fairy children, priests returning at midnight to say Mass in dark churches —'

The thirteenth man coughed a little between two sips of the yellow whisky. The twelve mourning men arose again and recommenced their circling dance. He said: 'I'm not as young as I look. I've heard most of those stories. Yet the truth is that when you turn around quickly in the quiet house you expect to see the Unknown.'

'I suppose that's true.'

'With an expectation that is fifty per cent fear. The Unknown! I am the Unknown.'

'Now that I've seen you I'm not so terrified. You may be the avatar, the mask for the Unknown. In fact, since you say so, I'm quite prepared to take your word for it. But to me at the moment you're the living image of a very charming young clergyman. And when you talk about the fear that is part of my expectation, you do leave something out. Fear of the Unknown is fear of the dark. A man gambles to prove to others and to himself, but most of all to himself, that he isn't afraid of the dark. A man is afraid of the dark because he has a guilty heart. Look at me, for instance —'

The thirteenth man did literally look, and with eyes of a disconcertingly bright blue, so that the gambler had to fortify himself with a sip of whisky, rolling it around in his mouth, then swallowing with a gulp that savagely resembled a bite.

'Look at me now.' With an effort he broke the link between those bright eyes and his own. 'I don't look like a man with a criminal record.' He had reached the condition of whisky in which every man falls back on his favourite topic: Adam discovering the road back to Eden, the great salmon returning to the red gravel where its life began, the desire in every soul for the dark original womb. 'But when I read in the paper that a woman has been found knifed in a flat in Soho or that a war hero returned crazy to civilian life has strangled and mutilated a three-year-old girl, then I'm afraid, because I'm the criminal. The police are pursuing me for stabbing the woman, and they will eventually catch me, nothing surer, they'll catch me. Or I've been sentenced and the rope is around my neck for the fearful murder of that beautiful little child. Somewhere, some time, some one of my ancestors stabbed with a knife or crushed with crazy fingers until life ended —'

'There's the story of a man and a woman, a serpent and a tree.'

'But who was the serpent? What fruit grew on the tree when you walked in the garden? And where in each one of us does the memory of the garden end and the memory of the sin begin?'

'For a somewhat similar situation I refer you to the Book of Job. You don't mind if I quote?'

'I suppose it's all right to quote from works inspired by yourself.'

'Well, you remember that after much talk Job admits he's beaten: *I know that thou canst do all things, and no thought is hid from thee. Who is this that hideth counsel without knowledge? Therefore I have spoken unwisely, and things that above measure exceeded my knowledge. Hear, and I will speak: I will ask thee, and do thou tell me. With the hearing of the ear I have heard thee but now my eye seeth thee. Therefore I reprehend myself, and do penance in dust and ashes.'*

'And when poor wailing Job was licked in the argument you felt so good towards him that you blessed his latter end more than his beginning —'

'With fourteen thousand sheep, six thousand camels, a thousand yoke of oxen, a thousand she asses, seven sons, and three daughters called Dies, Cassia, and Cornustibii.'

'That was decent of you. But suppose in my particular case I refused to play ball, refused to admit defeat —'

'You still couldn't stop me from doing what I'm going to do.'

'What are you going to do?'

'Tomorrow I'm going to baptize your third child.'

'You are?' They exchanged a long, hard glance. This time the eyes of the gambler didn't flinch, for he thought, with the blood angrily warming up in his face as if a rash was about to break out on his skin: this daft dialogue has gone on long enough. He remembered his message. He felt in his pocket the money given him by the wife's cousin.

'That was my purpose in being here, visible, and dressed in these clothes. A public house was the most likely place to find you in, and I follow men into all places, even into the poor house of artificial pleasure. And if I appeared at the baptism without clerical clothes it might cause comment. People might wonder.'

'They might indeed.' With a great effort he rose to his feet. The room was slowly circling around. Possibly it was too early in the morning for drink. Or had the whisky been violent with peaty poteen? 'You forget about the brother of the wife's cousin.'

'That will be arranged.' A brilliant blue-eyed smile, a wave of the hand circling as the room was circling, an outburst of singing from the twelve men, slow, deep-voiced singing like the burdened hopeful chant of pilgrims ascending a narrow path to the cold misty summit of a holy mountain. 'That will all be arranged. Everything will be arranged.' The beautiful voice was a bell, clearly and distinctly chiming, welcoming the pilgrims to the shrine in the clouds. The beautiful voice was a golden winged bird circling against the circling of the room, following him down the coloured steep stairway to the street, where in the blinding sunshine pilgrims passed on the way from birth to death, from darkness to darkness, from beginning to ending, coming from the unknown and returning thereto. He had been wasting the morning with a telepathic madman. He had been drinking fire and now in the bright day he was as drunk as an owl.

V

Look at it this way, he told himself.

He went not too steadily along the dazzling pavement. Noon heat struck upwards at his face. Odours divided the air between them: tar melting under the sun, fumes of petrol, different smells of people passing, little radiant typists racing for lunch. He couldn't remember where in hell he'd parked his car. He couldn't make up his mind whether or not to finish his journey to the uncarpeted, book-lined room where the priest who was the brother of the wife's cousin read and worked, prayed and slept. In staggering indecision he passed the brown closed door of the presbytery, passed the open door of the church, saw votive candles glimmering in a dark interior, felt coolness, and quietude like a settled bird.

For look at it this way, he thought, his lips soundlessly moving.

You sit down in a public house for a drink, something you've often done before, something you're perfectly entitled to do according to the laws of the country.

Twelve drunk men in mourning clothes are playing ring-o'-rosy around and around the floor. That is a little surprising, but still I've seen strange dances in public houses: an old woman capering with seven soldiers in a pub in a village in the Usk valley; a young plump woman with a shrieking voice wriggling and gesturing obscenely in a

Montmartre café; a clay-footed peasant, an American sailor, and two yellow-legged girls from the mercenary quays dancing a four-hand reel in a pub in North County Dublin. Yet there is something odd about twelve men dancing because somebody is dead, about their twelve oriental faces.

And who is dead? Nobody told me who is dead? Not even the wise, handsome cleric who knew so much, bought me drinks, set me drunk, told me without moving a muscle on his face that he was God.

What in God's name are you to make out of a handsome cleric, sitting where he shouldn't be, in a singing pub in a shabby street, buying you whisky, telling you your business, calmly asserting that he is God? He may be a lunatic, but he didn't look mad; and I'm a doctor, or I was a doctor, and I should know a madman when I see one. Or more likely he's a joker, but, if he is, he does it very well. Or perhaps he *is* God. For God is all-powerful and could take the appearance of a young cleric sitting in a wine shop if he wanted to, but why should he want to, and why should he speak to me, one of the damned, one of the fools who stake the world on the turn of a card or who stagger drunken in the sunshine when the world is ill lost.

What is he? One of three things? And why and why and why?

His head was whirling. Sunshine reflected from the street sucked around him like the flames of a furnace. The noises of the street increased, diminished, increased, diminished, until all the noises were one noise, an accusing voice, the voice of God shouting from a brazen mountain. The movement on the pavements threatened him like whirling water conquering a drowning man; and desiring to retch, desiring refuge, he cornered, hand on the wall, from the busy street to a shadowy cobbled laneway blocked with parked cars, slow-moving drays, dusty men carrying boxes. Above a narrow door he read the magic word: *Lounge*; and, hand still on the wall, he went along a dark passage, hollow boards echoing under his feet, as if some attracting magnetic force in the dark, deserted little room had drawn him away from the life of the dangerous streets.

This was certainly the most puzzling thing that had ever

happened to him. In the dim lounge with port-hole windows, modelled on a ship's saloon, possibly because the crowded cobbled laneway outside led directly to windy quays and the coming and going of ships, he sank down to a red-cushioned seat, relaxed, tried to give settlement and order to his writhing thoughts. No sound reached him from the street outside or from the bright room somewhere in the same building where men, elbows hooked on counter, drank slowly, talked noisily. He rested in an unearthly calm — the calm of the saloon in a sunken ship, all life gone except his own life wondrously preserved, a half-light filtering down through fathoms of motionless green water; and gradually his disturbed mind rested in indifference or acceptance, seeing the events of the morning as things that happened like sunrise or dew or pain or bushes swaying in the wind. He would understand when he was sober, and since nothing sobered a man like one more drink, he spread on the table before him some money that had lived for a while in the wife's cousin's handbag, and, reaching around over his shoulder, he found the bell-push. He pressed three times and heard deep in the bowels of the building the bell ring three times, three single notes, solemn as the tolling in the steeple when a coffin is carried from the altar to the grave.

A door opened in the corner behind him. A man came in briskly but no light came in. He stood in the middle of the room, looked flickeringly about him for a place to sit. Eyes focused to the shadows, the gambler saw a stout, red-faced man, middle age, middle height, wrapped in good brown tweeds that made his body look stouter and his face more rosy, wearing a loud check cap with the peak at a merry angle above his dark dancing eyes, carrying a huge black briefcase. A bookie? A commercial traveller? Or just one of those wonderful men who, hiding mystery behind merriment, sit all morning making valuable contacts over cigarettes and coffee in the public lounges of good hotels?

He saw something, said 'Ah! here we are', leaned over the gambler's shoulder, thumbed the bell-push. Fathoms deeper down, the bell boomed, a knell for sunken ships. Nobody answered. Nothing happened. He lowered the black briefcase to the red-cushioned seat, sat down facing the gambler across the table. He said: 'The service is lousy.'

'So I notice.'

'Passed through the public bar on the way in. Full to the door. Only one man behind the counter. Dead-drunk. Customers helping themselves.'

'Is that so?'

'Never saw anything like it. Drunk behind the bar is bad news.'

'Bad for business.'

'We could go out and help ourselves too. But, on principle, I wouldn't do it. Like to have things regular.'

'I'm not too particular myself. I feel I've had enough to do me for this morning.'

'Feeling down and out?'

'No. But I do feel a little drowsy. I had some whisky and then I was walking in the hot sun.'

'Nothing wakens you up like another whisky.' Once again he reached over the gambler's shoulder to the bell-push. 'One on me. Do. Have one on me. To make you laugh.' The bell tolled. Nothing happened. Nobody answered.

The man leaned sideways, knowingly twisted his mouth, whispered confidentially. The movement was the one that preluded the making of an important contact: silk stockings, watches, cigarette lighters, or contraceptives. But the whispered words were as shattering in the dim silence as a blast from ninety bugles: 'A little bird told me you were talking to the boss.'

The room rocked. A storm screamed over the wide waters and down deep in the guts of the sea the dead ship trembled, salt green walls quivered like jelly. The gambler moved away a little from the confidential stranger. He said: 'What the blazes do you mean?'

'No offence. Only somebody told me you were talking to the boss.'

'Who told you?' If this was a joke it was a most elaborate one. Somebody was going to a great deal of trouble to make sure it was a success. Somebody? That strong woman exacting vengeance for a slighted love and a shameful kiss? Or those six club-house sods exacting vengeance for debts unpaid? He repeated roughly: 'Who told you?'

'A dark horse. We'll mention no names. But he keeps trying to listen in when the boss is having a conversation.'

'Who are you?'

'Must I tell you?' The voice was coy, affectedly modest. Stubby, short-fingered hands, marked with two rings of solid gold, were taking a cheroot from a small scarlet case, offering the case to the gambler. 'I'm not much, really. I don't set anything moving. I come in at the end and buy up anything that's left.' The gambler, with a feeling that was half indignation and half horror, spurned the offered cheroot. 'To be quite honest, I'm a contact man. Can put you in touch with the boss. Or in touch with the dark horse. We'll mention no names.'

The gambler's black brows came together in one hard line and his jaws stiffened with anger. 'You'll mention your own name. I want to hear it. Just for fun.' From the lane outside a wandering wasp had found its way into the forgotten lounge and now hovered buzzing over the empty table.

'Okay so. If you feel like that. But you won't believe me. Nobody ever believes me.' He reached again for the bell-push, and once again vainly; nobody heeding, nothing happening, the distant bell tolled. He gestured with one short, red hand, a golden ring suddenly flashing in the shadows, then fumbled for a match to light his cheroot; and the lost wasp ceased buzzing, dropped silently to the desolate drinkless table, and lay motionless. 'I am Death,' he said.

A man could only laugh. A red face, warm tweeds, shrieking check cap, red, short-fingered hands, made more vulgar by two gold rings, a smoking cheroot. And when the first gale of laughter had passed a man could only make the inevitable pun: 'You'll be the death of me.'

'I will. Some day. You bet.'

'But you look and act so cheerful.' The second gale of laughter, an attempt to hide that bad-mannered laughter by turning again to the bell-push. Nobody answered. Nobody came.

'You mean I look so funny.'

'Well, if you put it that way —'

'Can't say I didn't tell you. Knew you wouldn't believe me. Nobody ever does.'

'Let's get this straight.' He would enter into the spirit of the thing. Getting angry would do no good. Somewhere, some time, the truth behind it all would be revealed to him. 'I always thought that Death would be a thin fellow, lean in the face and hollow in the jaw, a little like myself, in fact. Dark-haired. Cadaverous. That's what a cadaver is, isn't it? A body overtaken by death.'

Crisp lips around the cheroot parted in a smile, showing expensive false teeth. 'I do the overtaking. I'm Death. I don't die.'

'I think my opinion has been held by men since Cain killed Abel. Where were you then?'

'Around.'

'I find you, if you'll excuse me saying so, a fat little turf accountant of a man with a red case full of bad cheroots.'

'Why not?' False teeth gripping the cheroot left the stubby little hands free to smooth a paunch round as a football, to display with lingering deliberate pride a hideously yellow waistcoat. 'Amn't I the best fed man alive? Listen to this, for instance. This happened only yesterday. Over in America too. But, then, I move around a fair share.'

He swung the heavy, black briefcase up to the table, unloosened straps, snapped the catch, pulled out an untidy pile of papers, books, newspaper clippings. Two hard, white objects rolled from the table and dropped to the floor, and the gambler, groping in the darkness, found them, to his horror — two jagged fragments of human bones. 'Thanks,' the contact man said. 'I'd be sorry to lose those. Keepsakes.' Selecting a newspaper clipping from the untidy pile, he read: 'A twenty-eight-year-old ex-soldier killed twelve people and wounded five others when he ran berserk on a busy street in Camden, New Jersey. After forty-five minutes, police, using tear-gas bombs, captured him, and three hours later it was discovered that he had been wounded in his duel with the police. The shooting began early yesterday when the soldier, brandishing a gun, went into a chemist's shop on the street floor of the house. Screaming: 'It's a maniac. He's got a gun,' the chemist's wife dashed upstairs and locked her twelve-year-old son in a wardrobe. She was killed instantly by a bullet which hit her as she came downstairs. The chemist was shot as he tried to escape through a back door, and after wounding the chemist's mother as she lay in bed, the gunman went into a barber's shop and killed the proprietor. His next victims were the proprietors of shoe repair and dry-cleaning shops, and a young bride doing her shopping.'

The contact man paused for breath, wiped his lips. The flush on his face had deepened, dark eyes shone; he was a man remembering passion. He said: 'A nice touch, that. The bit about the bride. Real classy.'

'Virtuosity,' said the gambler, measuring with a subtle eye the distance through the shadows to the door. He was, or had been, a doctor, and he knew a madman when he saw one.

'That's the word. I'm proud of that touch.'

'You?'

'I was around, you know. In that street. Could describe it to you. Ever been in New Jersey?'

'Not yet.'

'Not a bad place. For myself or for the boss. But here. May I read on.' He read: 'The soldier went back to his room where he kept an arsenal of knives, clubs, and ammunition. After barring the door he went to the window and started shooting at people in the street. Among those he killed were a five- and a six-year-old boy and two men. One of the victims was a two-year-old boy who was having his hair cut in the barber's shop as he sat astride a hobby horse. Other victims of the shooting included drivers of motor-cars who had halted for traffic lights.'

He read briskly, his lips curiously jerking like the lips of a puppet, and the reading ended in dry, staccato laughter moving away slantwise towards the low, dark ceiling. The lips and the laughter had their own gift of dusty mechanical life. 'Eyes on the red light,' he said. 'Red for danger. Never knew what hit them.' The dry laughter went on, an almost visible, independent presence, until it became unnerving, and the gambler spoke merely for the sake of interrupting: 'That was great fun for everybody. But it only proves to me that you read the papers with a certain perverted appreciation.'

'You still don't believe me. Ah, well! You don't have to. Not for the present.' The bell-push, again pressed, provoked one hollow boom from some unseen, unheeding place. 'But, believe it or not, that sort of thing goes on all the time. Millions every day. Not to mention wars. I'm run off my feet.'

'Now wait a minute. I know all about that.' The gambler with an effort conquered a feeling of revulsion, a whisper of fear, a stir of anger at this preposterous joke. The life of the whisky still seethed in his head. He would be calm. He would be cool. He would cross-examine methodically this vulgar little japer, or this horrible little lunatic. 'I am, or I was, a doctor. I've seen you often at work. In the houses of the poor. In rich houses, street accidents, convents, slums, parochial houses, lunatic asylums, lock hospitals. The impression I got was that you always dressed in black. Like my own suit. A serious black, and never in bright colours. Mourners wear black. And here you are: tweeds and a yellow waistcoat and, merciful God, that cap.'

'A dying man doesn't look ahead into the dark. He casts his long, lingering look behind at the coloured things he's leaving. And in among the colour he sees me. Of course I'm ahead there in the dark as well. Waiting for him. I do keep moving around. That's a cute idea, isn't it?' He waited for appreciation. 'Occurred to me once when reading Pirandello. I read a great deal. Lots of time. All sorts of stuff. Not as ignorant as I look.'

'We'll never get a drink here,' said the gambler.

'Move out and help ourselves? Only thing for it.' He bundled books and papers tidily together. 'Talking of selves reminds me of the doctrine of the antithetical self. Listen to this.' He opened a large green book and read: 'I see always this one thing, that in practical life the mask is more than the face.'

'So the tweeds and the cap and the yellow waistcoat are only an outward show.'

'So are your own clothes. My advantage over you is that I have staying power and a choice of shapes. What would you like me to look like? A smart guy with a black jack in his pocket? A Government minister, a policeman, an executioner, a painted whore with disease and madness in her caress?'

'You're eloquent.'

'Most men die because of other men or women. People

kill each other all the time and no court could ever call it murder. I get all the blame, but I'm not really a bad type. I told you I come in at the end and collect the leavings. I don't make crazy idiots or dirty politicians send the people to war. I didn't ask that ex-soldier to run wild with a gun. People want to kill each other and I'm at their beck and call. Told you I'm run off my feet. No rest day or night since that Cain and Abel business, one wanting to kill and one asking to be killed. People want to live and die all at the same time. They even expect me to make up their minds for them. Look at yourself, for instance.'

The red face with the fervour of conviction, the panting expression of injured feeling, shone like a sunset. If he was one in the involved conspiracy of a practical joke, then he or somebody had given great thought to the part he was to play. If he was a maniac, then he could have his amusing moments. 'What about myself?' asked the gambler.

'This morning you were thinking of suicide, of rushing to meet me before I came looking for you. Taking me unawares. Piling work on me that I wasn't expecting. Was that considerate?'

Once again the room quivered. The shock of a storm passed, almost unheard and unseen, over the surface of the salt, unfathomable ocean in which all men were drowned. Another telepathic madman? Two in one sunny forenoon? Merciful Christ, this was beyond a joke, should be stopped immediately, was as obscene as an exhibition of mass hypnotism. He opened his mouth to speak, then closed it again, gestured into silence by the golden flash of a ring on one pudgy hand. 'Let me speak now. By your leave, let me speak.' Two pudgy hands shuffled among the newspaper clippings. 'I want to tell you something about suicide. To make a point. To give you an idea of the sort of job I'm up against, the sort of people I have to deal with.' One pudgy hand isolated one yellow-with-age clipping. 'Ah! here we are.' He read: 'Out of every one thousand infants born in the United States of America ten males and three females end their lives by their own hands. Fifty per cent of them do so when they are over forty-five years old. Experts say that statistics show that the motives for suicide include mainly age, weariness, disillusion, helplessness, loss of emotional outlets, business reversals. The rate of suicides is high among men and women of high standing in business or social life, or of intellectual or professional eminence who are labouring under nervous pressure.' Reading made his small, smart mouth moist. With a quick sweeping gesture he wiped his lips with a black silk handkerchief, shaking the folds of it open to display, with an ease that smelt of a carefully rehearsed stunt, a ghastly skeleton design stitched in white phosphorescent thread. He said: 'Why in the name of the dark horse would you wish to get yourself mixed up with people like that? Can't you take your ease and wait until I come looking for you?'

'My practice is gone. My reputation is gone. My friends, for what they are worth, are my friends no longer.' He stopped abruptly, a little amazed, a little angry with himself that he should be answering this little bookie's questions as if they really mattered. Then he added: 'I come home like a beaten cur, tail between legs.' It didn't matter what he said to this man, madman or joker.

'Then you kiss your wife's cousin and think you're a demon.' The shadows in the low-ceilinged room were sinister with crouching mysterious knowledge. If that woman had betrayed him she was the greatest bitch on two feet. But then, why should he be annoyed at betrayal, since he was himself a betrayer, one of the lost, one of the damned. 'You think you're a demon because you've destroyed a childish memory, a thing as fragile as a lollipop on a stick. Easy seeing you've never met a real demon, not to speak of the dark horse himself. Nasty people, even the least of them, let me tell you. I do jobs for them under orders from the boss, but I might as well say I don't like them. Always regret when I have to put anybody in touch with them.'

He took carefully from the pile on the table a thick red book. 'Now you think you've suffered this morning. But here, listen to this.' He shuffled the thin, closely printed pages, his lips moving like the lips of an old person who could read only with difficulty. He said: 'I like this particular writer. Long-winded, of course, but at moments he understood me very well. Or at least he understood what a fellow feels like when he's depressed. Have you read him?'

The gambler nodded. In sombre black lettering on the red spine he could read the words: *Crime and Punishment*.

'Then you'll remember this passage. I have a fair memory myself. But at times, between ourselves, it gets overstrained. You remember Marmeladov. A drunk. Loses his job. Daughter is a legalized prostitute. Gets his job again, goes blind drunk the very first day, crawls back later to beg his wife's forgiveness. Back to their slum room. He's stinking dirty, tattered, half-drunk. Listen to this.' He read, holding the book high, his arm rigid, his dark, squinty, crafty little eyes protruding and intent: 'A strange wife for Marmeladov. She had not heard them and did not notice them coming in. She seemed to be lost in thought, hearing and seeing nothing. The room was close, but she had not opened the window. A stench rose from the staircase, but the door on to the stairs was not closed.'

'A poor place to live,' said the gambler. He saw the white concrete of suburban roads, neat green gardens, red roofs, bright curtains, neat cases of harmless books in conventional sitting-rooms. He heard, laughing like flying snipe or chattering like concealed corncrakes, the small, merry, mowing machines mastering smooth lawns. It was all lost and far away and swiftly receding, suddenly and inexplicably desirable as the green land from which the water sweeps away the struggling, screaming, drowning man. Sour with nauseous sorrow, he listened to the reading: 'The youngest child, a girl of six, was asleep, sitting curled up on the floor with her head on the sofa. A boy a year older stood crying and shaking in the corner, probably he had just had a beating. Beside him stood a girl of nine years old, tall and thin, wearing a thin and ragged chemise with an ancient cashmere pelisse flung over her bare shoulders, long outgrown and barely reaching her knees. Her arm, as thin as a stick, was round her brother's neck.'

Through the half-open door of the garage he saw two children solemnly playing at houses, marking on the floor with empty petrol tins and blocks of wood the patterns of fairyland homes: two small, delicately featured children with dark curling hair, a boy in a sailor suit, a girl in a blue dress; and he was lonely for chirruping voices and little hands as far away now as flowers from the screams of the damned. This jackanapes with a black bag stuffed with books and bones was deliberately breaking him down, reading of horrors until the gambler's heart would squelch with sorrow for his own disgrace and ill-luck and poverty. So he tried not to listen to the pert little voice, but out of his own limited reading that terrible scene of man's degradation had stuck like the crabs in his memory, and he could see the wife of Marmeladov rush to assault her worthless husband; could feel the frenzy, hear the screams, see the woman gripping the man by the hair and dragging him around the room, and Marmeladov crawling after her, loving the blows, adding to them by striking his forehead against the floor, crying out that his punishment left him honoured and consoled.

'... shaken to and fro by his hair and even once striking the ground with his forehead. The child asleep on the floor woke up, and began to cry. The boy in the corner, losing all control, began trembling and screaming and rushed to his sister in violent terror, almost in a fit. The eldest girl was shaking like a leaf —'

The contact man abruptly stopped reading, closed the book, and restored it to the pile on the table, then took from his breast pocket a pair of smoked spectacles rimmed with tortoise-shell. He fitted them carefully to his eyes. He said: 'I find the sun sore on my eyes.' The shadows crouching in the cabin of a room were increasingly sinister, tangibly cold.

'I know what you're thinking,' said the contact man. 'That you're not such a cur as poor Marmeladov. That your wife isn't a virago. That your kids aren't starving, yet.'

'Wouldn't anybody think that?'

'Oh, don't take me up wrongly. I'm not blaming you. That's what I want you to think.'

'Why?'

'Because I want you to live. At least until your time comes. Not to do anything precipitate. Not to think that no man in the world was ever in a worse fix. For quite selfish reasons I don't want you to upset my schedule. But there's more to it than that. In other words, I've my orders.'

With a care and deliberate method that seemed curiously away from the character expressing itself in corpulent tweed and loud check, he was stuffing books and papers back into the black bag.

'You see,' he said, 'there isn't any need to rush to meet me. I'm with you most of the time. People walk hurriedly, trying to leave me behind. But for all they know they may all the time be rushing to meet me. You don't normally notice me. But I'm with you every time you cross a street or run down a stairway —'

'Now that you're visible I can keep my eye on you.'

From the quiet, shadowy room the gambler led the way out to the bright, noisy bar, coloured bottles and glittering chromium, customers helping themselves to drink, brown porter and green liqueur, occasionally dropping money into the open cash register. Dressed in blue shirt and long white apron, spread flat along the counter like a body on a sacrificial slab, was the sleeping, drunken barman.

'Keep your eye on me if you like,' said the contact man. For himself and the gambler he poured two stiff whiskies. Drinkers pressed around them, singing voices, popping of corks, occasionally the splintering crash of glass falling to the floor; bedlam. 'But you can't stop me from doing what I'm going to do.'

'I know. I know. I suppose you're also going to baptize my child?'

'No. Not exactly. I'm to be godfather.'

'Decent of you.'

'Don't thank me. It has all been arranged.' He raised the glass towards his red face and greedily sipped. 'It has all been arranged,' he said again. With one gulp the gambler emptied his glass. Bedlam closed in on him and went whirling around him, excited faces and raised glasses, circling like the dance of the twelve mourning men, around and around, his mind circling into darkness as if he had been drugged with ether; and booming regularly over bedlam the voice of the contact man said again and again: 'Arranged. Arranged. Arranged.'

VI

The booming voice eased gradually into silence. After bedlam and the circling whirling movement there was a vast motionless quiet, made more quiet by a faint monotonous humming like the sound of smooth engines working in a subterranean power-house and heard by men moving on the surface of the earth. Then, faintly at first, later a little louder, but all the time hesitating and faltering, the sound of the steps of one man moving came out of the silence. The steps shuffled slowly over rough cobbles. Once in a while the body swayed and groping hands touched cold, windowless, doorless walls. When the wind from the restless harbour blew suddenly about his face he awoke completely, knew the faltering shuffling feet were his own feet, that he was alone, that chill, empty night was over the city.

He turned his back on the ships and the open harbour. He went painfully westwards along the quays towards the brighter lights and the centre of the known city. The known and the unknown, he thought; and the things that had happened and the words spoken before bedlam and the triumph of darkness came back to him instantly. He stopped, leaning against one of the iron pillars of an overhead railway bridge, tried, until his head ached, to give order and reason to those words and happenings. The effort only brought him confusion, followed by a mental numbness in which he was conscious only of iron and stone, behind him the wind blowing from unknown oceans. So when he heard regular, heavy steps on the cobbles and saw thirty yards away a helmeted policeman, he left the refuge of the iron pillar, walked on steadily although his head was seething like a boiling pot, past the policeman, an occasional straggler, a line of high green buses parked in silence and waiting for the morning; past a newspaper office noisy with life and shining with light, windows crowded with photographs of weddings, football matches, pilgrimages, ploughing competitions, annual dances. Then, crossing a bridge, he was in the wide street that was the centre of the city. Statues on high pedestals, bright lights burning pitilessly for the benefit of the few waifs who never go home, vastness and emptiness, the known become the unknown, a clock striking four and not a taxi to be seen.

He recrossed the bridge and went towards the south. The streets here were windless and a mizzling rain was falling. Even Marmeladov, utterly ruined and conscious of sin, turned his face towards home. Once he hailed a moving taxi, but, crowded already with shadowy, shouting people, it went on, leaving him waving his right arm, angry and foolish. After that he walked doggedly, clenching his teeth, his feet lifeless and heavy. Once he leaned on a canal bridge, his forehead to the coarse cold stone while a fit of nausea crept down his limbs, leaving him shivering and perspiring.

Beyond the canal bridge a car overtook him, hooted twice, then pulled up beside him. The taxi returning, he thought, but it wasn't the taxi. It was a small green car, his own car — or the grocer's, with a woman driving, and when she opened the door he dropped automatically into the seat beside her, sat silent for five minutes while she drove southwards along skiddy streets glittering with rain.

'Thanks for the lift,' he said.

'It's a great pleasure.' He lighted two cigarettes, passed one to her through the circle of the steering-wheel. She said: 'I suppose there's no need to ask where you were?'

'Not much. Unless you can't recognize whisky smell.'

'I rang his reverence. He's laid up with a cold. He said some clerical friend of yours had rung up to say that all had been arranged about the baptism.'

He accepted the information with complete calm. He said: 'That's correct.' He was like a secret agent sent through Balkan cities with only partial information — a clue, a hint, as to the real purpose of his mission.

'I never knew you had a clerical friend.'

'I have friends in the highest places,' he said drowsily, and his eyes closed and he half-slept, leaning sideways towards her strong left shoulder. She sat erect, her eyes steadily fixed on wet asphalt. Once, the car jolting over a bridge, he sat up stiffly, gripped her arm, said: 'Am I dead? Are you dead? I killed you with a kiss the way Judas betrayed Christ.'

She shook her arm free. 'Stop raving,' she said, and then she closed her mouth firmly and gripped the wheel more tightly.

'Not raving. Not raving.' Then from the black pit of his memory a fragment of verse came up, and again slowly slipping sideways, he mumbled:

Death takes but little, yea, your death has given
Me that deep peace, and that secure possession
Which man may never find in earthly passion.

Trying to repeat the lines, trying to emphasize their meaning, suddenly lucid to his staggering brain, he fell asleep, and, his head on the strong shoulder of the wife's cousin, the gambler again came home.

First Interlude

'I am,' says the gambler, 'but how do you know where I am going or what is my business?'

'I am God,' said the stranger. 'Turn back and I will baptize your child.'

'I will not turn back,' said the gambler. 'If you're God you're not giving me a fair deal. When my neighbours are getting on in the world I'm going backwards, and on that account you'll have nothing to do with my child.'

He walked on, and it wasn't long until he saw another stranger drawing towards him. It was a big, long skeleton of a man, black-headed, with a sallow skin and a face like a corpse, just skin and bones. The gambler thought: 'There's little resemblance between yourself and God.' They saluted each other.

'You're going for the priest to baptize your child,' says the stranger.

'I am,' says the gambler. 'But I'd like to find out how you know where I'm going.'

'I am Death,' says the stranger. 'No person can come to the world or leave the world without my knowing. God met you before I met you and He offered to baptize your child. You should have accepted His offer. Turn back now and I'll be godfather to your child.'

The gambler and Death turned back until they came to the place where God was waiting for them. The three went to the gambler's house and God baptized the child and Death stood sponsor. Then God went away.

TWO

I

Priest: What do you ask of the Church of God?
Sponsor: Faith.
Priest: Of what does faith assure you?
Sponsor: Life everlasting.

The central church of all the churches in a city where they were as plentiful as cinemas was a small cathedral in a ragged, smelly street. No spires soared above it. It crouched, grey stone stained with the drifting of smoke, close to the ground, dwarfed by the red and brown brick walls of the high uneven houses where poor people lived. Within, it was congested with pillars and cumbersome inartistic statues to dead ecclesiastics; and the poor people escaping from the odours of the red and brown houses came there to pray, craning their necks to catch between the pillars a glimpse of the altar and the ancient ceremony of sacrifice. Among the poor people there were always wealthy people venturing into the lanes from the wide, bright street one hundred yards away. Occasionally there were foreign visitors from the great hotels.

Priest (making the sign of the cross over the infant to be baptized): Receive the sign of the cross both upon thy forehead and also upon thy heart; take unto thee the faith of the heavenly precepts, and in thy conduct be such that you may now be the temple of God.

The other churches of the city and the country revolved in concentric circles around that crowded, crouching cathedral. The first circle included on its circumference an italianate church with lavishly ornamented altar where ignatian men dealt cannily with the stories of troubled sinners, a romanesque church where white sons of Dominick preached resoundingly, a neo-Gothic church where crowds gathered to pray every Monday evening for nine successive Mondays, a convent chapel where the poor, twisting, grimacing oddities, always to be seen in the streets yet inhabiting their own exclusive world, gathered together every afternoon for benediction of the Blessed Sacrament; a church on the quays where greasy dockers slipped in for an occasional prayer; a church in a fashionable street where well-dressed women rested silky knees on kneeling-boards softened with green baize. That was the first circle, noisy all day with the business of the city.

Priest: I exorcise thee, unclean spirit, in the Name of the Father and of the Son and of the Holy Ghost, to go out and depart from this servant of God; for He commands thee, accursed one, who walked on foot upon the sea, and stretched out His right hand to Peter when sinking.

The second circle marked the fringes of the city: little churches of grey stone, fresh with good air blown in from neighbouring fields, churches of corrugated iron on sandy places by the sea, neat churches ringed by trees and overlooked by lonely uninhabited hills. At a spot on that second circle the gambler walked slowly along a concrete path, his back to the suburb hidden around the last curve of the road, his face to his parish church. Morning sunshine brightened grey stone. A lively wind played with the taller grasses around the ancient graves; played with the hem of the garment of the wife's cousin walking ahead of him and carrying in her arms his unchristened child. His eyes wavered between her ankles and flapping skirt, and the diminutive spire against the blue sky, and the tall autumnal trees. He walked behind her through the porch. The air smelt faintly of must. At the public font he dipped his fingers in the holy water, marked her high white forehead with the sign of the cross. Over the bundle of white shawls, containing as a pod holds a seed, the unchristened, devil-possessed child, she smiled at him, all anger washed away by the sacred water, the mark of his evil kiss gone from her lips. A hat rested uneasily on her springy dark hair. He walked behind her up a narrow echoing aisle, past the weeping women of Jerusalem, Veronica with her sacred, merciful towel, Simon of Cyrene, the afflicted mother, the judgement of jesting

Pilate. He had forgotten to mark his brow with the sacred water, so, hurriedly crossing himself, his head still confused with delirious memories of the previous day, he prayed without words that somebody would be there to baptize the child and somebody to stand sponsor, some credible, encouraging shapes, no brazen, handsome angels, or black, bull-headed, fire-breathing men.

She whispered over her shoulder: 'I wonder have your friends arrived yet.' He wondered too.

He walked behind her past a confessional, little angels cut in brown wood, heavy red curtains for secrecy, then through a gold-washed gate set in marble railings, into the little chapel where the baptismal font was. His friends were there and waiting.

Priest: Ephphetha, that is to say, Be opened for a savour of sweetness. *(With his saliva he moistens his thumb and touches the ears and nostrils of the child.)* But thou, Satan, begone; behold the judgement of God shall draw near.

The first thing he noticed was the contact man's solemn black briefcase resting on the mosaic floor beside the marble font. The contact man stood modestly in the corner behind the font and wore, for this special occasion, a shabby, dark lounge suit, sleeves a little too short, trousers frayed at the ends, cracked shoes radiant with rhythmical polishing. His hands were joined, fingers locked cradlewise, his eyes modestly cast on the ground, and without his check cap he was revealed as almost bald, a few dark hairs sleeked in parallel lines across the baldness, a pimple on the apex of his pointy forehead. A black-gowned verger fussed around the font. Through a high semicircular unstained window the gambler saw green and brown branches irrelevantly waving, flying like birds, the children of no earth-bound tree.

Priest: Do you renounce Satan?
Sponsor: I renounce him.
Priest: And all his works?
Sponsor: I renounce them.
Priest: And all his pomps?

Sponsor: I renounce them.

After that the father of the child was as irrelevant as the flying branches. He was only ears that listened, eyes that saw: the strong Latin words, drip of salt sacred water into the font, the sudden cry of the child at the taste of salt on the tongue, the voices of the wife's cousin and the contact man answering the responses, the tall golden-haired man magnificent in a white linen surplice, the verger's shuffling feet, and, later, the scraping of a cracked hirsute pen on the register in the sacristy.

Priest: I baptize thee in the Name of the Father and of the Son and of the Holy Ghost.

When he had written in the book, the priest turned away from the gambler, slowly began to divest himself of his snow-white surplice. Along a narrow passage that led from the sacristy door to a furnace room at the back of the building the gambler sought the verger, found him, slipped the expected silver into his crooked hand. Then he walked back quickly to the sacristy. The priest was gone.

II

Outside on the pavement the contact man, carrying his black bag, wearing a bowler hat, walked up and down, neat, quick steps in shiny shoes. The gambler's green car was parked at the kerb. The woman and the child were gone. There was no sign of the priest.

'She went on home at once,' he said. 'She said she didn't want the child to get its death in the cold wind.'

The wind came down viciously from the brown, empty mountains, sending a few dead leaves scraping along the dry pavement, threatening the lives of the green leaves still perilously attached to the branches. The gambler shivered. The hot sun of yesterday had been summer's last demonstration. He said: 'It is a cold wind. There's winter in it.' He sat into the driver's seat, unlocked and opened the door nearest the pavement. A pony pulling a cart, with a brown-coated man standing on his heels in the middle of metal cases of jingling empty milk bottles, came round the corner from the suburb and trotted off between swaying hedges.

'Can I leave you anywhere?'

'You could at least buy me a drink. After all, I'm the godfather.'

'I didn't invite you.' The cold wind, the ceremony, salt on the child's tongue, the white robe of innocence, the burning candle of faith, his own irrelevance — the irrelevance of the flesh, had set him shuddering with shingles of irritability.

'I didn't invite myself. I was acting under orders.' He drew back a step from the open door of the car. 'But I won't go where I'm not wanted. Not yet.'

'Sorry,' said the gambler. 'No offence meant.'

'No offence taken.' A pudgy, short-fingered hand waved the matter down the wind and two broad gold rings for a second attracted the sunlight. 'These little events are always a strain on the nerves of the half-domesticated man.' He stamped his feet as if inside the cracked shiny shoes his toes were frozen cold. 'By the way, you wouldn't mind a word of advice. A tip from the stable.'

'I'm always ready for a tip.'

'You shouldn't have let him walk off like that. At least a lift. Or maybe lunch. You won't often have the chance.'

'I meant to. But he went off so quickly.'

'That's the way he comes and goes. Have to keep your eyes on him. It's a pity, all the same. Be nice to him and he'll be nice to you.'

'Which way did he go?' The engine of the car hummed musically. Whoever or whatever the golden-haired man was, he was a clergyman and he had baptized the child.

'That way.' A pudgy, beringed hand pointed at the road narrowing between swaying hedges. 'Away from the city and towards the hills.'

'Had he a car?' If he was not the victim of madmen or jokers, the golden-haired man might have somewhere on the brown hills a flaming, flying chariot.

'When I saw him he was on foot.'

'Hop in,' said the gambler.

Like a swift green bird the little car hummed away from the suburb and the city. The wind blew sideways. The high unkempt hedges swayed backwards and forwards. Tall trees groaned and here and there a leaf crackled and turned brown. The contact man whistled a slow tune, slow military steps, four sad pipes wailing before a coffin, the lament for the flowers of the forest; and on his tight-trousered plump knees he nursed his black briefcase. He said: 'If you get a chance, ask him for something. He has plenty and you're up against it.'

'I'm not good at asking.'

'Don't be a fool. Ask all the same. This is an exceptional occasion.' He whistled a few more bars, sad pipers droned desolation around an open grave. He said: 'I like that tune. Goes right to my heart.' They passed a clean factory perched on a hill above a mountain stream. They passed a whitewashed school and heard above the hum of the engine the chant of children learning their prayers. 'There's no written law about it. But I think that on an occasion like this you're entitled to three special requests. If you like, I'll remind the boss. Discreetly.'

'You take a great interest in my affairs.'

'Pure camaraderie. Honestly. Not business. Not yet. I take an interest in lots of things. Books. People I like the look of. Lifts my mind from the old humdrum.'

They slowly turned a corner, the engine roaring in low gear; passed the last trees, saw above them stunted bushes fading into billows of brown heather, the long, empty curves of the white road.

'No sight or sign of him there,' said the gambler. 'He must have wings.'

'He's around somewhere.'

'He couldn't have walked as quickly as all that.'

'He's a fast mover. Still, I think I can guess where he is.'

So very much against his better judgement, the gambler drove his green car up the long desolate mountain road. The surface roughened and set the car bumping. The wind sprang sideways out of the heather, wrestled with the car, tried to drag it sideways again into the heather and down the steep shoulder of a hill to a deep valley where great trees grew around a diamond-shaped lake. Sheltering down among those trees the wind crouched and gnawed the crackling branches. The triumphant machine driven by the gambler went up and up in spite of rough road and wind. He was alone on a mountain with an odd little man, obviously mad, but possessing the power to give to his wildest words a dangerous, lulling credibility. One eye on the road ahead and the mountain above, he kept the other on the contact man.

'Great air in the mountains,' the contact man said, screwing the window open a bare quarter of an inch. Lips to the narrow opening, the wind puffed into their faces the smell of autumn heather, sullen black peat, green and brown fish in cold lakes. 'Very healthy,' said the gambler, and the contact man drew a deep breath and said: 'Nothing like it for the lungs.'

On a high stone viaduct the road leaped across a great gash in the buttocks of the mountain. Far below, a brown stream went restlessly on a bed of irregular grey rocks; and once across the viaduct, the road, sloping gently down to fall in some unseen place among flat midland fields, went on along the round sides of the range of mountains. But another narrower road turned sharply to the left, went climbing up a deep, dark glen: pot-holes and loose stones and the car rocking helplessly; long rushes leaning over the diminishing stream; the stream itself playing with the road, running beside it, darting under it, bursting across it. Beyond the stream furze grew densely. Above the furze dark, straight pine-trees stood in thousands.

'You could park here. This should be the place.' A path left the road, crossed the stream, cut through the furze, vanished upwards into the pines.

'Could I? Should it?' The gambler for a moment tightened his grip on the steering-wheel. Was this at last the meaning of yesterday's fantasy and today's sacrament: conspiracy between two telepathic madmen, a murder on the mountains, a dead body between the dark, heedless pines? But why? Not money. He couldn't lose money. He couldn't lose reputation. He could lose only life and find in this lonely place the true meaning and appearance of death; and in spite of yesterday's glorying in damnation and final ruin, the tightening of his grip on the wheel, the quick stooping gesture with which he scooped a heavy spanner from the floor of the car to the pocket of his overcoat, was the common gesture in which every man shows the desire for colour, warmth, movement, his horror before endless night.

The contact man, disdaining the diminutive bridge fashioned crudely from limestone slabs and softened with green sods, had leaped lightly across the stream. His cracked shiny shoes looked absurdly inadequate against furze and pines and mountain paths. He had not seen the gambler arming himself with the spanner, but he knows, thought the gambler, he knows; and silently he followed the other man up through the furze. He knows, and somewhere on this mountain the golden-haired priest knows, that for one moment, stepping out of the green car, I was afraid of them the way I'd fear ordinary criminals. They may not be real at all. They may not exist except in my mind, and this mountain may be a cloud in a dream that began in a drunken club-house, and all mountains may be clouds in dreams, and pines and furze have roots nowhere except in man's soul. His left hand on his forehead, almost as if he could feel bewildered thoughts feebly fluttering, he followed his leader through pricking furze into the shadow of the pines. Hidden in his pocket, his right hand still clutched the spanner.

Between the trees the wind was quiet; their feet were quiet on the brown, fallen needles. The path faded and they climbed blindly upwards, pulling along from tree to tree against the steep slope. One final strong pull, one breathless scramble and, free of the trees, they were out in sun and roaring icy wind. The heather was as high as their bellies. Holding aloft his black briefcase, the contact man waded through the heather. Close on his steps the gambler followed, eyes actively searching for a trap, a pit, a marsh, or a man hiding. When the contact man said: 'There he is,' the gambler was startled into one sudden shout, almost startled into pulling from his pocket the heavy spanner. They were out of the heather and standing on the edge of a circle of vividly green grass. The centre of the circle was a mound of grey stones, carried to that summit in some lost age to build a burial place or a temple to sun and wind.

'He likes altitude,' said the contact man. He called across to the man sitting on the sheltered sunny side of the ancient stones. The grey pile might have been a throne. His head was in the wind. Golden hair blew long and wild, catching the sunlight. High behind the stones a mountain ash grew, alone, feeding on the body of the mountain, abnormally tall but warped by wild weather. They went slowly, conscious for the first time of fatigue, across the grass. He watched them approaching. He said nothing. He didn't move. The palms of his hands were flat on his knees. He might have been part of the mountain.

'You went away too soon,' said the gambler.

'I like walking. On mountains in the morning and in gardens in the evening.'

'You made good speed too.'

'I got a lift.'

Below them heathery mountains billowed away, a brown sea, concealing all trace of the city and the flat green plain.

'By aeroplane?' asked the gambler. But his question went on the wind, ignored.

'Bracing place, this,' the contact man said. The tone of his voice was deferential. His bowler hat was in his hand, but his few ribs of hair were plastered so tightly to his bald crown that the wind, unable to find a grip, passed on roaring and left them undisturbed.

'I'm all for fresh air,' said the gambler. 'When I had a busy practice I was never done telling my patients about the benefits of fresh air. But I'm also a great believer in food. We came up to ask you to have lunch with us.' The dream that began in the sodden club-house was continuing on a windy mountain in the sober morning. He would no longer question the peculiarity of events; would accept them as men must accept the oddities of ordinary everyday life. The daftest incidents must in the end come to a logical, reasonable termination.

'We could always eat here,' said the golden-haired cleric. 'This grass is like a rich green carpet. There's shelter under the mountain ash.'

'Service would be a problem,' said the gambler, and the contact man, humbly interjecting, said: 'His reverence has certain winged waiters always at his disposal.'

The cold wind soaked with wild sunshine might have suddenly been tremendous with trumpeting angels. For the second time that morning the gambler was afraid, and although his hand in his pocket gripped the spanner, he was not at all sure that a short length of iron would be a sufficient defence. Who or what were his enemies? Two madmen? Two rogues? Or the sun and the wind and the deep heather on the wild mountain? So he said simply, wondering before he spoke would his lips tremble and shatter the shapes of the words: 'Come on. We'll go down.' He walked in the lead until they came to the circumference of the green circle, then waited modestly until they went before him into the heather, the tall priest walking easily and erect, the contact man struggling to keep his black briefcase on a level with his shoulders. In that order they went down through the shelter and quietness of the pines, along the narrow path between the furze, across the little stream to the road and the waiting green car. His hands on the wheel, that contact with normality, memories, routine, made the gambler feel for a moment that the meaning of the last two days was almost within his grasp. The mad mountain was behind him, dressed in pines and rough heather, the mystic circle of green revolving around a centre of ancient grey stones and a crooked giant mountain ash, the wind alive with the winged messengers of God. They passed again the whitewashed school. Children played in the concrete yard or perched on a low wall and cheered as the car went down the steep road. They passed again the two public houses. He saw with relief that the men on the scaffolding were still building the new house. They passed again the seven cottages, the falling mansion, the ancient graveyard, the clean factory, the church, swept through the suburb and down a long straight road to sink into the traffic of the city.

III

'Bortch,' read the thirteenth man, the golden-haired priest, the omniscient baptizer of gambler's children, the haunter of morning mountains and evening gardens, 'is a potage militaire russe composed of betteraves, céleris, oignons, choux en Julienne avec tomates en purée, cuit au bouillon de boeuf and servis with fresh cream.'

His French was excellent.

'That,' said the contact man, 'is the advantage of a continental education. Where did you go to school?'

'Possibly in Kildare,' said the gambler, 'with the Jesuits.'

With the appetite given them on the mountain, they ate thick brown bortch studded with cream. The little French restaurant was quiet, all noisy crowds kept at a distance by the price of the food, the gambler looking three times in succession into his wallet to assure himself that he had in his possession enough money borrowed from the wife's cousin to carry him through the settlement without shame.

They drank a middling red wine.

'Côtelette Maréchal,' the thirteenth man read, 'is aile de poulet désossée, fourrée au beurre, panée, cuite à la friture and garnie de pomme-paille et légumes divers.'

'Sounds good,' said the contact man. His bowler hat was in the cloakroom, but his black briefcase was safely within sight of his eyes. He moved his right foot and touched the case with a shiny shoe. He said: 'My trouble is I can only speak one language at a time.'

With evident relish they ate Côtelette Maréchal. At a distant table, as distant as it could be in a small restaurant, six men sat conspiring. They were eating and drinking, too, but the food and the drink were less important than the words they spoke, when simultaneously, like six puppet chickens in a child's toy, they bent heads over plates and secretively whispered: the draper and the grocer, the university professor, the bookie, the factory owner, and the professional golfer. Once in a while one of the six would raise cunning eyes and steal a glance at the gambler and his two companions. Conspiring against me, he thought. One of them saying: I own his overcoat. Another saying: I own his motor-car. All saying: he owes money to every one of us, debts of honour; and then at the mention of the word honour they would all sit upright in their seats, spoon their soup, feel rich and strong and righteous. Cunningly under his black eyebrows he watched his two companions, watched their eyes for any glance that might indicate an understanding with the six conspiring men, felt the air with his mind for any current of common feeling passing between the two tables. The contact man was neatly and methodically putting the finishing touches to his Côtelette Maréchal, rinsing his mouth and softening his dry, mechanical lips with wine, then lowering the red liquid in reckless thirsty gulps. 'Took the liberty of suggesting to our friend here,' he said. Another gulp at the wine. 'That on this special occasion.' A drop red as blood trickled down his chin to stain an already-stained shirt collar. 'A certain tradition entitles him to ask a few favours.'

'Blinitzki,' said the golden-haired priest, 'is described as crêpes à la russe, fourrées de confitures, ou flambées à la liqueur.'

'The liqueur is the hard man, the man for me.' The wine glass was emptied in one final assault.

'You're quite correct about the tradition. I think, unless my memory fails me, that on special occasions like this occasion I'm more or less expected to grant three requests. Within reason, of course. And only if the person asking the requests desires them with all his heart.' His strong beautiful hands played with the stem of the wine glass, and the wine glass, like a shell holding the sound of the sea, seemed to live and tingle with the music of his voice. Really a handsome man, thought the gambler. Women would worship him in pulpit or confessional and pray like burning saints for his sake and never know from what strange land, red cities in high mountain places, the wind came warmly to blow across their souls.

He finished eating and turned to his coffee, laced with lively brandy. He said: 'Well, seeing that you've so decently made the offer, there are a few things I'd like.' Now was the time to test his dream, to test his companions, madmen or rogues or something strangely outside all his previous experience. He almost said: 'Of course I realize this is all a game.' But he thought: Creation was a game and God putting a man and a woman in the testing garden was the first gambler, and all gamblers must be close to the heart of God. Across the restaurant the six men had finished their meal, folded their napkins, paid their money, shuffled out in single file through a door that connected the restaurant with a cocktail bar; and sickeningly he realized that he was lonely for their conspiring enmity; lonely for their gambling friendship. The pack of cards, still warm in his pocket, weighed him down with loneliness and desire.

'As you probably know, I'm a little given to the cards.' The priest smiled. The contact man picked his teeth. The gambler spoke slowly and distinctly, his heart beating rapidly. Asking these mad requests was a gamble. The fever was again alive in his blood. 'My luck has never been all that it might have been.' The dining-table with three cups of brandy-strengthened coffee was gone. He saw a green field where kings and queens and jesters in two different colours, red for blood and black for death, lay on beds of red diamonds, dark trefoil, bleeding hearts, the heads of black spears. 'I've concentrated. I've studied methods, read books, read articles in the newspapers — all written by experts who never played cards in their lives — but I never could find the tune to whistle to bring luck to me like a terrier at my heels. I blame nobody. And recently things have got so bad that I've decided to give up the cards. My overcoat doesn't even belong to me. I lost it at cards. The car I drove up the mountain and down the mountain isn't my own any more.' He was about to, but didn't mention the money borrowed from the wife's cousin, for even in a gamble he wasn't prepared to show his soul utterly naked to a quiet, smiling priest and a friendly little tooth-picking spiv. 'Now you, your reverence, if you're everything you say you are, and if you honestly mean to give me what I ask, then give me this.' The door between the restaurant and the cocktail bar slowly opened. The head of the grocer, shaped like a turnip, blotchy skin, a tuft of grey hair standing erect, looked in through the opening and then quickly pulled backwards and vanished. It was all that was needed. The gambler sternly pulled breath into his lungs. His opponent's card was on the table. He said each word as carefully, lovingly as if he was reciting a charm. 'When I sit down to play, let me always rise a winner. Give me good luck with good cards and good luck with bad cards. Give me smooth fingers in dealing so that the cards will flow out from my hands like milk from the udder of a cow. Give me a steady eye to stare my opponent into fear. Give me victory every time and all the time, night and day, in the club-house and everywhere else.'

'It's a poor request,' said the contact man. 'The will for power has the world the way it is.' He swallowed the produce of his methodical toothpicking. 'Where does power get you in the end? Look at Hitler.'

'I'm not interested in Hitler.'

'If you'd even asked for sense to keep away from cards altogether.'

'Which of us is doing the asking?'

'Sorry. Sorry. Only trying to be helpful. Only trying to put you wise.'

The thirteenth man, the odd number, silenced the argument. 'I'm inclined to agree with my old friend here. It is a proud, foolish thing to ask. If you're always certain of winning, where's the fun in gambling?'

'I've had the fun. Now I want money.'

'Since you asked that request you can have it. It's too late now even to change your mind.'

'I've no wish to change my mind.'

'So be it.' A graceful waiter presented on a plate the monstrous bill. The gambler took it, folded it outside a wad of *her* money, handed it back to the waiter, and told him to keep the change. 'You have two more requests,' said the thirteenth man.

'As you probably know, I'm a doctor by profession. When patients still came to me I flatter myself that I was a very good doctor. Kind and knowledgeable. A general practitioner, but every bit as good, and by no means as expensive, as the specialists in their high, fashionable houses in the centre of the city. You mightn't credit it, but I was the most brilliant student of my year. Took to dissection like a duck to water. At practical exams I never thought the hoary old case of general paralysis of the insane was really suffering from influenza.'

'That was astute,' said the omniscient stranger.

'Heard of you many a time,' said the contact man. 'Many and many a time. Saw you too. You fellows don't make my work easier. You create suspense, doubt.'

'But people don't come to me any more to tell me their relatives are sick. They don't like a doctor whose front garden is like a jungle. The front of my house hasn't had a lick of paint in seven years. They don't like a doctor who's drunk two times out of three.'

'Between friends, can't say I blame them,' said the contact man.

'I don't blame them. But it breaks my heart. You see, I liked my profession. I liked helping sick people. I liked the look on their faces when they knew they were getting better.'

'Don't dislike it myself. Within certain fixed limits. Saves me the trouble of making arrangements. Advance bookings and all that.'

The handsome, golden-haired priest knitted his fingers together on the table, studied them from under drooping eyelids, listened to the gambler talking and the contact man interjecting; the just judge hearkening to the importunate widow, waited for the prayer, the second traditional request.

Thou hast granted me life and mercy, prayed holy Job, and thy visitation hath preserved my spirit. Although thou conceal these things in thy heart, yet I know that thou rememberest all things. If I have sinned and thou hast spared me for an hour: why dost thou not suffer me to be clean from my iniquity.

'I want my practice back,' prayed the gambler. 'Not only do I want my practice back, but I want always to be able to cure my patients. I want to be able to bring life into dark, weeping rooms. I want to have power over —'

'Me. Over poor me. Not that I care much. Don't mind me. You're only one man, only one doctor. You can't attend the whole world. But remember, it would look a little peculiar if none of your patients ever died, not even of old age. People might begin to talk. It isn't centuries since doctors were in trouble for witchcraft.' He spoke respectfully across the coffee cups to the silent priest. 'Excuse me, your reverence, but as a member of this little luncheon party, all friends together, I think I have the right to propose an amendment.'

One barely perceptible nod of the golden head. A few slow words: 'You have the right.' From the cocktail bar came the sound of six voices raucously and derisively singing:

> I'm a rambler, I'm a gambler, I'm a long way from home.
> And if you don't like me, well, leave me alone.

'Here's my amendment.' To the gambler he half-whispered out of the corner of a twisting mouth: 'No offence. As much for your good as for mine.' The six voices taunted:

> I'll eat when I'm hungry and drink when I'm dry,
> And if moonshine don't kill me I'll live till I die.

'When our friend here enters a sick-room to see a patient I'll be there waiting. The sick man or woman may not see me. The people of the house may not see me. But our friend knows me now, and I'll manage things so that he'll always recognize me.' He swivelled around in his chair, aimed his words directly at the gambler. 'Imagine yourself walking into a room. Bag and full medical equipment clutched in the right hand. Here's the invalid stretched on the bed.' A gesture of his left hand indicated the bed of pain, the suffering person. 'Here am I, the old firm, the old contemptible, everybody's humble servant, sitting on my bum or perhaps standing quietly on my two feet. If I'm at the foot of the bed, you're laughing. Heal your patient, take your money, and go home. But if I'm at the head of the bed, let me have him. Or her, as the case may be, even if I'm not a lady's man. Is that a bargain?'

His hands were out before him, the left with the palm up, the right with the palm down, ready like a dealer in crooked horses for the hearty bargaining slap.

'Let his reverence here arbitrate.'

'I suppose I have some experience in arbitration.' He was a smiling, well-dressed cleric. He was Minos. He was a voice speaking to sheep and goats in the deep valley of judgement. 'To me it seems a reasonable bargain.'

'And if,' said the contact man, 'he breaks his bargain —'

'I don't break my bargains.'

'All men are weak,' said the arbitrator. 'And although I avoid personalities as a rule, there are three broken bargains already in the book against you.' He ticked them off on the fingers of his left hand. He said: 'So far away from files and winged secretaries, I may make a mistake. Correct me if I'm wrong: a marriage vow broken in the heart, a gambler's word twice broken.'

The gambler's long, dark face was sullen with suppressed anger. He wouldn't be weak. He wouldn't reach across the table and strike at that calm face. He wouldn't yield to the black revolt in the blood that had set men smashing images and spitting in the face of God. He would play this crazy game to the last move, accept it all as normal, not surprising; the sort of thing that regularly happened to a man; the sort of conversation that went on every day in the week between friends in hotels, offices, shops, church porches, public lavatories, suburban houses.

He asked: 'If I break my bargain?'

'Then,' said the contact man, 'yourself and myself will get down to business.'

'It's a deal,' said the gambler, and he slapped his hard, cold palm against the soft, moist palm, and felt the gold rings on the stumpy fingers. 'I suppose in the nature of things we'd get down to business some day or other, sooner or later. If I break my bargain I die.'

'I'm glad to see,' said the arbitrator, 'that you take the sensible view. You've another request left.'

The gambler took a look at his life, years and years of it in the past; so many things gone wrong, a hundred moments of brief happiness, so many things desired in vain. Then he looked at the present. Desires by the dozen whirled in pattern like dancers before a sultan, moving so fast and so much in unison that the most intently watching eye could isolate only the sheen of a thigh or the whirl of a tantalizing veil. No dancer, no desire, could be chosen from that pattern except by a random choice that might in the end prove how a veil could cover a wicked heart or how the face above the shining thigh could be the face of a noseless hag. The present circled around him: houses, streets, London theatres, holiday hotels on French shores, horse races, coral islands, wind in high New Zealand trees, faces and figures by the thousand; two faces that now he could neither love nor hate with a mind absolutely at ease; all things possible and impossible moving within reach of his right hand. Could it be true that the impossible was now also possible? And, suffocating with desire to handle the world as a child handles a coloured cloth ball, he pitched choice to the winds and grabbed blindly.

'This, then, is my third and last request.'

His choice would cock a snook at all choosing, all hope, all desire. It would be the joke of generations of wry peasants who had imagined the devil thwarted and imprisoned in the crooked branches of an apple-tree.

'Before I make this request,' he said to the contact man, 'I think it had better be strictly private between his reverence and myself.'

The little man wasn't angry or embarrassed. He accepted his own exclusion with a nervous little smile that stabbed across his face and then vanished. He said: 'This always happens to me. That's what comes of being too friendly.' Carefully he picked up his black briefcase from the floor. 'Find me in the bar,' he said, and for two minutes after the door closed behind him, the gambler, ashamed, didn't speak. No sound of singing came from the six conspiring men. They must have gone home.

'My little green motor-car,' said the gambler; 'did you like it?'

'It runs smoothly. As smoothly as anything on the earth could.'

'It has seen a lot of service. It isn't bad for its age. But when my practice expands again and my gambling debts are paid I may need something more elaborate. One of those big American yokes that looks as if it's going in two directions at the same time. A Cadillac. A Buick.'

'Why not?'

'Why not, indeed. When I buy this car I want one special favour in connection with it. If any man other than myself sits anywhere in that car, let him stay there until he has my permission to leave, and let him be subject to my orders while he stays.'

'I've heard something like that before.'

'It's not exactly original.'

'The other requests were proud. This one is lunatic.'

'It's what I want.'

'Do you realize all the chances you're throwing away? Everything man has ever desired — with a few reasonable exceptions — might be yours, and you're prepared to throw all away for a fantasy.'

'I'm a gambler.'

'I'm a gambler myself. But, then, my bank is unlimited.'

There was silence, a straining struggle of wills. Then the gambler said: 'That's my request.'

'So be it,' said the odd number, and looking up suddenly, he showed a face no longer absolutely free from wrinkles, no longer so healthily handsome, a little lined about the temples, tinged with grey along the cheeks. 'So be it.' He stood up. 'Thanks for the lunch,' he said. 'Our friend will be lonely in the bar.'

The door of the bar swung shut behind them. The contact man sat drinking alone in a lonely corner. The six conspirators were gone. The barman was reading a newspaper.

IV

In the late afternoon, with dusk just around the corner, they walked, breathing wine into chilling air, in a public park. They entered the park under a high arch lined in gilt lettering with the names of men killed in some ancient war. They walked by the edge of the still lake, seats crowded with people to their left hand. They leaned on the stone parapet of a little bridge. Six quiet children flung scraps of bread to contented ducks. A keeper fed pigeons, birds crowding the path around him, birds perching on his shoulders and on his peaked cap. They stepped off the path to avoid disturbing the pigeons, walked across a level stretch of grass where riotous children played. They came to a green seat in a quiet place, beside the seat the statue of the rich man who had once, out of his riches, given the park to the people of the city. His bronze image was set in a semicircle of beech-trees because in his life, the lines on the pedestal said, the rich man had loved children, beech-trees, and the poor.

'Leave me here for a while,' said the thirteenth man, 'I

have some reading to do.' He opened the black covers of a breviary. The thin pages marked with holy Latin words fluttered in the wind. They left him reading and walked for twenty aimless minutes around the maze of paths in the park, knowing that when they returned the green seat by the bronze statue by the beech-trees would be empty.

'I wonder where he's got to?'

Drying leaves rustled whispering on the high beech branches. A rich man in bronze looked sternly out at the playing children that a rich man in blood, bone, flesh, and spirit had tenderly loved.

'Not far,' said the contact man. 'He'll turn up again.'

He might be a noisy child playing between the beech-trees and the bridge or a quiet child scattering bread to the ducks or an old man talking with old men on a bench by the lake or a beautiful girl walking out of the park under the gilt-lettered archway. But the gambler didn't know and the contact man was giving no hints and the keepers, ringing mournful hand-bells, were driving the people from the park to make room for darkness.

Through crowded, lighted streets they walked back to the cobbled lane where the gambler had parked his green car.

'Can I drop you anywhere?'

'No. I'll find my own way home.'

'Good luck. Nice knowing you.'

They shook hands around the handle of the black briefcase.

'See you again,' said the contact man.

'*Au 'voir.*'

He didn't switch on the engine until the sound of the contact man had gone off down the lane. The soft, shiny shoes made little noise on the dull cobbles, but for a long time he could hear the shrill, slow whistling, sad pipes wailing, the flowers of the forest scythed down and withered. When he could no longer hear that eerie music he drove his car out of the cobbled lane, out of the confused city, along a great highway between flat fields, passing little cottages with friendly bright windows and high white gables like conical hats. Under the last light of day he saw dry dunes, cold sea, flags fluttering on greens, the bulk of the club-house. From this moment out, he thought, there is no feeling of damnation. The defeated is now the conqueror. But parking his car, a domino among dominoes, on the gravel before the club-house, he had one moment of doubt — or sanity. If this were a dream? Or a joke? Or the work of two madmen?

With one foot on the gravel it's too late to turn back. My effrontery in returning will leave them silent. Here I am, not to pay my debts, but to win back all I've lost, and more, and more. Here I am, step after step across the gravel, into the club-house, into that warm, heavily curtained room; six faces staring like six amazed masks; not all amazed, not utterly, for deep in their dirty guts they were expecting me, a soul from hell, a ghost from the grave. A square deal and thirty minutes' credit? They'll give me that. They're afraid to refuse. Thirty minutes' credit on a green field among kings and queens, diamonds, black spears, dark trefoil, red bleeding hearts.

V

When he awoke in the morning she was bending over him. He had no dull headache, no sour taste in his mouth. Instead, his soul was inflated with a joy like the joy in a child's heart wakening on Christmas morning to expected gifts, and there she was bending over him — dressed as if she was going out or had just come in; a dark costume, a short, warm coat of rich brown fur. Quickly awakening, he saw how her dark eyes were soft with anxiety.

She said: 'So you did come home after all.' She straightened up quickly. He knew that she wanted to hide the look in her eyes.

'At four-thirty. I let myself in quietly. I didn't want to disturb anyone.'

'You mightn't have bothered. There was nobody here to disturb.'

Heaving himself up to a sitting position, pulling his buttonless pyjama jacket together to conceal his dark hairy chest, he digested the significance of her words.

'You mean she's gone.'

'Taking the children with her. Last night. When the whole

day had passed and you hadn't returned from the baptism.'

He didn't ask: 'Where to?' He knew that his wife and his three children were now in the house of the dowager duchess. He did say: 'I suppose you think she was right?'

'I don't take sides. But, dear Lord, you could have come home just once to see if we were living or dead.'

He almost said: 'I knew Death couldn't have been here in my absence' or 'I spent the day with God and Death'. Yesterday it had all seemed as ordinary as that. But he checked the words in time. She could only think that drink and misfortune at cards had driven him mad. Had it not been that misfortune had gone last night like straw or dry sand before the wind that blew over the dunes, he must have doubted his own sanity.

'She wasn't fit to travel.'

'She wasn't. But she went all the same.'

'Under strong leadership?'

'Don't be nasty.'

She snapped up the window blinds. He watched yellow autumn light rush past her like a torrent, outlining her tall, desirable body. 'If the neighbours see you standing there.'

'You're worried about the neighbours?'

'From now on I am. I've turned the new leaf.'

'Looks very like it. Where were you last night? I searched the town for you. Never saw the insides of so many pubs in my life.'

'Wasn't in a pub.' Straining over the edge of the bed, he reached his jacket, heavy with the wonderful weight of his stuffed wallet, and pulled it to him. 'I was in a club. Making money.'

Every note in the stuffed wallet was a five-pound note. He peeled one from the wad, held it up to the light flowing from the window, studied the design as a forger might carefully study the produce of his genius.

'Isn't it a sight for sore eyes?' He counted out four notes, reached them towards her. 'I owe you this.'

She stood without moving, her back to the window and the movement of the fluid light. 'How did you get that?'

'Oh, you needn't worry. I didn't rob a bank. I haven't taken to forgery. No, my dear, my luck has turned.'

'The next time it may turn the other way.'

'I've better hope. Won't you give my new luck a trial? Say, for three months? Take that money now, anyway. I owe it to you.'

She took the money with reluctance. While he was poor and broken and in her debt she felt happily that she owned a share of him, a piece of wreckage. She said: 'I'll cook something for you if you get up.'

'You're an angel. I'd be lost without you.'

She knew that mood, hard and light; the mood of a gibing boy helping a girl to wring sea-water out of her underclothes; of a young doctor doing well and recently married to a fluffy, pretty, plump girl. Yesterday in his despair he had come so close to her, even if years of training and some innate horror of the love that was not sacramental had made her strike out in protest against his kiss. Now she was an angel and he would be lost without her, and she could have wept — would have wept if she had not been a valiant unweeping woman — because she felt that his words were hollow and rotten, without life, empty of meaning. When she was at the door of the bedroom she said: 'Do you want me to go over and argue her into coming back?'

'No. Not this time. I'll go myself. By God, she'll come. Her place is here. We can't have you making a skivvy of yourself.'

In the kitchen she took off her coat, tucked up her sleeves, tied an apron around her waist, washed and cut and cooked, laid the dining-room table, made a skivvy of herself. It seemed the most natural thing in the world. She heard him whistling as he shaved. Yesterday he had said, with a little mockery and some seriousness in his voice: 'Come with me when I take to the roads.'

When he came down she was ready to go. She poured his first cup of tea, placed his plate on the table before him.

'Going so soon?'

'I have to work.'

'Some night we'll go out and do the town. I want to thank you for all this.'

'That'll be fun.'

She walked quickly away from him, then stopped on the threshold of the dining-room. 'Before you bring the children back there's something you might do. Their little brown pup is dead in the kennel.'

'Dead!'

'Yes. Even dogs die. It looks to me like the result of a fit. You should have him out of the way before they return. It would break their hearts to see him dead.'

'What'll I tell them?'

'Say the vet. sent him to hospital and he'll be back some day.'

She closed the door behind her, annoyed that he hadn't walked with her to the threshold, gripped her arm with his strong hand, looked at her with dark eyes that said more than dry words could ever say. She didn't know — how could she know? — of the thoughts her words had set boiling in his head, so that food turned tasteless in his mouth, so that later, tearing away damp tangled grass in the corner of the garden under the boor-tree bush, digging in the packed, neglected earth until his muscles ached, he was forced to halt repeatedly, not because of weariness, but because he could not work away those mad thoughts.

Death visited here when I was playing cards and winning five-pound notes. So that I would remember my bargain? He left this memento, a dead dog, as a visitor would leave a visiting card.

Above his head the narrow boor-tree branches were whispering doubts about his sanity.

I have no friend to confide in. What friend could listen to such a story and not think the storyteller wandering in his wits? It may have been a dream, and yet I won all that money. With bad cards too. I tried once to lose and I couldn't.

Gently he lifted the dead puppy dog from the straw of the kennel. The underside was still slightly warm and moist. But there was no doubt about its being dead. He knew death when he saw it.

I'll know him when I see him, at the head of the bed, at the foot of the bed, some day at the head of my own bed.

Carefully he wrapped it in a piece of sacking and carried it to the corner under the boor-tree bush. Six inches down, the ground was stony and difficult to dig. Because the dead puppy was bigger than he had reckoned, he had to widen the hole. He tore until he perspired at the stubborn earth.

Everything changes when a man seriously begins to consider God and Death:

He knows Death to the bone —

Man has created Death.

To the jabbing rhythm of another of his quotations he finished the digging. Then he lowered the dead dog into the hole, scraped the earth over it, concealed the brown wound by scattering grass and boor-tree twigs. His fears fled when the work was done. A man must accept the things that happen to him. Perhaps he had buried ill luck for ever in the corner of the damp garden.

Second Interlude

The gambler and Death turned back until they came to the place where God was waiting for them. The three went to the gambler's house and God baptized the child and Death stood sponsor. Then God went away.

Says Death to the gambler: 'It wasn't right for you to let God leave you without asking a request from Him.'

The gambler went off after God, and when he came as far as Him, God asked him what he wanted.

'I am seeking a request from you,' says the gambler.

'What is the request?' says God.

'Give me victory in card-playing over the whole world,' says the gambler.

'You will get that,' says God.

The gambler, satisfied, turned towards home. Death met him on the way and asked him had he seen God.

'I saw God and I got my request,' says the gambler.

'What was that request?' says Death.

'A good request,' says the gambler; 'that I should have victory in card-playing over the whole world. And now I will win again as much money as I ever lost, and more besides.'

'It's a bad request,' says Death. 'Follow Him again and ask a good request from Him.'

The gambler set off again until he came as far as God, and he asked another request from Him.

'What is the request?' says God.

'Give me victory in healing over the whole world,' says the gambler.

'You will get that,' says God.

Joyfully the gambler returned, and when Death met him he told Death about the other request he'd been granted.

'It's a bad request,' says Death. 'Follow Him again and ask a good request from Him this time.'

The gambler went off again after God and asked Him for a third request.

'What is the request?' says God.

'Growing in my garden,' says the gambler, 'I have an apple-tree, and when I'm out card-playing by night the children of the neighbours steal the apples. I ask that if any person puts his hand on an apple his hand will stick to the apple and the apple to the tree until it is my will to set them free.'

'You will get the request,' says God.

Then the gambler went back to Death and said that he'd got a good request this time.

'What is it?' says Death.

'I won't tell anybody,' says the gambler.

'Fair enough,' says Death. 'You have now victory in healing over the whole world and that suits me poorly. I'll make a bargain with you about that request. When you go into a house in which a person is ailing, if I am sitting at the foot of the bed, heal him, but if I'm sitting at the head of the bed, let me have him — or I'll take yourself instead.'

'It's a bargain,' says the gambler.

THREE

I

This was the pillow-chat of a certain respectable grocer to his inadequately perfumed wife on the night, or the morning, he returned from the club-house with empty pockets:

'You'd never credit it, dear. The hard neck of that fellow. I'm a business man, as you know, not a professional gentleman. In my game you need push and go. But if I had the shameless neck of that fellow I'd be as big a man as Gordon Selfridge. I'd sweep every shop in the world into one monopoly and paint the front of every shop the same colour, a very nice light green with cream decorations and gilt lettering three feet high.

'We never expected to see him again. I know you think it was wrong for us to allow him to go as far as he did, and to take the overcoat and the motor-car from a doctor who needed them to keep up his professional standing. I ask you, what professional standing had he left? His practice went to pieces long ago and it's a miracle that the fellow still has his name on the medical register. You know there were some nasty reports about cases he neglected or mishandled. Of course, these doctors get away with murder. Anyway, if a man was mad enough to stake his car and his topcoat, it wasn't our business to stop him. Cards are like the grocery. You have to take a risk now and then, and every man takes the risk he thinks he can afford.

'In he walks as brazen-faced as an impertinent domestic servant, and says he: "Here I am, boys, to pay my debts." He throws the topcoat across the back of a chair and says: "That's a better coat than was ever made by underpaid employees in a factory in a back lane." Before anybody had time to object to the tone of that remark, he wheels on me, looks hard at me, raises the big eyebrows halfway up his forehead, glares at me — sometimes I've an odd feeling the man isn't all there — and shouts: "Your car's outside. The tank's full. You'll be able to drive it home if I don't win it back."

"Win it back," says I. "Not so fast. There's a little matter to be settled before you sit down to cut cards in this room."

'He looks from face to face, sizing us up, and naturally he picks on the professor. A soft young lad that! "Can I play or can't I play," says the boy to the professor, and the soft slob, he says, "I don't see why not, suppose we put it to a vote."

'I never was a man for putting things to votes. He either had a right to play with us or he hadn't. In my view he hadn't, and a vote couldn't change my opinion. I voted against him, and so did the factory man, but the other four, I regret to say, voted in his favour. So what could we do except get up and walk out, and there wouldn't be any sense in that. It was agreed that we should postpone payment of the money he owed us, and allow him to sit in if he had more than two pounds in his possession. He whips out a fiver, puts it down on the table. I'd like to know who owned that fiver. Between ourselves, dear, I had it from you-know-who at the last meeting of our trade association that that fellow has his mother-in-law paying for the groceries for himself and the wife and children. No shame in him at all.'

The grocer's wife, like all wives who had to endure long monologues, had cultivated to perfection the technique of pretending to listen while she was softly and deliciously asleep. Sooner or later he always discovered the imposture, ceased talking, also fell asleep. Closing his eyes and turning his bottom towards his wife's bottom, he reflected, with the satisfaction of a man who loves selling at a good profit, that he had said his say on the question, except that he hadn't had the opportunity of pointing out how bad his cards had been for the remainder of that fatal night.

The young professor had a rich, resonant voice and a handsome hollow-jawed face that reminded six out of seven of the undergraduate girls who attended his lectures of the voice and face of a popular film star. A large number of these girls were in love with the young professor. His fiancée had once been an undergraduate girl and had been overcome by the melody of his voice telling of the Medici Popes, Gustavus Adolphus, and the relations between Church and State in Tudor Ireland. She loved his voice still, because when she danced with him he could, unlike most other men, make himself heard without getting red in the face in an effort to shout down saxophones and coloured crooners. That was the way she heard him telling how, because he wanted to marry her and because he'd lost two months' salary in one night, he'd decided to give up gambling. Using the identical words, he told the story to a taciturn colleague across the fire in the common-room during an interval between lectures.

'I can't say honestly that I was sorry to see him again. He is an intelligent fellow, more interesting to talk to than that crook of a grocer. You see, the trouble with this country is that we pride ourselves overmuch on a certain sort of morality, sixth and ninth commandments, you know what I mean; and we have absolutely no notion of common honesty in business dealings, no commercial morality whatsoever. In that respect our neighbours, the British, are our moral superiors. Of course I know you'll say there are historic reasons for that defect in our national character and, by and large, I'm inclined to agree.

'But there I go, dear, digressing again.' (In the common-room version he said: 'Pardon the digression, my dear fellow.') 'What I meant to say was that when the grocer objected I stood up for the other fellow. The professional, he's a quiet fellow, but he was the first of the group to take his stand with me. You can always depend on the sporting type. My own natural sympathies are with the aesthetes, but after that give me the athletes; and while the professional isn't an educated man, he is, *sine dubio*, a —'

'— sport. I repeat, sport is sport. I don't have the gift of the gab the way the professor does. He's one of the smart guys who get paid for talking by the hour. I'm paid for sport, for playing a game, and if you want to know what the game is, well, the game is golf. That's how I make my living. Putting a tiny little ball on a green, holing it in the smallest possible number of strokes. Sometimes I win. Sometimes I get licked. I'm always game for a comeback, though, and I don't see why I should grudge the chance of making a comeback, at cards or golf, to my fellow-man. Them's my principles. The professor endorses them. So does your man the bookie. He doesn't know any more than myself about Latin or Greek or history, but he's a sport. He's made his pile out of sport, and he knows how much everything depends on getting a chance and taking it, and then upon —'

'— luck. All I say is the blighter has luck. Six favourites in the field and he beats them all by twenty lengths. Nothing like it since Tipperary Tim. Dropped fifty quid myself. But no grudges. I always pay when I can afford it and, thought I don't boast as a rule, I can afford it nowadays. No man better.'

Across a counter in a draper's shop two drapers compared their own trade to all other branches of trade and industry. The results of the comparison were in favour of drapery. As men who sold food, one draper said, grocers were perhaps of equal importance with men who sold clothes. The second draper said that the repute of the grocery was ruined by the repulsive personality of one grocer he was personally acquainted with. 'A member of the golf club I belong to,' he said, 'although how he ever became a member is the eighth wonder of the world. No class. It gave me great satisfaction to score over him a few nights ago in the club-house when he tried to keep the doctor out of our game. Sure enough, the doctor did owe us all something. His luck had been awful for weeks and weeks, but he came back and faced us like a man and asked for one more chance. He was rewarded for his courage. Never saw anything like it. He played as if he was a magician and had us all bewitched. The grocer didn't like it. Neither did one of our leading industrialists. There's always been some secret little feud between the doctor and the factory man, something that makes the doctor say the most impolite things — and get away with them too. Our industrialist hasn't as much resolute courage as you'd imagine from the speeches he makes at Rotary luncheons. Did you see the report in this morning's paper? Look, here he's demanding tariff protection from the Government, firm action against strikers. I bet the doctor'll make some comment on that speech the next night we're all in the club-house. Although the same seven men will hardly ever be together again. The young professor's getting married soon. He was so badly cleaned out the other night that he's sworn to his bride-to-be he'll never play cards again. Anyway, if the doctor's luck goes on like this we'd all be wiser to stop. A man has his future to think of, and his wife and children.'

Across the counter in a shop soft with cloth, the two drapers agreed that gambling was fine, up to a point; that drink was also fine, up to a point; but that men should never forget the future and the welfare of wife and children.

II

The draper was a prophet. The young professor never came to the club-house again. The professional golfer got himself another job with another club where a man might have a chance in a game of cards. The bookie stayed at the bar and never came near the room where he had lost so much money. The draper said honestly that he couldn't afford it any more. The grocer and the factory owner whispered together, stopped paying their club subscriptions, stopped playing golf, fell ill from lack of exercise, and sent in panic for the doctor to come and cure them. He came and cured them. His fame as a healer was spreading. So many patients were coming to him to be cured of so many different ailments that he had little time left for gambling, and he ceased to worry when he could find nobody, except elderly clergymen in trains, to gamble with him.

Men and women frequently wrote letters to their friends in praise of the doctor who had restored them to health; and sometimes the friends sent those letters to the doctor. As a general rule, of course, patients attributed their recovery to their own foresight in sending for the doctor in time, and to their prudence in not completely obeying his instructions. But out of the letters he received he preserved some because they brightened a memory or restored a mood. He gave a special place to a letter from one poor woman to another telling how one night in a deep slum her baby had almost died of gastroenteritis. That was the first case he had attended on the night of the day on which he buried the dead dog. He had spent the afternoon and evening and a portion of the night in the club-house adding to his bank balance. He valued that letter greatly: the coarse paper, the blotchy, dirty ink, the mis-spelling. It went like this: 'Dear Cecilia, A line to let you know we are all well, baby also, thank God and a very kind and good docter. That awefull night that Maisie told you about we were neerley demented the poor wee thing as pale as a ghost and its eyes staring as big as saucers and the green dicaree coming like water out of a downspout. So I says to himself run out like a hero to the public telefone and ring up a docter and he hadn't two pennies in his pocket and no more had I twopence in the house and Uncle Willie coffing and spitting with his cote on him in the house hadn't twopence no more so at this stage my poor man says I'll run from here to the bus stop and no conducter bad as they are will have the heart to put me off on such a night when he hears my errand even if I haven't the price of my fare. It was the worst night that ever fell and the lane or the avenue as the landlord calls it was six inches under dirty water and says my poor man to Uncle Willy any chance off a lend of the old coat, and Uncle Willy sitting selfish with his grey face screwed up like a button on a tea chest at the foot of the child's cot coughs again and pulls the old rainproof so tight around him it neerley split across between the shoulder blades. But not a lend would he lend only looks at the fire and spits and takes the holy name and says he's perished there is no heat offa that fire. So my poor man runs to the main road in time to see the last bus vanishing away towards the city and it full of people snug and dry in showerproofs and with the money to pay their fares. So he sets off to walk as far as the docter's and bye-and-bye along comes a motor car and he says here's for luck and sticks up his hand and the car halts and the driver opens the door and says hop in if it's a lift you want. Just as he's getting in he smells drink and only for at that moment he thought of the wee shirtbutton of a face of the ailing child he'd have closed the door firmly for the things that drunk drivers do are in the papers every day. But says he very polite to the big man in the car I'm deeply indetted to you for my wife's infant is on the point of death and I'm running for the docter and the man stares hard at him and says he where's your house I'm a docter myself and in two ticks my husband is leading the docter up the stares to our room. He is a big black man with thick eyebrows and a long black face like the divil and he takes an extra cross look at Uncle Willy on the teachest and says he so there you are and Uncle Willy just coughed and cleared his throat at the fire. I see that the docter had some drink taken and I wasn't feeling happy in my mind but how and ever he examines the infant and gives it a white pill from a box. Says he the quicker this child gets to hospital the better. Well as you know no mother likes to hear the hospital mentioned in connection with her child and my face must have showed my feelings for says the docter to me as if I was a grand lady cheer up madam your child will live and out of his hip-pocket he whips a bottle of brandy and makes me take a sip and gives my poor man a sip and then turns to Uncle Willy and holds the bottle to his lips and puts a hand on his shoulder and says my man you look like death. God sees that was a true profesy for Uncle Willy the heavens be his bed crabbed as he was didn't last a week and the child is now well and strong even if it is a bit pale. It shows you that docters know more than people give them credit for and that night he wrapped the poor infant in the rug out of his own car gave me a five pound note and stayed in the hospital until he saw the child getting treatment with his own two eyes for you know in some of those places they're not too partickular about the poor and when I said I dont know how to thank you docter all he said was I should thank you for you have helped to set my mind at ease. God only knows what he meant but dear Cecilia I've written down his name and address and all this rigmarole so that you'll go and see him yourself about your own little ailment for none of us are as young as we were and the years are hard on women but a bit of an operation and a whiles rest in hospital would make you like a girl of sixteen.'

When Cecilia went to see the doctor she brought the rigmarole with her as a letter of introduction, and he kept it. He kept also a letter from a soldier who had literary aspirations to another soldier, telling of an incident that had taken place on a western roadside near a summer military camp. That letter provided him with evidence that other eyes had seen her with him on that happy night. It had been a night cut off from all other nights, separate and apart from his life as a grown man, a fulfilment of all the delicious desires of boyhood. The road from the seaside resort to the market town cut through dry dunes. Occasionally the lights of the car picked out white, neatly thatched cottages. Fifty yards beyond one cottage they picked out the bleeding soldier prostrate and roaring on the middle of the road.

'I'm telling you, Jerry,' the soldier's letter said, 'that red-headed boy never was a fellow to drink with. When I read the newspaper you sent me I thank my Saviour that I'm a living man to write this letter. We arrived safe at the summer camp the year I had the trouble with him, got our stuff under canvas, fixed our beds, and had medical inspection. The camp is on a wide flat place between the road and the sandy hills and the hills there are all notices for danger on account of the firing ranges. A bad place for coorting couples. You might get a bullseye where and when you would least expect it. I shared a tent with the ginger boy. He is a decent spud when he's sober but walking death with the whisky in his guts. When everything was settled to the captain's satisfaction we had the night to ourselves so some of us walked the two miles east to the market town but most of us hobnailed the two miles west to the seaside resort, since it was the height of the season. The girls, the air and the salt sea waves are salubrious and in the pubs they sell a local dark ale that at one draught eases both the mind and the budget and makes harsh voices melodious. Since we were paid on the previous day we were all carrying a plentiful supply of hard cash and myself and the red-headed gentleman settled down to the ale in a certain house of worship. All was well if his holiness had not taken it into his head to insert one small whisky into every half pint of his ale, to liven it up he said and he was dead right. When we struck the road to walk the two miles east to the camp we were near to being what you might call footless. We carried with us six bottles each of ale to keep the thirst at arm's length, and as we wobbled along we knocked the tin caps off the bottles and drank out of two tumblers borrowed, without his consent, from mine jovial host. Then when the ale was finished our friend of the golden locks got cross. He said there was no God and as that is a matter of opinion I let it pass. He said he could beat a certain portion of the anatomy off any man under canvas including myself and the captain to whom he applied a certain adjective that I would spell for you if I knew how. I let him talk but when he said he knew how sailors used the jagged ends of bottles for in-fighting I kept my eye on him carefully. He later stated that he considered me a louser and that he had a strong suspicion my mother never had a wedding ring to call her own and let fly at me with an empty bottle. I saw it coming and ducked. That bottle is still reclining in the sandy hills that is if it didn't drop ten miles out to sea for it was travelling like a bullet. As it was the last of the twelve bottles and as your man isn't as hot as he thinks with the bare fists I took defensive action by knocking him down with a welt on the face. But alas and alack I had forgotten that the jagged end of a tumbler is as handy a weapon for a dirty fighter as the jagged end of a bottle and the next thing I knew I was on the hard road picking splinters of broken borrowed glass out of my jaw-bone and the bright boy was about to ply the boot on my belly when he was interrupted by the lights of a car. By the mercy of God the driver of the car was a doctor from the city on a holiday with his wife, a fine well-built dark-haired woman. This I saw later, even though my jaw was bleeding like the proverbial stuck pig for the doctor and the red-headed butcher carried me to a farm-house on the roadside and there, while the farmer lowered the lamp to throw light on the proceedings and while the doctor's wife and the farmer's wife heated water and cut up an old shirt for bandages, the doctor stitched as neat a job on my dial as was ever done in a well-equipped casualty ward. They stretched me out like a gory corpse on the bed in the kitchen and the lad with the red hair sat on a box at the foot of the bed, his head in his hands, and once the doctor took a hard look at him and said you're sitting in the right place anyway. It looked as if he was going to address some stern words to the culprit but at that moment the dark ale and the whisky rise in revolution and mister redhead says jasus I'm sorry and makes for the door. Bad as I was I could hear the din he made getting sick at the edge of the road and I can't honestly say that he had my sympathy. Well, the doctor's lady bathed my face and cleared the ground for action and then in moved the doctor with kit and weapons ready to do a bit of needlework. The lady sat down on the box at the foot of the bed and I kept concentrating my glance on her bust and thinking of the fun the doctor must have. But all of a sudden the doctor bellows at her don't sit there. She looked a bit taken aback but she moved all the same. He might have spotted me giving her proportions the wishful eye and it could be that he wanted to save me from bad thoughts. He was an odd laddo even if he was a damned fine doctor and when the needlework class was over he gave me a pill that sent me off into deep and dreamless sleep. Then he drove the red-headed hero back to the camp, told the captain who and what he was and fixed things up so that the captain let us off with a caution and a day's fatigue. I must say for poor unfortunate ginger that he offered to the captain to take the whole show on his shoulders. He was a decent spud when sober and I was sad and sorry even if I wasn't surprised to read the bad news. I always knew that some day he would meet his waterloo and I thank my God he wasn't carrying that sailor's knife the night himself and myself had the disagreement. It was unfortunate for the poor lad he stabbed and for the wife and child he leaves behind him. He must have struck him a furious blow to put a knife like that clean into the heart. But as you know that was what I said always — walking death when he had the drink taken. . . .'

This letter from one private soldier to another fell into the hands of the captain who, remembering the doctor, sent him the letter as a curious example of the things that went on under a uniform cap. The doctor preserved it for another reason.

III

A Dialogue Between Two Women

A: You know your heart, my dear. I can't presume to advise you on a matter so important. But since I am a little older than you —

B: Not much older —

A: How charitable you are. Four years. And my hair has a premature grey that laughs at all lotions. And your hair's so dark and shiny. Lovelier than it was when we were little girls in school and you used to wear it long, hanging down to your waist.

B: Razor-cutting made it curl. It was always straight when I was young —

A: He's a fine man, of course. I'd like nothing better myself. But there are complications. The children and the wife. Even if she is your cousin, rumour has it that she's a bit of a bee.

B: She's as good as she can be. The marriage should never have taken place. It's my fault that it ever did.

A: You're such a dark horse. You kept all this to yourself for so long. When did it all begin?

B: Well, strictly speaking, on the day his last child was born. He was very much down on his luck then. I loaned him some money and then without any warning he kissed me. I was horrified. But then, when I thought it over it felt as if something hard inside me — like a block of stone — had begun to melt.

A: I've had that feeling so often, my dear.

B: That wasn't really the beginning. You see, when we were children his parents and my parents went every summer to the same seaside resort. A little place in the west. He wants me now to go back there with him. He has some foolish notion that if we got back there we could begin at the beginning all over again.

A: A romantic type. He certainly doesn't look it.

B: He was a lovely little boy, though. Not smelly, as most little boys are, and very daring; always ready to take a chance at climbing trees and leaping streams. I'm afraid I was a terrible tomboy. I remember one lovely sunshiny day we went walking in a grassy place by the edge of the sea and he took a running leap across a little stream and dared me to do the same. I tried my very best, but my legs were too short. When I crawled out dripping he helped me to wring the water out of my knickers.

A: That was the age of innocence.

B: He remembers that still. He often mentions it.

A: I could imagine that. Does he want to make a fresh start by the edge of that stream?

B: Please don't be nasty about it.

A: I'm sorry, dear. I don't mean to be nasty. But there are times when you're as innocent and trusting as a two-year-old baby calling to daddy to come to her cot. And you look so competent and strong, so much a woman with her career made. Not like me, a dithering female, easy game for two out of three men.

B: You're too hard on yourself.

A: Oh, no, I'm not. But being easy game for the last six or seven years taught me something. I'd like to give your strong innocence the benefit of my experience of being weak.

B: I'd love to have it.

A: If you go away with him you know what it means.

B: I can guess.

A: Guessing is a good beginning. He won't ask you from here to there just to hold his hand.

B: I've held his hand.

A: You've been breaking ground, so.

B: It seemed so natural to be more to him than a childhood's friend or a relation by marriage. We've got into the habit of meeting privately in quiet places. Just to talk. We could meet publicly if we wanted to. No scandal-monger even in this city could say a word against a man being seen at a theatre or in a bar or a restaurant with his wife's cousin, the woman who introduced him to his wife. But there was something different about meeting in quiet corners where you never saw a familiar face. Then he was so gentle and so kind. Something came into him the day he buried the dead puppy in the garden. It's from that day I date the beginning of his prosperity. He paid his debts and rebuilt his practice. He stopped gambling because he was so lucky that nobody would gamble with him any more. Still, it wasn't the normal sort of prosperity. It left him as if he was wondering and afraid, like a new boy or girl in a boarding school looking around for a possible friend —

A: For you?

B: Perhaps. There's no love in his life. Except the children.

A: He doesn't, I hope, tell you that the wife doesn't understand him?

B: Nothing so vulgar. He says that no person ever understands another.

A: I've heard that one too. What I honestly cannot fathom is how and why you ever allowed him to marry that woman.

B: Things happen that way. You know a thing and you feel it, but you never never say it. We stayed dumb too long and he was as bad as I was and she had a word for every occasion. You see, I was reared in a queer house; a quiet father and mother, a sickly sister doing the dying and making me her slave because she was supposed to be in ill-health; no visitors coming and going; not even a radio to break the silence; just coughs and monotony and family prayers. It took me a long time recovering from the things that house did to me. My only bright memories were two sunshiny weeks every summer by the sea. When I met him afterwards I couldn't tell him how he was part and parcel of my only happy memories of what they call girlhood. Girlhood! I was never a girl, or, at most, only for one fortnight out of every year. Now he tells me he always thought me a masterful sort of person.

A: Mistressful?

B: He was afraid to talk to me. She came in between and talked and talked. That was how it happened.

A: Just like that?

B: Just like that.

A: Now at last you've spoken to each other and you know your own mind. If I told you not to go, you'd go all the same. You wouldn't have asked my advice if you'd thought for a moment that it would have been: don't go, don't give yourself recklessly, throw nothing away. I can only envy you, dear. You have so much to give, so much to find out, like a child climbing a gate into a green field. . . . Or am I being silly? Of course, I've always been silly, from the moment I came to the age of reason.

She remembered that conversation the night he attended the wounded soldier and then drove to the hotel in the market town; darkness over the dunes and the wide estuary, darkness over the green fields. She remembered it in the morning when he drove away from the town, past the market square crowded with tilted carts, over the bridge with the grey stone plaque to the memory of the local poet, up the long hill by the sleepy railway station. She looked down a slope of green fields to the silver river, the leaden-coloured wedge of the eel-weir, the bright red brick of the county hospital, the restless white foam where the river cried outwards from a cold, dark gorge. Her life was like that on this morning, a river escaping from rocks, a child running zigzag across a daisied field.

Two miles outside the town a petrol lorry with defective brakes came, scattering screening stones, down a steep side road, ending for ever the journeys of the little green car. The woman died there on the side of the road, the green grass her death-bed, her head on the knees of the gambler.

IV

The Monologue of a Forgiving Wife to a Dark Husband

Look, darling, if I were in your shoes I'd stop worrying about the business. It was a shock to all of us, but what's happened has happened and a long face won't mend matters. Since I'm prepared to forget and forgive, I don't see why you should go on worrying and acting sometimes, honestly, darling, as if I was responsible for the whole affair. I wasn't, you know. When I came back with you from my mother's place I never thought I'd be brought face to face with tragedy. You made such a scene; said you'd take the children and charge me with desertion; you even threatened my mother with a prosecution for abduction or kidnapping or something. I was certain that from then on you were determined that our life in future would be as smooth as glass, with no drink or gambling. I know now that there are worse things than gambling, but I'm not going to make an issue of it, and I don't see why you should, darling. Nobody could be more sorry than myself about her death. She was my best friend. She always helped me out when you were being difficult, and, no matter what happened afterwards, she did bring us together in the beginning. It's very easy to forgive her and she's dead now. People do the oddest things, and, darling, since you'd probably have been foolish some time with somebody, wasn't it much better that she was the woman and not some mercenary slut of a waitress, with a scandal following the children all through their lives? As far as the neighbours are concerned, you had a perfectly sound reason for being there with her at that time. You were exonerated from all blame and the driver of the lorry lost his licence and got jail. It was early in the morning, so there wasn't even any suspicion that you were driving while drunk. Think of the things that could have happened scores of nights when you were driving home from the club. You have your new car now and your practice was never better. We're much better friends than we ever were, darling, aren't we? You can't have everything the way you want it. Mother always says: lucky at cards, unlucky in love, and what you lose on the swings you gain on the roundabouts. Death will come to all of us some day, darling, and her death was mercifully sudden. No lingering pain. I think when my own time comes I'd honestly prefer a sudden death, but for the sake of the children I hope it keeps away until I'm an old old woman.

V

For seven years of increasing prosperity and fame the gambler kept his bargain with Death. He purchased his magic car. He moved from a small house in the suburb near the mountains to a large house in a suburb by the sea. He established himself in consulting-rooms in a high house in a Georgian square. He healed the sick. He visited hospitals and hot, hushed rooms, and Death was always there; sometimes at the head of the bed and sometimes at the foot, at times a shadow, at other times a charitable visitor, an anxious relative, once or twice a weeping child. But always, by a word or a gesture or a glance of the eyes, he knew Death and kept his bargain.

Third Interlude

'It's a bargain,' says the gambler.

Death went off about his business and the gambler went off card-playing, as he was accustomed. He won as much money as he had ever lost, and more besides, until in the end he could find nobody to play with him. Then he took to the doctoring.

He kept healing sick people until he had his riches made. His reputation went farther than his foot ever walked, and his fame was that he was the greatest doctor in the world.

There was a rich man living in Spain and he fell ill.

FOUR

I

The teenagers had a wonderful party in the doctor's house the night before the French boy went home again to France. They had the house to themselves. The doctor and his wife came home early the next morning from a party in the professor's house; a farewell party too, for the doctor was going to France with the young French boy to see that he got safely home. The doctor's son was also going to France, to live and learn French in the French boy's home, as the French boy had for two months been learning English in the doctor's house.

For teenage girls living in a suburban seaside road on a rainy island, a French visitor in his teens is an experience. His face is brown, his features smooth, his hair dark and crisply curling, his accent like Charles Boyer, his eyes subtly glowing with the suggestion that he's older than his years and knows more than he says. And the French are the French — even if his two uncles are Jesuits in Lyons, his seven aunts Dominican nuns in Lourdes, his father and mother Franciscan tertiaries living in a château somewhere near Pau and keeping disciplines hanging on nails behind the doors of the visitors' rooms. The French boy, enjoying his first holiday away from his grimly sanctified parents, was escaping from a way of life as rigid as the Cistercian rule. He kissed a girl that summer for the first time in his life, subconsciously attributing the absence of immediate thunderbolting divine punishment to the moist island air. For the first time in his life he smoothed his lips around the sweet sounds: *Je t'aime.* The sixteen-year-old girl that he kissed felt Paris around her like a hot climate, and from a hearsay knowledge of what happened when you were married, she tingled to the tips of her toes. Her regular, island boy friend, square-faced, square-toed, slow-spoken, slow-witted, who at the age of sixteen and a half carried a rolled umbrella, was worried for a while by the French invasion.

Pierre arrived on the last day of May and the sun was

shining, a silver echo of the golden sun that in Basque country had burned his skin brown. Next day it rained steadily and a cold wind blew in from a high, grey sea. Pierre and the doctor's son went in the afternoon to a cinema in the city, met Miriam and the doctor's daughter. (The doctor's third child, a daughter, was only seven years of age, too young to go to the pictures.) Miriam is a tall, brown-haired girl, boldly featured, with a slight tendency to pimples which will vanish as she slips adolescence off her body like a tattered set of undies and grows up into handsome womanhood. Pierre said in stiff English: 'How do you do?' and she answered him in schoolgirl's French, and everybody laughed, and before the picture ended Miriam and Pierre were holding hands in the darkness.

Next day, also, the sun shone, and Miriam and Pierre went bathing. He tasted his first kiss in the shelter of the dunes, his second in the snowy whipping surf, his third on the sand in the silver sunlight. After that day the month of June went past in twenty-eight strides, alternate sun and rain, and kissing whenever practicable. In July the doctor drove all the way across the country to a seaside resort in the west, taking a party of seven other people along with him: his wife, their two eldest children, Pierre, Miriam, and Jane on the invitation of the doctor's daughter, and Joe — for once without his umbrella — on the invitation of the doctor's son.

They went all day across the country, the weather changing abruptly, showers scattering up from the south-west, and then brilliant sunshine. The sky was high: bright radiant blue varied with white, curling clouds, darkening suddenly when the showers came. Pierre admired the white, roadside cottages, the yellow thatched roofs, the brown stretches of bogland. He talked of the vast, sandy, silent pine forests below Bordeaux. He exclaimed with enthusiasm when he saw long, restless lakes, hills dissolving into mist on distant shores. He admired the rushing rock-torn western streams, still full and brown after recent rain, and told how the rivers came down blue-grey with flood-water from the high places around the Pic du Midi. Everything was lovely until they were a short distance from a market town close to the seaside resort. The doctor's wife said: 'This is the place, isn't it, dear?'

and consolingly she touched her hand on her husband's arm. He shook off the consoling hand with obvious roughness, broke off in the middle of the story he was telling, and was morose all the time they sat at dinner in the hotel in the market town. With his shock of hair gone grey in the last few years, with his long, hard face, his bushy eyebrows still dark, he could be a chilling companion. It wasn't until they had resumed their journey that he became again companionable. To the right of the road hundreds of white tents shone in the day's last sunshine. He parked the car close to a roadside cottage, said 'Back in a minute', went into the cottage, leaving the engine running. The young people and the doctor's wife stayed chatting in the car. A light shower blowing in from the sea whipped at the closed windows, streamed diagonal-wise across the windscreen. Fuchsia bushes growing by the drystone wall beside the cottage tossed their blooms in the moist wind: Japanese dancers dressed in red and green and purple. The doctor and the farmer-fisherman who lived in the cottage came out stooping under the low lintel, stood chatting for a while on the brown flagstone before the door, then shook hands. The farmer-fisherman closed the half-door, leaned on it, stayed pipe-smoking and waving a hand until the car moved away. 'Once upon a time,' said the doctor, 'I patched up an injured soldier in that cottage. I wanted to see if the place was still the same. But the people are new there now. They've new furniture and fittings and a modern range instead of the open hearth. Everything changes.' Everybody, even the doctor's wife, was silent for a while, because the doctor's deep-voiced words were spoken as if in solitude, seeking no answer.

They had a fine time, bathing, boating, dancing, tennis, picnics, walking by the light of the first harvest moon — if it hadn't been for the way jealousy developed between Miriam and Jane, who could never keep her nose out of another girl's business. Joe was civil and decent about it. When Jane and Pierre went night after night walking together, slyly slipping away from the rest of the party, poor Joe went on dancing, as if he hadn't a care in the wide world. He didn't even attempt to console himself with Miriam, who was looking pale, pimply, and wretched, and who would have welcomed Joe both for his own sake and for the opportunity of getting her own back on Jane. Always a little older than his years, Joe developed a close friendship with the doctor, walked with him and talked with him for hours on the green flat where a small stream twisted sluggishly towards the sea. He never mentioned, nor did the doctor, what they talked about on those occasions, but from the doctor's words the boy seemed to gather strength and an equanimity that annoyed Jane, who had a liking for feeling herself desired. Miriam had no similar source of strength. The storm broke on the night of that farewell party, with Jane saying to Miriam: 'You're all pimples' — an obvious truth; and Miriam saying to Jane: 'You're all padded' — a hidden truth, for Jane was the child of a modern mother who had initiated her daughter into certain tricks and techniques for making mountains out of molehills. Then Jane cried out before the whole assembly: 'Anyway, he's asked me to marry him,' and Miriam clawed Jane and Jane clawed Miriam, and they gripped each other's party hair-styles and held on.

Pierre laughed at the tugging girls because they were mauling each other for his sake and he had all his life been entombed in a decaying château . . . and then he saw the château so plainly that he became serious with leadership. He disentangled the two girls. He was brisk and efficient. He kissed Jane gently. He kissed Miriam gently. He stood between them with the easy composure inherited from men who had ruled men harshly and managed women adroitly for sunny centuries. He saw the three turrets, the high-windowed walls, strong stone soaked with sun, the steep slope down to the grey torrent, vineyards on the slope, the slow, yoked oxen, in the valley, maize plants denuded and drooping, poplars lined like graceful, green giantesses along the river, in the distance cloven peaks in the clear air.

II

The doctor, Pierre, and the doctor's son saw the château in reality three days later. They had a solemn, courteous welcome, presided over by one of the Jesuit uncles who was on a visit from Lyons. High above the valley and the grey poplar-guarded torrent the doctor spent two pleasant days considering the adaptability of his son; the rapidity with which a man's children grew up around him; and marvelling at the sights and sounds of a strange country.

On the third day he packed his light luggage and boarded a train going towards the Spanish frontier. He travelled alone, wanting to see Spain for himself. Beside the railway a road lined with walnut-trees went, rapid with scurrying cars, all the way to Perpignan. At Bayonne his eyes closed in sleep as the wheels clanked over a long metal bridge and opened again heavy with sleep to see fertile coastal land, white hotels, and villas, the waters of Biscay blue in warm peace. He took off his light alpaca jacket, opened the front of his shirt, rolled up his sleeves, opened all the windows.

He tried until he was tired to suck coolness out of the idea that a train moving at seventy miles an hour must create a refreshing air current, or out of the reflection that down deep under blue Biscay water fish swam in coolness like that of white foam tossed in summer on the dim island shores of Britain and Ireland. It was no good. He sweated as if the compartment was a Turkish bath. He slept uneasily, awoke drenched with perspiration, saw low, crouching hills where France and Spain locked arms around a small bay and across a slow river. With infinite weariness he saw ahead of him hundreds of mountainous miles of arid, burning Spain. He remembered all the horrible tales he had heard from truthful travellers about the railways of Spain, about officials who, with Moorish imperturbability and indifference to the passage of time, said *No se puede* to the most rational request. Then the train slowed and stopped. He saw written large the name of the last French town. He grabbed his luggage, leaped to the platform, presented his ticket, walked across the blazing street to the hotel. When he had filled in the official form he sat in the cool, darkened restaurant, sipped watery yellow ale, talked with three Basques and a Parisian railway official who played a card game that was Gallic cousin to poker. When he had the hang of it he took a hand, won easily for half an hour, provoked much laughter from the players and the proprietor and the proprietor's three sisters at the luck of the uninitiate stranger. Then they drank and sang until darkness dropped slyly from the eastern mountains.

III

The four days spent in that town were happy. He had found rest and peace, losing all desire to cross the river and look at Spain. Once a man loses all desire to go round the hill or over the river or outside the door of a room or inside the door of another room, he tastes in calm without motion the green oily drink of happiness.

In the mornings, shaved and dressed, perfumed as the men of the place perfumed themselves against perspiration and the sun, he sat, feeling like an oriental prince, on the balcony outside his bedroom window. In the comparative cool of the morning the place buzzed with life. Men in Spanish uniform and men in French uniform moved briskly around a little platform built outside the main station. Traffic went up and down on the street below the balcony: south to Spain, north into France, south to Africa, and north and east across the patch-work pattern of Europe. He watched the people who stepped out of parked cars, sipped drinks or ate snacks at the red and green tables below. He overheard their talk: French and Spanish, which he understood; German and Swiss German, Dutch, Portuguese, Basque, Italian, which he recognized; other languages which he neither understood nor recognized — floating upwards to his ears sometimes as the words of angels, sometimes as the sputtering noises of men creeping like animals out of unknown jungles. His balcony was a throne and he was an emperor surveying his people. His balcony was high heaven and he was God looking down on all nations and tribes. This was how a golden-haired God — was it Aengus dressed in the clothes of a priest of Christ? — might feel on his rainy Irish mountain: moveless, undisturbed, and the world going past like the wind.

The sun flexed his muscles, stretched out his neck until he glared over the roof of the hotel and down directly on the balcony. Sheltering in the back of the café, four steps lower than the street and as dark as a cave, the doctor sipped for his aperitif the rich local liqueur, grass-green, sweet, and almost viscous, smelling of nodding flowers and apple blossoms swinging in cool mountain valleys. The gamblers gathered around his circular, marble-topped table and once again he was a gambler among gamblers, winning every game with absurd ease.

A great place for peace, he said, walking the long street that sloped up from the railway station to the square, when the sun had exhausted himself and was running, a beaten bully, from relentless shadows. Two miles to the left, beyond a maze of railway tracks, a belt of tufted Eastern trees, a calm corner of the sea, was the first headland of Spain. A great place for eating and for drinking tall bottles of red Irouleguy and dainty glasses of the green fire made in guarded secrecy in a clean distillery beside the parish church. Upstairs, when he sat at dinner, the swirl of southern music, the measured sounds of agile feet, the clicking of castanets, as some of the girls of the town under the leadership of the mayor's daughter rehearsed for a dance festival. A great place for sun-ripened, little women, he thought, seeing three in particular: two dark-haired ringleted girls standing one evening at the barrier by the bridge, twin sisters probably, alike even in their lithe way of walking, white blouses slipping down off smooth, brown shoulders; and a fair woman, neat shorts and thighs the colour of rich wheat, seen once, as storytellers once glimpsed Helen, walking around the red-sanded town square.

Bats soared and descended, looped erratically around the plane-trees and between the high houses of the square. All day the shutters on the thin windows were closed against the heat, but at night they were flung open, as if the town gaped through a hundred mouths to suck coolness from the sea-wind. He sat on a red chair and at a white table before a café in the square, deeply drinking red Irouleguy. From where he sat he could look between trees and across clean red sand to the Moorish outline of the parish church and the brightly painted walls of the distillery. An old man who sat every night in that café, drinking the liqueur made at the opposite side of the square — a finger-depth of green fire diluted in a tumblerful of Vichy water — talked of the Spanish war and of Basque refugees crossing the river from Guipúzcoa.

On the doctor's last night in the town — he didn't then guess that it was going to be his last night — the old man, pouncing suddenly, captured between aged skeleton hands a bat that had dropped fluttering wildly on the white table. Then, lifting his feet high as if his leg muscles had been contracted by rheumatism, the ancient stepped out to the centre of the red sand, opened his hands, and hooshed the bat upwards, offering its awkward body, half mouse, half bird, to the spirit above the velvet night. Something in that action — the pouncing capture, the theatrical mincing walk, the absurd gesture of release and oblation — snapped a spring in the doctor's gambling soul; set him shouting laughter with and at the old sloppy-slippered Frenchman; set him drinking until the sand was gold-dust, the plane-trees whispering people, until he and the old hobbling man were boys together. They sang as they made their way through a maze of lanes towards the sea. He left the old man safely on his own doorstep, promising to meet him again on the following night. He walked home alone by the edge of the water, seeing the faces and the meaning of the people he knew more vividly now that, walking in a strange country, he was separated from them by restless miles of ocean. One face he saw with exceptional, frightening clarity. The ocean rolled between. The clay for years had covered that face. Decay had long ago destroyed the features. From this foreign night, wind rustling in exotic trees, lapping Biscay water, the distant lights of Spain, the red lamp shining in the parish church in God's eyes, he could not extract the meaning of her life, of her calamitous death. He passed a high building, dead except for one living lighted room, where four people sat card-playing. The window was open and uncurtained. He looked over a low hedge and railings, tempted to call to the gamblers, to ask for a hand in the game; deterred because he knew that there he would find no clue to the mysteries surrounding him: her life and death, his own strange powers, those two mad, distant days in Dublin, a priest saying: 'I am God,' a contact-man saying: 'I am Death.'

Was the secret hidden here in the settled peace of the town up on the hill, by the edge of a pear-shaped bay set in between France and Spain like rich fruit between greedily closing hands? Or had he missed noticing it in the church where his child had been baptized, or above the pines on the boggy mountain, or in the tavern where the bell rang and no answer came, or in that other tavern where twelve men danced in a circle to celebrate a death? Or for his third request should he have cried out: Tell me how? Tell me why?

On a grassy patch beside the road a couple made love elegantly. Was his secret there in their graceful embrace, or in an old dodderer catching a bat and offering its blind, slimy body to the skies, in any incident anywhere, in things as trivial as a child dropping a penny on the pavement, a country musician tuning a fiddle, a bird whipping across the sky, a girl dancing? Or was it to be found in violent, horrible things: a drunken soldier gashing with jagged glass his companion's face, an old man spitting death by the bed of a sick child? Would he know everything on the day he broke his bargain with Death?

The walk by closed, empty hotels had deadened in him the joy of wine. Tired, thirsty, depressed, he crossed the square again to the café; sat drinking until the place was empty except for himself and the proprietor. Then they bade each other good night, and the doctor, a red bottle tucked under each oxter, went singing through the deserted town. He sang old Gaelic ballads made by people who lived in small cabins in lonely places by Atlantic seas. He staggered, shouting, over the railway bridge, finished the emptying of one red bottle, some of it into his mouth and some of it on the parapet of the bridge, then tossed the empty bottle whirling to smash with a tremendous explosion on the maze of railway tracks. Beyond the bridge a woman, young and slender against the yellow lamp-light of her room, looked out from a high window; and young again himself, defying death, he waved to her, called to her lovingly; crossed the road and, reckless of knives of husbands and brothers or of police batons, hammered on the heavy door. But the house remained silent, and when he looked up again the lamp was no longer lighting, the lady gone from the window. He stood swaying by the unresponsive door, wondering who she might be; lovely or ugly, happy or lonely, or had he seen her ever on the sunny streets, or was she the wheat-thighed woman who walked like Helen, or one of those twin white-bloused girls with tanned bare shoulders. Maudlin with drink, he turned away from the door to see a man watching him from the other side of the road.

It was one of the gamblers from his own hotel: a hungry-faced, hawk-nosed, witty-tongued man who had served as a soldier in Indo-China. He crossed the road to meet the doctor, raised his right hand, holding his beret in salute, took the doctor's arm in his, and turned with him towards the hotel.

He said sympathetically: *'Tu es cuit, ma parole.'*

'Another bottle here.'

'There are other houses more suitable than that. If you so desire.'

'No. No. Only a passing fancy. The wine.'

'The wine is a great breeder of fancies.'

'I saw a woman at the window.'

'Ah, *oui!* That woman. So sad. She is beautiful. But she is so alone.'

'Why alone?'

'Once she loved. A fine handsome fellow. A friend of my own heart. But he is killed. In an instant. Like that. Eaten by a machine in a factory. When she hears a step in the street she looks out. Hoping, perhaps? Perhaps she does not sleep.'

A passing fancy had set him knocking on that door. He sat with the hawk-nosed man on a bench outside the railway station. Death had once come knocking at that door, bringing news of a body mangled in a distant factory; a handsome man eaten by a steel machine. Even in this place of peace, sunshine, wine, old men and bats, oily-leaved trees, green fire, red sand.

'There are other houses,' said the hawk-nosed man. 'Two of them. Down by the shore.'

They drank, turn about, out of the last bottle. The road sloped up from the station, vanished over the hill, across the bridge to Spain. Here, or in Spain, or in London, or in Ireland he must go on to the breaking of his bargain.

'No. No other houses.'

The hawk-nosed man emptied the bottle. *'Très bien,'* he said, and the doctor, standing at the door of the hotel, watched him walk lightly up the road towards the bridge.

Tomorrow he would go that way himself, put his feet on the ground of Spain.

IV

In the sluggish water of the river small fish with big heads played at acrobatics. The girders of the bridge scorched at the touch. The sun in his power had no mercy on rivers or mountains. But walking in the sun's full heat was now less to the doctor than the restless horror of desiring to cross a bridge, or a road, or an ocean.

This was the best way to pass a frontier: on foot and alone, unencumbered by any baggage. His one case was in the hotel to be called for, or, if not called for in three weeks, sent back to Paris. He had no plans, was free to walk at his ease, seeing how two countries grew out from one river like a multi-coloured leaf on its stem.

From the frontier to the first Spanish town the road runs straight, shaded by closely planted trees, raised high on an embankment above flat riverside fields. A lizard takes the sun in a shy corner where the town's first wall commences.

The children are clean and curious. The men are magnificently dressed. The women are big in bottom and bust, bold in the eyes.

For two hours he sat in the shade watching the main street: some old houses, occasional wrecks — like rotten teeth in a sound mouth — where shells had landed, blocks of high modern buildings, some of them nakedly new, others still ugly with scaffolding. Two-by-two, soldiers and policemen walked past, weary in heavy uniforms, burdened with ugly machine-guns. Little brown men in berets and dark dungarees sprawled in groups on the ground wherever a tree or a jutting wall made a patch of shadow.

Whether a man runs or walks or swims or sits down or flies in an aeroplane, he moves always at the same speed towards the breaking of bargains.

Was there one person walking here in the sun or sitting in the shade who shared his experience?

A cart drawn by two slow oxen goes creaking down the

street, a barefoot man walking in front holding the long goad solemnly at the perpendicular before his nose, turning at intervals to tap directions with the goad on the yoke between the horns of the oxen. Their eyes shaded by fringes falling from the yoke, they follow docilely the movement of his bare feet.

If she had lived he might one day have attempted to tell her that he was a man who had talked with God and looked into the face of Death. Even if his story led her, as it must, to fear for his sanity, he could still depend on her discretion and sympathy. But she was dead these six years, and there was no one alive who would understand: not his wife, nor his children, nor the men who were supposed to be his friends. How could one expect them to understand? In seven years he had learned the high cost of singularity.

Could he tell his secret in French or in Spanish, to some chance acquaintance made preternaturally wise by the constant pitiless sun, or by the mysticism of his race, or hardened for ever against madness and strange stories by memories of some night of war flattening his home, killing his people. His eyes searched the street for a listener. That thin woman with the lines of some loveless experience about her mouth? That workman more quiet than his fellows, a ravenous anger in his dark eyes? One of the passing gun-burdened guards, the careless waiter, any one of a dozen spotless staring children? So, searching for a listener, he went restlessly up the street, his hat-brim pulled down over his eyes, staring at every face, being pleasantly stared at in return. That little Basque girl, perhaps, whose eyes for a moment touched his with a divine inquiry? He turned and walked the way she was going, loitered outside a shop while she bought some sticky sweets, feeling that here in the sun such a pursuit was as natural as in some ancient Grecian wood, as it could never be on rainy pavements in a northern city. Outside the dirty, bullet-marked railway station she boarded a tram and he followed — suddenly, unreasonably as gay as a boy absorbed in his first flirtation. It was the world's worst tramway: bumping and jerking along at two miles an hour as if it was flying at eighty, swinging out at every corner as if it would leave the tracks and jerk over a wall into somebody's garden.

After a long time they left the suburbs behind. She sat opposite him. Once, when the tram leaped like a hooked fish, one of the two conductors lost his footing and expostulated with the crowding passengers. She smiled at that, a quick little smile coming and going like a touch of a breeze on the skin of a deep lake. Recovering slowly from his first frenzy, he knew that the smile was as little interested in particular persons as the sun or the wind; and he noticed that she was short and stout and probably not more than fourteen years of age. Swaying, now uncomfortably, with the cracked antics of the tram, he thought: an old fool is the worst fool.

High red-roofed houses with blue and white shutters. In the semi-darkness of the ground floors the shapes of chained, stall-fed cattle. In the main street of the fishing village, where the tram came to its terminus, the odours of onions, garlic, fish, stale wine, thickened in warm, still air under motionless trees. A statue of the Virgin brightened with gaudy colours a niche in the white wall over a Moorish archway.

Without emotion he watched the girl walk away from him through the archway. Very slowly he went in the same direction, through narrow streets overshadowed by similar high coloured houses, the air always liquid with warm smells, until he came out above the deep sand of the shore. Hundreds of children played on the sand or jack-acted around boats floating in shallow water. A pair of oxen with patient effort dragged their cumbersome wagon over the yellow yielding earth. Fishermen, home from the sea, smoked and argued by the long wall above the strand. He sat with them on the wall, looking out across the bay at France — a headland of dark trees jutting over the water, or looking inland at the high, narrow streets of the village. Higher still and isolated on a soaring rock, a great white house with round windows stood solitary and proud.

He'd almost forgotten he was a man with a secret, with another life as a famous doctor in a distant city, with a son in a château learning French. Men for centuries had gossiped on this wall, forgetting their real lives. Their musical speech, sometimes Basque, sometimes a Spanish he couldn't understand, the shrill calls of running children, soothed him as the meaningless sounds of a lullaby soothe a child. It needed hunger and thirst to recall him to time and the truth that in an hour the sun would drop like a red coal sizzling into the water.

V

The outside of the café was a curious imitation of an English cottage. He passed through a creaking gate, along a narrow paved path bordered with sharp sea-shells, went stooping through the doorway into a dark cluttered shop. The smells of the south stopped abruptly on the threshold as if repelled by the curious alien appearance of timbered walls and red-tiled roof. Some Spaniard or some Basque had travelled to England, or captured the idea in a glossy magazine, or married an Englishwoman, and then startled and amused his native village by building this disguise for his café. It was only a disguise. Beyond the dark shop was a space of yellow sand, partially roofed for shade, whispering with oily trees, tables tucked here and there in corners, somewhere the faint jingling sweetness of a hand strumming strings. He walked to the far edge of the sand, through a maze of tables and little trees to the white ironwork railings. He picked a chair at a table from which he could see a corner of the life of the village: armed soldiers supervising work on a breakwater; four boats and twenty splashing, shouting children; a triangle of tall houses; a pointed arch framing against the light a group of gossiping fishermen. Above all that, the great white house balanced on the edge of the rock.

He settled himself comfortably in his chair, waited for the waiter or the waitress, listened to the faint suck of the sea against the wall below the white railings. Then, looking around, he saw a few yards away, at a table in a corner between two trees, a woman sitting alone.

It was her seclusion, her immobility, hands lying in her lap and clasped tightly, that made him look a second time. Her bright red hair made him look a third time. Although her eyes seemed absorbed by the sun poised above the wooded headland, he felt that she had watched him with interest from the moment he'd entered.

She said: 'You're a stranger here.'

'I'm a great stranger here. But I like it.'

She was somewhere in the middle thirties, a small, oval-faced woman.

'The few strangers who come here always like it.'

'It's peaceful.'

'Always peaceful. Even when the war passed through the great town to the bridge.'

'It's as if one's normal life didn't matter any more.'

'When you live here your normal life is part of the place.'

'Part of the peace, then.'

'No. No.' For the first time she moved, shaking her head sadly, emphatically, raising her hands, breaking the grip that had bound them closely together, letting them fall separately, palms down, on her knees. Her skirt was a sombre unshining black.

'Peace,' she said, 'is a thing a stranger sees in passing. A homeless man walking through the street of a village peeps in at a window and sees peace in a lighted room. He walks on lonely, remembering that room, desiring peace. But there may be anger in that house; fear, hate, or death in a dark room above the lighted room.'

'What could you know about death? You're too young.' She was beautiful in a bony, intense, fragile way. Her red hair and pale skin seemed in that place as exotic as the woman of a romantic poet's dream walking among fishwives.

'That is true.' A fat waitress came between them, bowed respectfully to the little woman, listened to the stranger's order with fidgety attention, shuffling her slippered feet on the sand. 'That is true,' the little woman said again, inclining her head, politely agreeing, when the waitress had gone. 'I have known nothing of death. My father and mother are still alive in Madrid. I was an only child. No person dear to me has yet died. I have never seen a dead body. Even when the war came and my people were killing each other, I seemed to be protected from the sight of death. That is why I find it now difficult to look day after day on a man slowly dying.'

Her small hands had come together again, creeping on

her dark skirt like white animals coupling or crouching for warmth. In a moment of silence, the shouting children gone, the workers stepping carefully shorewards along the jagged teeth of the uncompleted breakwater, he could hear her knuckles cracking with agonized pressure.

'You're in trouble.'

The last man in the line of workers leaped from the last tooth of the breakwater to the firm shore, shouted his jubilation at the day's work ended and the feel of rich sand under his feet. The sun was quenched as he leaped and shouted. The woman in the shadows remained silent.

'Could I help you? Who is the dying man?' When she didn't answer, he said: 'Perhaps I shouldn't ask that.'

'There is no reason why you shouldn't. You look wise. I could talk to you, and I can talk to nobody in this place. You are a stranger passing and you see peace.'

The fat waitress shuffled back over the sand, pressed a hidden switch, and lights glowed, coloured rose and green, in the hearts of the little trees. She left wine, bread, meat, and shuffled away again.

'Tell me, then,' he said.

'Ah, there is not much to tell. He is my husband. He is a very fine man. He was chosen for me by my parents. There was no madness in our love. We were at peace for ten years. Even when the war happened, when his wild brother was driven out over the bridge with the refugees. Then my husband fell ill. That was two years ago. Up there now he lies dying.'

Her right hand, clingingly, reluctantly, parted company with her left, pointed rigidly over the railings, and upwards. The last light, rising from the sea at an angle over the dark headland, brightened the walls of the great white house.

'The doctors say it is useless to hope.'

He was mesmerized by the way the pointing hand returned to find and grip its fellow, as if fingers twining tightly with fingers kept her from throwing her arms wide, crying to, beseeching the hot, dark-purple heavens.

'What are the symptoms?'

'Our doctors here are not so good. They say they do not know what the disease is.'

He had read in ancient books about the antics and eccentricities of the doctors of Spain: Sangrado's phlebotomy; the surgeon's fatal stab regarded, by a people used to bull-fights, as one of those inevitable things — *Cosas de España*: country curates and quacks furnishing incantatory remedies; a drink made of a hundred herbs, *centum herbae*, and claimed to be capable of healing all ills; pulverized stones sold at Manresa, where Ignatius did vigil, and swallowed as physic by the faithful. But years had passed since those books were written, often by unsympathetic travellers. Wars had happened, revolutions, modern science, new drugs, social reform, welfare states, microbes, and Maeterlinck's diseases ill and in prison in the caverns of night.

He said again: 'What are the symptoms? If the doctors here are not so good, why don't you send somewhere for a specialist?'

'Yes, a specialist. Two of them came on the same day. One from San Sebastian and the other from Madrid. They argued a long time and used great words in several languages. My husband said pains, dreadful pains in the left arm and side, and they looked at him and tapped him all over, and used more big words. They told him to rest. They told me to abandon hope. It is difficult to abandon hope. I do not blame them. It is just that doctors are helpless when Death makes up his mind.'

'Death has been cheated before now.'

'I have never watched it happen.' Abruptly on the far headland the lights of France danced like frosty stars. 'I have never seen Death cheated. I have never seen him have his will. But I have sat by a bedside for months and Death has sat with me, waiting.'

He knew now why he'd lingered in peace in that French town, why the peace had finally been shattered by wine, a woman at a window, a hawk-nosed man walking up the road towards Spain. He knew why he'd followed a too-mature child, like a satyr pursuing a sound in the grass and brambles; a memory of the white breasts of a fleeing nymph. The lights of France knowingly watched him. He said: 'In my own country I'm a doctor.' The small oily trees rustled. The water with the regular beat of a Latin chant lapped the stones below the white railings. 'May I see your husband? I might be able to help him. And you.'

In the long silence that followed he counted the beat of the sea nine times against the wall, nine long waves smoothing deserted sand, rasping in distant shingle.

'You are a stranger. I have never seen you before. You will go from here and never return. Yet, since you walked into this place and sat down at that table, I have felt that I could trust you, that you would know and understand. But I am afraid that if you walk with me up there —'

The two hands remaining locked together gestured towards the sky where the high white house, outlines now fading, showed two round lighted windows and a pale blur of wall.

'— I am afraid that with every step upwards my hope will grow until it bursts my body.'

'I offer you no increase in hope.' Power over Death when Death or his sign sat at the foot of the bed. Power over Death when Death or his sign sat at the head of the bed. Except that the use of that power breaks my bargain. 'But I can see your husband if you so wish. There's always a chance.' Some day or some night, in Spain or in Ireland, in Paris or in London, a man must break his bargain.

'Come with me,' she said. 'It is a great climb. It is high up a steep winding road.'

'My limbs are equal to it. I've dined.'

Side by side they treaded the sandy maze between little trees glowing with light. The leaves were quickened by the air from the sea. She was taller than she had seemed when sitting down. At the counter in the cottage he paid for his meal. She walked before him along the path between the rows of sharp sea-shells. He reached around her to open the creaking gate. They were together in the dark street, breathing the same warm clogged air, walking a little apart from each other, not talking at all.

VI

It was a great climb. It was high up a steep winding road, chiselling at first through sheer walls of moist, threatening rock, then coming out on a perilous ledge looking away from the village. A few miles distant the lights of the town on the Spanish side of the bridge reddened the sky. The road, just wide enough for one car to go without risk between the face of the rock and the protecting railings, went around and around, gradually ascending, passing under buttresses built at intervals to guard against falls of soil and stones. Now they could see, below, the dim, tree-smothered streets of the village, the glowing trees in the café, beyond the bay the dancing French lights. A turn of the circling road and they saw only dark water, the headland, spotted with lamps burning in lonely houses, lying down on the sea like a brooding monster. Another turn and again they looked south towards the hidden immensity of Spain and the red glow in the sky.

She stopped by a small door opening in the solid rock. 'This is a shorter way. It is all steep steps, but it is direct.'

'You're my guide.'

'You trust me a great deal. I might be leading you to your death.'

'You might indeed. You might also be walking round a rock in the company of a strangler.'

'We must then trust each other,' she said. 'You are a stranger to me. I am a stranger to you.' She opened the door on impenetrable blackness. 'Even if I am walking in my own place. Even if this rock is as familiar to me as the face of my mother.' She stepped forward, vanishing, her dark skirt, her dark shawl, her red hair, into the blackness. He heard the shuffle of her slippered feet on dry stone, the rustle of her clothes. He took one cautious step towards the sound, heard the click of a switch, was startled and dazzled by a line of lights leaping upwards like a curving constellation, illuminating a steep stairway tunnelling through rock towards the white house. He followed her stiffly, not as agile on stairs as he once had been. The years were gripping his knees, tightening sinews and muscles. He counted the steps. Seventy-nine. He counted the soaring lights. One light for, approximately, every eleven steps. His ninety-fourth pace from the foot of the tunnelling stairway left him standing by her side on the threshold of the white house.

White walls. The stone was cold as marble to the touch.

A great door of oak studded with brass. It should have been opened by two bowing servants, but she opened it herself with a quiet key. A passage floored with smooth stone, walled with smooth stone. He followed her past three protruding pillars, touching each pillar to assure himself of reality, and under two arches. When, through a third arch, he could see in a dim patio the sparkle of fountain water rising and falling, phosphorescent in the night, catching and again losing glimmers of light from unseen windows, she turned to the left, ascended a curving staircase on steps of wide polished oak. Taking two steps at a time, he followed. It wasn't easy to keep up with her quick jerking step. She whispered: 'Do I walk too quickly?'

'No question for a young woman to ask an ageing man.'

'You are not old.'

'Thank you.'

'It is the truth.'

Then, as they came to the top of the stairs and another long passage, open and pillared like a cloister, on the side overlooking the patio and the fountain, she said: 'You must eat and drink in our house.'

'I've dined.'

'My husband, if he were well, would wish every stranger to be suitably welcomed to his house.'

'First of all, let me see your husband.'

'I will see if he sleeps.'

Night air, as they walked, came cool between the arches. They went now side by side along the cloistered passage. The water of the fountain rose and fell, a seething, tinkling, lulling sound. Water has a hundred voices. 'A lovely place,' he said.

'It is a fine house. It is old. It was built on this high rock by my husband's great-great-grandfather. The world has changed so much since then.'

'Servants are scarce. Labour's dear.'

'Servants are different now. A house like this is a weight on any woman in any country. I have only one servant. She is a little girl from the village.'

They turned the right angle of the cloister. A few yards ahead a door opened and closed. Nobody came out or went in, but a bar of light dropped almost audibly across their path, then vanished again as the door closed. 'That is his room,' she said. 'The captain must have heard our steps.'

She had only one servant: a girl from the village. Her husband was bedridden. But the door had opened and closed as they approached, released for a moment a bar of light, then recaptured it greedily. The captain had heard their steps. 'I hope I'm not being too inquisitive,' the doctor said, 'but who's the captain?'

She gripped his left biceps with the small fingers of her right hand, so swiftly, so sharply that through thin jacket and silk shirt-sleeve she nipped his flesh. The fountain down below sang with a score of water's hundred voices: voices of velvet darkness, of the light that leaks out of even the darkest sky, of the yellow lamp-light lancing out from some unseen window. It was as if on the sacred floor of a temple he had spoken the unutterable word, the one dreadful syllable symbolizing the unseen. The door was still closed. No light came through. The light that lanced and melted into the rising and falling singing water must come from the window of the room where the one servant, the girl from the village, undressed for sleep. The little woman said: 'Perhaps I should have warned you.' Her eyes were fixed on the closed door. She was rigid with pride, concealing a fear that might if yielded to, if admitted, have set her limbs quivering. But he wasn't deceived. He'd seen so many brave people concealing fear, rigid in their wrestling with fear.

'Today, earlier, I may have mentioned my husband's brother. He was driven out with the refugees.'

'I think I remember.'

'He has returned. He is hiding in this house.'

'Perhaps you shouldn't tell me this —'

'It does not matter. Even if I knew you were a secret policeman I think I would still tell you.'

'You don't like the captain?'

'I could kill him if I was not afraid of seeing Death, if I did not fear that his end might also kill my husband. I could betray him. I could watch him burn or die of thirst.'

She hissed, whispering into his ear, standing on her tiptoes, gripping his arm, her body rigid, but not now with pride concealing fear.

'Why not, then? The village is alive with men with guns. They're leaning against the wall at the corner of every street. They'd be glad to hear of the refugee's return —'

'I cannot. I cannot. It cannot be done.' It was the traditional phrase used by unwilling officials. But it came from her lips electrically, alive as an eel, poisonous as an adder. 'My husband loves him because he thinks it is sacred duty to love one's brother.'

'I see now why you hate him.'

'No. You do not understand. How could you? You are a stranger. You think this is a peaceful place because there are no black ruins, no unburied bodies lying in the street.' She walked back a little the way they had come, and leaning against one of the pillars, looked down into the patio where the fountain, wavering, whispering, rose and fell. He stood beside her. 'You do not think to ask me why my husband's brother has returned into danger. It is real danger. There is proof that he killed a man in the town by the bridge.'

'In a war men kill and get killed.'

'This killing had nothing to do with war.'

Somewhere in the unseen room the girl from the village quenched the flame in the lamp, snuggled her brown body between sheets as cool as the white walls. The fountain sang now only with the seven voices of darkness, the seven voices of secret phosphorescent light leaking from the velvet sky.

'I waste your time,' she said. 'I spoil your holiday. I should never have brought you to this unlucky house. Death is here waiting.'

He touched her small hand, like a tiny, cold animal against the cold pillar. 'If I could help you it would be no waste of time. Shall we go to see your husband?'

'You are very kind. But first I must tell you. You must understand about this brother. Trouble has always followed him. It is not his politics. It is himself. He has returned here because —'

Her back was to the pillar, her face a blob. Her breath was warm, smelling like rich milk. Her odd red hair had been washed and dressed in some liquid as sweet as apple blossom; and in one instant of desire, towering above her, he tasted red wine, green fire; felt the sensuous sun, saw ripening bodies, trees rich with oil, the cool paradise of the sea. This was a house, a night, and a happening to drive a man mad, to restore life to a charred log, a dry nettle.

'— returned here because —'

She lingered on the words. Did she sense the madness that had touched him for a moment?

'— because he wants me.'

He was ashamed of his madness, his grey hairs, the stiffness behind his knees, the realization that he was common clay with the evil captain.

'Even with his brother dying here in this house he speaks to me as a man might speak to a girl in a brothel. If I tell the police he is here I save myself, but I hasten my husband's end.' She walked towards the closed door of the room where the sick man lay. He walked beside her, feeling old and miserable, shame dredging his soul for memories: two children, a green place, a strong, dark woman who was dead, and, strange because most poignant, memories of three children, a clubhouse, six friends, a suburban house, a pretty, selfish woman. 'If I tell my husband the truth I have still only hastened his death. What can I do? If my husband were well. If the truth were not strong enough and wicked enough to kill him!'

Her small fingers searchingly touched the wood, as if she were trying to read through their sensitive tips some meaning in oaken carving, some ease for her fears, some answer for her questions. The doctor gripped the knob, turned it, pushed the door open on the room, the captain, the dying man.

VII

High on mountain slopes above flat valleys, with poplars lined beside slowing torrents, above small vine patches and shining villages, but below the beginnings of the bare rocks, the oak-trees grew. Woodsmen of two countries hewed them down. The saw-mills of two countries smoothed and shaped them. Craftsmen of two countries worked the wood with confidence and precision, expressing images and patterns native to the sun-soaked land. Now as the door opened the doctor saw a room in which skilful men had caught the secret of those mountain forests: the strength of the trees, their beauty in age, their straight lines forceful enough to hold up the sky, their muscular curves threatening to break the deep grip of the roots in mountain soil.

For a moment the room blinded his eyes to the sick man on his bed. Carven images of plants and blossoms flowered on the foot of the bed as if the brown wood were alive and growing. A settle with similar carvings stood along the wall beside an empty, gaping fireplace, partially hidden by a jarring, grotesquely modern washstand. The round windows, draped with light curtains, were open to the air.

'This is the new doctor,' she said, speaking neither to the invisible captain nor to the dark head above the bed-clothes, but to past generations and a lost host of servants.

'A new doctor is always welcome,' said the captain. He didn't rise from his concealment in a deep chair between the wall and the head of the bed. His voice was high-pitched, querulous, protesting against his fate, cracked a little with the vexation of futile villainous love. 'From Madrid?' he asked.

'From London,' lied the doctor. Closer to the bed now, the room and the forests it interpreted in grotesque carvings, in panelling and furniture, faded from his eyes. The lamp-light was reflected dimly from old dark wood. He saw a thin, wasted face dirty with two days' beard, hair that had gone sparse on the high crown and over wide temples. The eyes were closed. Without stooping down he could hear the rasp of troubled breathing, could smell faintly the smell of a body imprisoned for a long time in the same bed in the same room in a hot country.

Power over Death when Death sits at the foot of the bed!

'From London,' the high-pitched voice said. 'I was in London once. I came back to a grateful country.'

'We are not interested,' the woman said.

'But I must tell you. In London I was poor and alone. The skies were dull. But my country offers me the sun even if I am denied liberty.'

The voice leaped a note to shrill laughter. 'But you have never been in exile, my beloved beautiful sister.' He had not risen from the chair. He was hidden by shadows and the high carven bedstead. Lamp-light sinking and drowning in the depths of old wood. The doctor listened to the captain's voice. But he looked only at the sleeping face in the bed. He wasn't anxious to see too clearly the captain in the high chair.

'Is he asleep?' he asked.

She stood close behind the doctor, placing his long, hard body between herself and the horror of approaching death and the unwelcome desires of her husband's brother. 'He may be asleep. But often he lies like that without moving, for long times. Perhaps he is too weak to open his eyes.'

'The greatest of all poets was an exile, just as I was an exile. Here in the shadows I read his verse while I wait for something to happen.'

'The doctor will be busy now.'

'My eyes are sharp. I can see clearly in the shadows. That's because the nights in Spain are brighter than the days in London.'

'You must go out of the room while the doctor attends to my husband.'

'I must not, dear sister. I must sit here in my chair and see what this strange doctor does to my brother.'

'My husband.'

'My brother. Can you trust a doctor, met an hour ago in the village?'

She said quietly: 'Filthy snake!'

'Please, my sister. We do not speak so to each other before strangers. If he dies this rock is mine. I'm responsible for the treatment he gets.'

'How do you know where we met?' said the doctor, looking fixedly at the still face in the bed.

'I was there.'

She whispered: 'Liar.'

'Where then did you meet, sister? When?'

She didn't answer. The doctor gently took between his fingers the dying man's wrist. The pulse was faint.

'Don't you agree with me, Doctor? Isn't it my duty as my brother's brother to stay here?'

'Please yourself,' said the doctor, feeling the faint pulse, looking steadily at the unshaven face. Behind him the door was opened, slammed shut again. The woman was gone from the room. The voice explained:

'My sister's hasty. She doesn't love me.'

'I couldn't blame her.'

'Oh, perhaps I'm not a pleasant fellow. But I've suffered. War. Killing. Destruction. Exile. I liked exile least of all. They may not welcome me here, but I love the place. The sun. This rock. This house. That woman. I haven't the fortitude of that greatest of great poets. He could harden himself, find consolation. I never could.' In the shadows between the chair and the head of the bed the pages of a book were rustled. 'Please, Doctor, don't say you're not interested. If my sister only understood how much it hurts when she says she's not interested.'

The doctor kept his eyes fixed on the face in the bed. He rested the thin hand, wrist marked vividly by blue veins, on the white turndown of the sheet. 'I'm very interested,' he said.

'Thank you. Thank you.' The voice shrilled gratitude, the voice of a troublesome, petulant child softened by an unexpected concession. 'Then, may I read to you while you work? I'm fond of reading. I love to read aloud. But in this house I can read aloud only in my own company, and that's an imperfect joy. My poor brother couldn't hear me. The servant wouldn't understand. My sister will never listen.'

'Read away, then.'

'Thank you. May I read you what the great poet who walked in hell and purgatory and heaven said about exile?'

'You may.' For a flashing second he thought the eyelids of the face in the bed fluttered. But he was mistaken. Some slight puff of wind from the sea had squeezed through the circular windows, set the lamp-flame trembling, light wrestling with shadows.

'I'm not as proud as that poet. He could under certain conditions have returned in peace to his native place. He refused. He would return only on his own terms. But I, like a beaten dog, was glad to creep back secretly with no safeguards, no conditions. Naturally, I'd have loved to walk back on flowers and under red flags, have my sleep cushioned by the choicest maidens —'

'Read your poet.'

Again in the shadows the pages rustled. The thin voice read: 'Shall one who has preached justice and suffered injustice pay money to those who have injured him, as though they had been his benefactors? That is not the way to return to my country. If any other way can be found that may not be derogatory to Dante's reputation and honour, I shall not be slow to accept it.'

The doctor, arms and fingers rigid, moved with effort one step towards the head of the bed. Unseen in the oaken shadows, the captain read on: 'Can I not everywhere gaze upon the mirror of the sun and stars? Can I not everywhere under heaven mirror forth the most precious truths, without first making myself inglorious —'

Two more slow steps. The doctor's hands were on the carvings living and writhing above the dying man.

'— nay, ignominious in the sight of the city of Florence? I shall not want for bread.'

'This has happened before,' said the doctor, and, reaching into the shadows, he touched the captain's shoulder.

The reading stopped. The captain, visible now as a lean brown figure crouching in the high chair, didn't move. But his voice said: 'You surprise me. What has happened before?'

'This. This smell. This feeling. This surrounding silence. The book is different. And the place. But everything else is the same.'

'Doctor, you've been walking in the sun.'

The doctor didn't argue. A man argues only to destroy his doubt, and he had no doubt. Alive with mysterious certainty, he stepped quickly across the room to an oaken pedestal on which the heavy, dimly burning brass lamp stood.

'The lamp won't show you what you expect to see.'

'Should it show me a nine-horned bull or a serpent or a greyhound or a bathing beauty, I'd still know you were there.'

'Sure thing I'm here.'

'You're not the brother of her husband.'

'The light of the lamp will hurt his eyes if you bring it closer. That's why she keeps it dim.' The doctor paused, his hand on the warm brass, looking for a moment at the black, irregular edge of the ill-trimmed wick. Then he faced back towards the bed and the shadows, his eyes for a while less able to penetrate those shadows because they had looked into light, into the flame's centre. 'Anyway, as you should know,' the captain said, 'I'm not afraid of light.'

'It's you, then?'

'I might as well admit it.'

'What do you want here?'

'Need you ask?'

The man on the bed breathed deeply, air rasping through his nostrils, stirred uneasily, then lay quiet again. The doctor once more touched the carvings writhing on the head of the bed, looked steadily into the shadows until he could see in the chair a slight, thin man in a brown duffle coat, hood pulled up monkwise on his head, his face narrow and hollow-jawed, eyes hidden behind large rimless spectacles; the face of a studious revolutionary, believer in impossible things, lamb among wolves; the first victim when fighting revolutionaries stab, without scruple, their knives in their brothers' guts. Long delicate hands lay as if half-dead on the arms of the chair. The open book rested on a black briefcase that rested on his crossed legs. His feet were bare. 'You're astute,' he said. 'I wondered if you'd know me in a new shape. Or if you'd think I was only one of my own signs.'

'You still have the black bag.'

'Never move without it.' His hands caressed it. 'My books. My little items of news. My gew-gaws of keepsakes. Where I go they go. My only consolations.'

'The old spitting man had no bag. The soldier who opened his friend's face —'

'Visiting cards. Signs and symbols.' The voice sharpened with a trifle of contempt. 'The chalked cross marked on a wall or a gatepost by children playing hare and hounds.'

'The dark woman . . . my wife's cousin? She sat where the drunk soldier sat.'

'I was sorry about that afterwards. My weakness. I couldn't resist the artist's touch. The little bit of virtuosity. But remember — I didn't kill her. I only knew she was coming my way. The play was written. I was only assistant stage-manager. Don't hold it against me.'

'I won't.'

'That's the spirit. We could get along together, Doctor, yourself and myself. We could make bargains and keep them.'

'We have made a bargain, and kept it.'

The book was snapped shut and forced among books, shuffling papers, brittle keepsakes into the stuffed black bag. 'True enough.' The thin voice mimicked the joy of discovery, of memory not unpleasantly jogged. 'I'd almost forgotten that.'

'One thing,' said the doctor; 'I've never understood about that bargain of ours.' He sat down on the edge of the bed, his eye on the circular windows, his back to the man in the shadows. 'I've known your wishes by symbols. And I've kept my bargain.'

'Like a gentleman and a sport.'

'When it was permitted me to cure, I cured by the orthodox methods, known to every general practitioner.'

'A wise course to follow.'

'But what I want to know is: did the granting of my request give me the power to cure by an effort of will, a sign in the air, the imposition of hands?' The sea-wind ruffled the curtains. The dying man breathed with effort.

'You're looking for dangerous knowledge.'

'Have I that power or haven't I?'

'Yes.' Lingeringly. 'I regret to say you have. I needn't tell you, but I believe in being frank.'

'You're lying. You wouldn't tell me if you didn't have to.'

'To be quite and completely frank, I wouldn't. It's no good for you to know or do such things.'

'Why?'

'I needn't answer that.'

'And you won't?'

'No.'

'If I make that effort of the will is the cure instantaneous?'

'Find that out for yourself.'

'You won't tell me?'

'No. I'm your friend. If you go about doing things like that you know how you'll end. With the world as it is today. Long ago, perhaps. The ages of faith.'

'People always have faith and hope. They can't get rid of them. They don't want to be rid of them. Haven't you ever found that out?'

'Dangerous subjects to argue about.'

'If in any one instance I'd been foolish enough to break my bargain, could I still have cured, in spite of you, just by an effort of the will?'

'You're not thinking of being foolish?'

'Can you stop me?'

'No. Every man has the power to break his bargain. Those are the rules. I didn't make them. Far be it from me to criticize the man who did.'

'Can I, then, cure in spite of you, merely by willing to cure?'

'I won't talk. For your own good.'

'That means yes.'

'I refuse to say.'

The curtains, in a wandering increase of air from the sea, flapped, brushing against the wall, like silken wings. In the bed the dying man moved a little, drew up one wasted knee to make a hillock in the bedclothes, wearily mumbled a few words that fell apart, like a handful of pebbles carelessly released, without sequence or meaning. The doctor waited silently, almost breathless, for sentences with relevance, for a third voice to give light and guiding to the sullen argument: the voice of a golden-haired priest on the windy summit of a mountain, or in a lounge bar where mourning men danced and sang, or in melodious Latin in a cold, salty baptistry, or granting requests over a round table in an expensive French restaurant. But no third voice came. The flame pipped in the lamp, sending up towards the invisible ceiling a puff of sooty smoke, coiling like a dancer. The doctor stood up, walked towards the lamp, screwed the wick up and screwed the wick down until the flame rested. 'Where, then, is her husband's brother?' he said, not turning again towards the shadows. He looked into the flame, searching for sanity, reality: a pretty, selfish woman, three children, a green place by the sea, a memory of childhood when death wasn't worth a second thought and God was a picture on the wall.

'Killed six months ago. By some enraged fellow-exiles. I suppose in a way he deserved it.'

'How?'

'One of those innocent fellows who ask to get murdered. A poet. An idealist. A lover outside the prescribed rules.'

No matter how deeply his eyes sank into the yielding flame, he saw nothing but red burning fantasy, dreams, delirium, Death wearing as a mask the body of a lover and a poet.

'Poor boy. He came to me in bad shape. You should've seen what his friends did to him. With blunt instruments too.' The voice from above the bed softened a little with pride in conscious benevolence. 'I found him suitable lodgings where he was going.'

'And borrowed his body.' The world dissolved in flame: houses, men and women, high towers, mountains, deep forests, dry deserts, and endless plains. Death had a thousand masks.

'More or less.'

'For your own use.'

'Wait a minute. Wait a minute. You do me wrong.' Above the bed, feet shuffled on the floor, clothes rustled as if legs were uncrossed and recrossed. 'Not completely for my own use.'

'For whose, then? Mine? Hers? His in the bed?'

'Now look. Take it easy for a minute. I don't know why I should explain. But it isn't often I get the chance of defending myself. I'm always being misunderstood. This brother, for instance. This poet. He comes to me, as I hinted, in very bad condition. In some ways he's an unpleasant boy. His voice, for instance. Did you ever hear anything like it?' He stopped for a while to give the shrill notes of the dead man's voice time to circle around the room, to die abruptly — steel blades snapping against thick walls. 'Believe it or not, it goes against my character to be as unpleasant as that boy could be at times. Particularly in matters of opinion. Insanely stubborn.'

'Why, then —'

'Wait now. Hold on. In some ways he wasn't a bad fellow. Took my advice on a lot of things. When he realized that politics or the party didn't count where he was going he was amenable enough. He did at first make a little fuss when he found out he'd have to live under a dictatorship.'

'Which dictator?'

'Ah, now! My client's secrets. But the poor fellow . . . his body was a little the worse for wear. The things men do to each other! With words or knives or, as in this case, with blunt instruments. What a mess! That's why I wear a duffle coat. Very concealing. That's why I sit here in the shadows as much as possible. I'm inclined to be a little self-conscious about such things.'

'But why? But why —?' The flame expanded and contracted like a living thing. One day it would expand to burn up the world. 'Wait a minute now. Hold on now. Being a poet and a lover, the boy had ideas and desires.'

'What could you know about the desires of a lover?'

'Now, I could resent that remark if I was the resentful sort. But we'll let it pass. I see a lot of people. Look after them at the greatest crisis of their existence. Lovers, too. Young and old. Men and women. Beautiful and ugly. Give me credit for experience and a sort of natural sympathy. The poor boy came to me with his one great desire unsatisfied. I listened to his sad story. I thought of a way in which something could be done for him.'

'So you're here.'

'So I'm here. But don't go thinking for a moment that I could get any kick out of gratifying the poor poet's desire.'

'You're his proxy.'

'Don't be cynical. Look at it from my point of view. Be fair. That's all I ask. No misunderstandings. Here I am in a borrowed body pretending for the sake of an unavoidably absent lover to be burned up with a desire that doesn't affect me in the least. I have to pretend to wish to possess just because he, where he is, hasn't yet recovered from being alive. It hurts me to annoy the woman. I'd rather leave her in peace. The game's too lively for me; not in my line. She'll be on my hands soon enough. In a different way altogether. But I promised that fellow —'

'You always keep your promises?'

'Always.'

'You sit there because you promised a lover, unhappily absent, you'd do something to set his heart at ease.' His eyes still soaked in the flame, he heard the movement of the bedclothes, knew that something was happening behind his back; and, quickly turning, he saw, dazzled, at first only thick blackness; then blackness broken by flashes of crimson; then, propped on elbows in the bed, the gaunt body of the dying man. The lips moved. The throat sucked for breath. The doctor, lowering him gently back to the pillows, could smell sickness, see the thin body half-exposed, hear the words he fought so bitterly to say: 'He sits there . . . why . . . he fears to look me in the eyes . . . he . . . like a rat in a hole . . . my brother . . . who hated me always . . . hated me when we played as children . . . always wished to see me dead . . . a murderer . . . to see me dead . . . .' Wasted hands gestured weakly as if they would beat and scratch at the doctor's face, at the hidden enemy, at the whole world. A long sigh. A shudder. The eyes closed again. The doctor waited motionless for minutes, then said: 'He's asleep.'

'Never properly asleep. He heard most of what we were saying.'

'He didn't like it.'

'Can't say I blame him. He doesn't mean me, though.'

'I suppose not.'

'No. Not really. It is horrible. Inhuman. To think of that other brother, deep down in his flowery poetic heart, wishing an end to the days of this fellow. So that he could have his rock and his wife. Makes you think.'

'It does.'

'I made my promise to the poet, nevertheless. A promise is a promise.'

'It is.'

Rasping breath assured the doctor that the man on the bed still lived. He said to the shadows, to the night outside, to the sea: 'Can't I cure this man?'

'You know the bargain.'

'If I break it?'

'Ah, well.'

'What would happen?'

'Please don't ask me. You can guess. I'm your friend. Don't embarrass me.'

'Wait one moment,' said the doctor.

VIII

When he stepped out to the cloistered passage and closed the door of the bedroom behind him she was standing a few yards away whispering to the one servant. He accepted it as part of the day's jigsaw that the servant should be the ripe-breasted child he, like a satyr or an ageing suburban man, had followed into the jolting tramcar. That brown-faced, deep-eyed child. A glimpse of running beauty leading him into the deep, ravenous forest. A quivering marshlight drawing his feet to flounder in murderous sucking bog.

Pacing slowly towards the whispering couple, watching the girl move slowly away as if frightened by the presence of a strange man, his heart turned in anger in his body. His heart was a salmon slapping and twisting away from a grazing hook. Someone unseen had set that girl before him in the hot street, had beckoned him on, led him under the arch to the Spanish shore, to a bizarre cottage concealing a café and a waiting woman. With the shivering instinct of an animal scenting a trap ready to spring or a pointed gun or a pit in the ground, he thought: why should I break my bargain? If I do, I don't even assert my own will. I merely move when pushed like a piece on a draught-board. I do a step in a dance for the pleasure of some unseen fiddler whose music is too low and horrible for ears of clay to hear. Sinews and muscles feel it and the heart, like a sponge, soaks it out of the air. So he looked over the woman's shoulders at the retreating girl and said savagely: 'Your husband is beyond hope.' He thought: Death's a decent fellow. He doesn't want trouble; wants everybody to come quietly, but only when they're called for. Death's only another piece on the board. Death's another dancer. He watched the retreating girl because he knew if he looked he would see, even in the poor light, and have his resolve shaken by, the pallor of the woman's face. He thought: she's afraid of sorrow, and it's part of the game planned by somebody else, a bar in the tune played by the hidden fiddler, that I should die to set her fears at ease, to postpone for her the first cut of sorrow, the vision of Death triumphant. I'll wreck the game, crash in on the tune with the discord heard first when angels wrestled in the clouds. But when he had finally steeled himself to look at her face he was shaken in a way he hadn't expected. The pallor was there, luminous in the gloom, but no sorrow or fear of sorrow, only weariness, acrid weariness; despair in man's stuttering, crippled lack of power. 'Death is so strong,' she said. 'We are all so weak against him.'

In the shadows at the head of the bed a lean man crouched, hiding a mutilated body in a brown duffle coat, clutching a black bag of books, newspaper clippings — keepsakes and souvenirs.

'No,' said the doctor, 'Death is a harmless man and we kill each other.' He thought (the fish accepting the hook, the piece on the draught-board obeying the pushing finger, the dancer cavorting to the will of the unseen fiddler): We can also kill ourselves and go unexpectedly to Death, jarring the tune, distorting the pattern of the game. He thought again, one thought qualifying another: Do we really jar the tune or twist the pattern? Or are we most subject when we think we are most independent?

Her voice was a hoarse whisper: 'Is there nothing can be done?'

Think for a thousand years and you know less than you discover in two cracking seconds of action.

'You must love him a lot.'

'It may be simply that I do not want to see Death.'

'Some day we'll all see Death.'

'Some day the sun will go east. I ask you to heal him and you speak what the world knows. There must be some way of halting Death. I will give anything. I will do anything.'

Once again her gripping hands sought strength from each other, rose upwards together as if she prayed to him, a dark power, an image in a wizard's cave. 'Don't be foolish,' he said, holding her arms, feeling how strong they were, how smooth.

'I have money.'

'So have I. Your money's no good to me, anyhow. Currency control.'

'I have jewels.'

'Think of Spanish or French or British or Irish customs officials searching my small-clothes and finding your jewels.'

'What can I do? What can I give? Look, I have myself.'

'For an ageing man with memories that would leave him unhappy in the bed of Helen.'

'Can I do nothing to persuade you to keep Death out of this house?'

'Are you certain I've the power?'

'When I saw you in the village, I said: if he cannot help me, no man can.'

'Why did you say that?'

'A child looks out of the window in the morning and sees a blossoming tree, and then sees a bird flying, and says, if the bird rests on the tree I will be happy today, and if the bird flies on without resting the child is unhappy.'

'Dreams. A child's dreams.'

'If he dies I will never walk into that room to look on his dead face.'

'It's better to talk to Death as you'd talk to a friend.'

'That is madness.' Her body tense, rigid, supported now by his large, hard, hairy hands, was living on nerves, hungry for life. 'I will never lie still in a smelly, heated room, watching Death approach.'

He could see her some day rushing to meet Death as one fighter goes against another. A self-inflicted wound, a leap from a bridge or a high building, or from a steep rock; no struggle, no scream, down on the roofs of the village. Nothing he could do or refrain from doing would weaken the steel spring of her soul, would affect her absolute refusal to accept the inevitable or to wait with patience for an end; and, touched by her clenched recklessness, he said: 'I can cure your husband on one condition.'

'The condition?'

He held her arms more tightly. 'It may be hard. But no harder than a leap to meet Death. Death should be met quietly, drinking in a darkened room.'

'The condition?'

'That I must be left in that room with only your husband. That you must go in there now, not tight and contemptuous and angry, but smiling like a girl going for the first time to meet her true lover. That you must bring away with you, and keep away as long as you can, your husband's brother.'

'How can I do that?' But crouching violently away from him, crossing her arms on her shrinking breasts, she knew.

'I don't tell you how. But you must do what I ask.'

'Now I know that today a devil walked into this village.'

'I'm no devil. I'm too old. I've offered to help you.'

'The bird the child saw flying was a foul, black crow.'

'Have it your own way, then,' he said, taking two steps away from her towards the door, the descending stairs, the circling road; but she held him and cried in her agony: 'Devil or dark bird, I will do what you order me to do.'

'Without fail?'

'I will do all that is possible.'

He pushed her away from him, afraid if she stayed a moment longer — small, neat body, red hair — he would hold her for hours silently in his arms, guarding her against pain, sorrow, death, as a man might guard his own daughter. So he waited in the shadows while she was in the room with her dying husband and her husband's brother; waited hiding in the shadows while she walked away along the cloistered passage. With her went the shuffling, shapeless man, hooded like a capuchin and carrying in his hand the black, incongruous briefcase.

Does he know I'm here in hiding? Does he go with her impelled not by her beauty but by his own promise? For a man must break his promise, but Death never can.

When they had gone into the darkness and a door had closed behind them, he came out of the corner where he had hidden, tiptoed to the bedside of the owner of that white house. For certitude his soul demanded a symbol, so, as quietly as he could, he dragged to the foot of the bed the chair on which the man had sat, pushed the bed, slowly and gently, until the heavy carved wood touched the wall. Then from his hip-pocket he took a small silver flask, screwed off the deep hollow cap, and filled it with burning liquid. Prising open the invalid's mouth, he poured in the contents of the cap, refilled it, poured again, thinking, willing: death or life, life or death. When the eyelids opened and the eyes with new, clear understanding looked at him and the voice said: 'Who are you? Where is my wife?' he knew something irrevocable had happened. 'Rest a while,' he said. 'I'll tell your wife to come to you,' and again he tiptoed, as if tiptoeing could conceal the thing he had done, from the room. But once outside in the passage, he put the burning flask to his own lips, drained it at one sucking gulp and, with bravado, walked to the door that concealed the beautiful little woman and the shapeless man. He touched the door with his fingers. For the truth was that never since the dark woman died on a road near an Irish sea had he met any one who seemed to fit so easily into the corners of his irregular heart. Touching wood with the tips of his fingers, knowing a truth that he could never tell her, was an ill way to say good-bye. But to tell her that truth would only make her old with horror, that the spectre she dreaded so much had really entered her house, had been cheated by sacrifice and a broken bargain.

I may never look on beauty again. I said that, too, when the dark woman died. I may never again know the fulfilment of desire. But because of me she has not yet understood death. In her I touch life, through a wooden door, over a boundary river and tapering mountains, across the plains and forests of France, across the restless dividing sea. When she walks out in the morning and sees a bird resting on a blossomy tree she may remember me, and in her memory I'll live, even under the boards, even under the clay.

He went in the darkness down the steep steps, the circling road, through the close, stifling village streets to the last lighted, rumbling tram, to the great town where hammering builders and the sun had ceased, where women sang in dark doorways. He went past weary officials, over the linking, dividing bridge to his balconied room in the hotel across the street from the railway station in a French town. In the morning he awoke, shaved and washed, dressed, heard the nations passing up and down the street, pulled aside the flimsy curtains, stepped out to the balcony, saw Death in a duffle coat sitting on a luggage truck outside the station, close to the place where the doctor himself had once sat drinking with the hawk-nosed gambling man.

Fourth Interlude

There was a rich man living in Spain and he fell ill. The Spanish doctors attended him, but they weren't able to cure him. His relatives came and advised his wife to send for the gambler to attend her husband. They got ready a ship and a ship's crew and sailed for Ireland to bring the gambler over to Spain.

When the gambler entered the room where the sick man was lying he found Death sitting at the head of the bed. Death scowled at the gambler and the gambler scowled back at Death.

'Can you heal my husband?' says the great lady.

'I cannot,' says the gambler.

''Tis a pity we sent to Ireland for you,' says she, 'if you came over only to put a scowl on you.'

She showed him a box filled with gold.

'If you heal him I'll give you the contents of that box,' says she.

The gambler coveted the gold. He asked her to bring in four of the servant boys. When they came in he asked them to grip the four posts of the bed and to turn it around. They did that, and Death was left sitting at the foot of the bed. Then the gambler gave a healing herb to the sick man, and he rose up as sound and healthy as he had ever been.

The servants carried the box of gold to the ship for the gambler, but Death came after them on the road and gripped the gambler by the throat.

FIVE

I

He didn't waste a minute on wine, luggage, or bread. He passed a bundle of crumpled franc-notes into the cupped hands of the placid *patronne*. When she went down the three steps into the dark kitchen to change his money and receipt his bill he slipped out by the back door of the hotel, saw a bus passing along a side-street, ran and leaped and went with it.

The side-street became a road corkscrewing into the hills. He stood strap-hanging at the back of the bus, jolted this way and that by the antics of a furious driver, bumping his left shoulder against the broad back of a bloused labourer, his right elbow against the pneumatic body of a tightly corseted, rigidly uplifted woman. Life swarmed in the bus as maggots swarm in ripe cheese, and feeling life around him, minds thinking, tongues talking, hearts pumping blood, coffee and wine and bread churning and splashing through soft unseen machinery, he felt content and secure. The mounting heat of the sun sizzled on the roof and the windows, set the air smouldering, bodies sweating. His white, wide-brimmed hat fell to the floor. He groped for it clumsily, clutching wildly, as the floor of the bus tilted up and down like a see-saw, around large male feet and trim female ankles. The tightly corseted, rigidly uplifted woman had neat, lovely feet, and the realization that he was still capable of noticing such things set him laughing, thinking he had the courage to face the consequences of what he had done. He was still alive among the living. But an hour later, when the bus had emptied a little and he was able to sit down, watch the countryside rearing and galloping past, listen at his ease to the jabber of gesticulated talk, he knew that his hands were quivering and his heart beating with a terror unknown since the days of his childhood.

The hills had grown up, changed their colour from brown of burned grass and drying trees to blue of bare rocks and some coarse flowering shrub. The road ascended a bare, lonely valley. He didn't care much where exactly he was going, content for a while in the knowledge that he was going northwards away from the sun and then westwards to wet islands. Out there he could fight better.

Was he only a child running from terror to the soil that had mothered him?

How pleasant to wake up and find myself back in the club-house, the morning — a chill, repellent girl — slipping between clay-brown curtains, the dark woman still alive; to know again the joy of a simple monetary ruin with no lunatic mysteries, no bones broken or lives lost in bad bargains.

The bus, almost empty, struggled, choking and chugging, slowly to the end of the climb. The bare valley ended as if sliced with a knife. Ahead the land descended and widened like a coloured majestic dress, blossomed and richly bore fruit and crops, prosperous houses, neat villages, sucked life from a slow, winding river consecrated by poplars. Ten miles away the first of the great mountains leaped up and shouted in the pure air. Four square, white farm-houses crested the ridge. The bus stopped. The last of the other passengers stepped stiffly down to the powdery road, and stiffly the doctor followed. For one hour the doctor sat and waited in a shady corner beside one of the white farm-houses where the enterprising farmer had made a rest-house, where his wife and daughters carried food and wine to hungry, thirsty, dusty travellers. The wind swished over the ridge, ran out of the fertile land and halfway up the slopes of the barren hills. The other waiting passengers sat like happy people while the doctor looked and looked again at his watch, saw one minute follow another like soldiers in single file advancing along a muddy road into enemy country. I must take a grip on myself. No panic. Death can't stab a man here in the white light. The food is good. The wine is good. The wind is healthy. For miles to the north and miles to the south I can see the road, and nowhere in the sun is there anything moving.

It needed all the restraining power of such reasoning to keep him sitting in his chair. For eating, drinking, dressing oneself, talking casually to the neighbour had become as irrelevant as whistling down a bottomless pit or spitting into a Himalayan abyss. It needed all that reasoning restraint to keep him from walking up and down the road, stamping his feet on the brittle dust, waving and walloping his arms as he had once seen a grey-coated lunatic wave his arms — walking with a silent chewing crowd of his fellows and five blue keepers on a road near a high-walled madhouse. The other waiting people, figures cut in wood, sat erect in their chairs, and he thought he could hear, approaching in the hot silence, the footsteps of something as high as the distant jubilant mountain. But when he tiptoed to the corner of the house and looked to the north-east the mountain still stood in its place and there was nothing moving except, far away, a travelling cloud of dust that might contain the other bus. He went back to his table, sat down, gripped the wooden edge, and held on. Was this the way a man felt in the silence of a condemned cell? Except that the condemned criminal knows what's coming, knows when, has a rough idea of how.

All the world's my condemned cell.

He held hard to the table because otherwise he might have raced shouting down the road to meet the bus, perhaps to lie down in the dust and wait for it: ending all waiting and wondering. If he did that and looked up and then saw, clarifying its outlines from the cloud of cutting white particles, not the bus, but something else. Something else?

When the cloud settled by the four white houses, the bus, hot and dusty, was there in the middle of the road. Stiff passengers, their faces to the south, descended and hirpled across for food and drink. The waiting people stood up, walked out into the sunlight while the driver turned the bus to face back towards the north. The farmer's wife and daughters came out bearing food and drink for the new arrivals. From the seat he found in the front of the bus he watched the mountain grow, lean forward, brood over the widening land. Then one by one other mountains stood up: some laughing giants jundying each other, crowding together; some stony, bitter, virgin giantesses; some black, bullying, broad-backed monsters.

Village after village. Cream-coloured oxen in goaded toil in the vine patches. A long straggling town. More and more passengers until the bus was crowded. A fat woman filled the seat beside him, overflowed from the seat, the air smelling of the musky odour of her vast body. His nostrils not unpleasantly filled with that smell, life and warmth, he fell asleep, woke after twenty minutes with a new odour in his nostrils, a sense of danger in his mind. They were dustily leaving the village where, probably, the fat woman lived, where somebody else now sitting beside him had joined the bus. Ahead, overshadowing the road, a mountain ridge, prickly with stunted dark trees, rose towards the north. He swivelled his eyes until he could see the clothes of the man who sat beside him: dark trousers tight across round thighs, thin dark blouse unbuttoned in front to show an obscenely plump hairy chest; no concealing duffle coat. The bus drove straight at the mountain ridge as if it could rise like a bird and curve, wheels whirring, high in the air over rocks and hunch-backed trees. Turning a little in his seat, pretending to watch the high mountains shouldering each other away on the far side of the road, he studied his neighbour's face; not thin, neither scarred nor marked, a plump, cunning face, a mouth used to whispering sideways, a face that jogged the doctor's memory. The eyes were closed. He couldn't be sure. The bus began to climb. The road curved up over a saddle in the ridge, visible here and there ahead in white dusty streaks, but hidden mostly by trees and overhanging rocks. He was vaguely uneasy with the sense that he was in prison in that corner of glass, wood, thin metal, with a formless suspicion that the face of the man sleeping — or was he sleeping? — beside him was dangerously familiar. Steadying his nerves with effort, he thought: the world is all familiar faces; I might see on a street in Moscow the shadow of a face seen in a Mayo village. But turning once again, genuinely to look at the distant mountains, to occupy his mind with their height and their monstrous joy in their own size, he caught his neighbour's eyes open. For one instant only. A flickering instant before the eyelids again cunningly dropped. But in that one instant he knew; he remembered a shadowy room shaped like the cabin of a ship, a bell tolling and no answer coming.

So this bus was a vibrating prison driving him to his doom. He must escape; floundering and falling over two round thighs, over baskets, parcels, protruding feet; struggling with the gesticulating conductor, hearing the startled voices of the other passengers as a meaningless babble, pushing the conductor away and leaping from the bus, falling forward, saving his face but scorching and skinning the palms of his hands, running upwards to the shelter of trees and rocks. Behind and below, the bus came sputtering to a halt, voices shouted, strange melodious vowels that might for all he knew or cared have come from the cracks in the bark of the dry, black trees. Possessed by panic, he ran blindly, a child on a dark road, a soldier with nerves shattered by the persistence of battle, by the recurrent shell-shriek threatening destruction. He fell again, rose again, ran again, dodging rocks and trees by staggering instinct, falling a third time, lying exhausted where he fell, thinking: This is the way a man goes mad. What have I done or what has been done to me that I should run like a lunatic away from harmless strangers, or see in the oily face of a French villager the reflection of my own daft dream in a Dublin lane? Should I, after that baptism, have told somebody — a policeman or a prudent priest — about those two men? Or should I have asked some wise man of my own profession to tell me whether I was mad or sane?

Sobbing out the perplexities of seven years to moveless rocks and old bent trees, he noticed abruptly the quietude of the world — no shouting voices, no sound of wind or river, no bird song or animal's cry — nothing but the humming of the engine of the bus, faint in the far distance. He was alone. Or was he? Would they tell the police in the next village that one of the passengers, a tall, dark man wearing light grey clothes and a wide, white hat, had gone mad and raced for the rocks? Would the police send out a search-party with long sticks and lanterns against the coming of night? Or would the policeman who listened to the story raise his hands, palms upward, crooked fingers asking a hundred unanswerable questions, and droop the corners of his mouth, as Latin men did when they heard of the oddities of other men, Latin or otherwise? Or now in the dusty, vibrating bus, were they laughing at dohel jokes on the incidence of dysentery among touristing strangers?

Cautiously then to his feet, to stand, his back protected by a high bare rock, listening in the silence for the crack of a branch or the rattle of a rolling stone. No sound. Nothing moved. He wouldn't return to the road because somebody — the villager with the oily face? — or something might be waiting there, because one step backwards might drag him on step by step to the white house high above a Spanish village. I cannot run away. I cannot evade. I can go nowhere where this man, this thing, is not able to follow, to be there before me, waiting, an owl on a dark tower, an assassin with a knife. Perhaps later, panic will pass. I may learn to turn, see him or it in the distance, and step steadily towards the event.

A path went straggling northwards between the trees. It rose as the road had been rising, towards the saddle of the ridge, and wearily he followed it, walking for two hours until he was certain the path had risen higher than the rising road. But always all around him trees and rocks blocked the view. He could not, would not, retrace one step; and worn out at last by walking and heat and hunger and thirst, he lay down and slept, plunging into sleep as a suicide leaps into a flood, rasping around in his drowning mind for fragments of his reading that spoke to him of his present predicament: an onanistic Dane screaming out that sometimes there was in his head a tumult as if hobgoblins had lifted up a mountain to dance in its iron bowels; a morbid Frenchman frothing that the great passions were solitary, that to fly from them to the wilderness was the surest way of rushing into their power. So through his restless dreams hobgoblins danced and passions as high as the mountains walked on red desert earth that steamed under their deformed feet. He awoke sweating; wondered where he was; then remembering, he marvelled that he had had the courage to close his eyes; and rising slowly to his feet, heard, as a soul in hell might hear a whisper of God's mercy, the sound of far-away music, jigging strings, the pleated jauntiness of an accordion.

He ran towards the music. Voices. Singing. The clapping of hands. Laughing and talking. Life is there and happy people. Friendliness, perhaps. Going still upwards along the path, coming suddenly out of the forest of warped trees, he saw the dancing, singing people and thousands of feet below a spreading valley. There were twenty people dancing on a flat rock. The two musicians danced as they played — a country dance, still figures moving in patterns, only feet, ankles, calves, and occasionally clapping hands, agile. To his eyes, dazzled with joy as lunatic as the fear it had driven out, they seemed to dance perilously on the sharp edge of the world, for all the time, climbing on the path through the trees, he'd been drawing towards the edge of an escarpment. The women wore coloured skirts and white blouses. The men wore black silky trousers and white shirts. The valley below was a huge green hand sticking five long, twisted fingers into the flesh of the mountains.

He was very glad to see moving, living people; to be certain that the music and singing didn't come from the mouths of unshapen hairy monsters or from the crevices in the rocks. But he stood steady for a long time, his left hand touching the dry, warm bark of one of the crooked trees, loath to leave these crippled things that for some hours had given him real protection. He could have kissed the black, ugly wood — a kiss of friendship and farewell — to leave for ever there the mark of a man's lips, a charm for lovers and for wandering men. But a dancing girl, twirling long blonde hair with the suppressed passion of the stiff rhythm , saw him, pointed, shouted. The music stopped as if somebody had slashed the strings and punctured the accordion. Twenty faces turned. Forty eyes looked at him as he approached: a tall, dark-faced man stepping out quietly from the rocks and the black trees. Fifty years ago their grandfathers might have gone armed, graips or spades or knives or clubs, or with holy water and the suffering majesty of Christ on His cross, to meet such a man. But now in these places they were accustomed to tourists and looked on strangers with mild, friendly curiosity. When he said: 'I am a tourist. I've lost my way,' and when they saw and heard how differently his mouth shaped those words, they said with one voice: 'You go to the town?'

'Yes.'

A small dark man who looked at the blonde girl as he spoke, said: 'You have gone walking and perhaps lost your way?'

They were helpful, friendly people.

'Yes. I followed for a long time a path through the trees. I'm looking for the shortest way to the town.'

Which town? And after that another town, other towns, the château, his son, Paris, Picardy, white lighthouses at Calais, the sea, white cliffs at Folkestone, London, Crewe, wild Wales, death in Ireland.

'The shortest way,' said a second man, 'is a way for birds or angels.' He was a tall, round-shouldered, mournful man. He gripped the doctor's arm, led him to the edge of the precipice, waved a watery hand, indicated the town. It shone white in the green wooded wrist of the valley, only four miles away, but four thousand feet down. 'To walk, you must go back the way you came.'

'No. Not that.' The trees might not be friendly a second time. Night would find him stumbling along under their wry, dark branches. Back where he'd left the bus someone or something might still be waiting — a policeman with a lantern, or an ape crouched on the grass. He must never turn back.

'To be a bird with safety you must fly by the *téléferique*.'

He led the doctor down a circling flight of steps cut in solid rock, curving around the edge of the cliff and away from the flat place worn smooth by generations of dancing feet. The dancers stood friendly and smiling, respectfully silent while the doctor followed his guide down the steps. Then the music began again, a slow sorrowful tune, and a man began to sing. The steps cut in the rock ended and steps of smooth concrete commenced. Just at their feet, hidden in a nook for shelter when the wind blew wild in winter, the *téléferique* station clung like a bird's white nest to the face of the precipice: a little concrete house where the engineer lived, a restaurant with a wide bay-window perched high above splintered rocks, thick walls of solid concrete to house the machinery, and, swinging out into the air, the two cables supported two thousand feet down by a rock pinnacle, then going in one last sheer swoop to the level of the valley.

'Below there,' the mournful man said, thinking perhaps of the eyes of the little dark man following the supple movements of the blonde girl, 'a bus will take you to the town. They are frequent.'

'Thank you.'

'You are fortunate to be able to travel.'

'Perhaps,' the doctor said, measuring nervously with his eye the extent of the cable's two swoops from the mountain to the valley. A slip, a snap, and bones shattered and blood and brains spattered on the pointed rocks. He shook hands with the civil, mournful man, and as he descended the last few concrete steps the machinery began to growl and far below, the tiny car, gripping the cables together with its iron claws, swung upwards on the first part of his journey. From his seat by the window of the restaurant he watched it swing into view over the supporting pinnacle. The wine was white and sour, the meagre blood of small white grapes. He ate sandwiches made from coarse brown bread and raw fat bacon, chewing with fierce hunger, gulping the sour wine. The car dropped for fifty feet when it had topped the pinnacle, then, the growl of the machinery narrowing to a shrill annoying whine, came up towards the summit with the directness and energy of a soaring bird. He'd drink this wine until his mind was numb and drugged against the giddiness of the descent. The sun still shone on the green, five-fingered valley. The fields by the winding river were velvet smooth in contrast with the jagged mountains. In the farthest distance were pointed peaks isolated from the earth by white evening clouds, gathering and hanging motionless above high, lonely farms. The car on its cables drifted gently, the engine cut off, past the window of the restaurant. He could hear it settling to rest, a bird of wood and iron on a nest of iron. It would descend in seventy minutes, and for seventy minutes he drank heavily until his mind was sodden and the sour white wine like beauty to his tongue.

Walking from the restaurant to the car, he muttered to himself: 'I'll not be afraid. I've left my fear behind me on the path through the dark wood. Am I worse off than any other living man? For in the mind of each of us is the memory of a bargain broken and the chill certainty that life will end. So I'll challenge Death, shouting defiance at him over rocks and crabbed trees, daring him to come upwards at me, winged like a bat, out of those deep, tree-grown canyons. A broken cable, a body broken on the rocks is an intelligible end; a paragraph in the papers; a story my people will understand.' And in the descending car he shouted and waved his arms to the intense discomfiture of the other three passengers and the man who collected the fares. Gaelic words, forgotten since childhood, came up-roariously from his lips, telling the French mountains how much better it was to drink and shout than to hoard guineas; telling about a houseful of handsome women in the city of Waterford and wine and punch plentiful on the table. Then, growing melancholy as the pinnacle was passed, he chanted the slow words of a poet who had promised gently to sing of Death's adventurous ways and of Grecian battles in Troy where princes fell.

From the platform where the cabin jolted to rest, he walked to the road where the bus waited. His eyes looked straight ahead. He didn't for a moment dare to glance around. He was a child shutting its eyes tightly and saying: 'You can't see me.' He was a discharged murderer walking, protected by a police cordon, from the place of trial, afraid to look at the watching people, to see in their faces curiosity or contempt or amusement or fear or hate or pity. He'd dared Death drunkenly in the air over the high mountain and he was still alive. He'd shouted challenge at the enemy and the enemy hadn't even answered. For the discharged murderer is really afraid that the watchers may read on his face evidence of his compressed diabolic joy in evil done with impunity. The child with shut eyes is locked into a secure little heaven.

He stared at the ground and nursed his joy, not caring to look to find out if the driver of the bus concealed a mutilated body under a duffle coat, if any fellow-passenger carried a black briefcase. He didn't lift his eyes until he heard the town around him — chaotic traffic, pilgrims coming and going around a lighted grotto, a point-duty policeman high on a platform gesticulating with a white baton, sudden dusk in the streets. Hotels were plentiful. He found one easily. A room. A bed. And sleep.

II

When he awoke in the morning the man was sitting by his bedside reading a newspaper. The man said: 'They told me this was your room, so I came right up.' He had a deep musical voice.

'That was decent of you.' A brittle, calculating silence. 'But I don't think we've met.'

'We certainly have met. We're old friends.'

'So,' said the doctor.

'Just so,' said the man, and he stood up, walked backwards and forwards by the foot of the doctor's bed. Bars of morning sunlight came in between the slats of the brown cane blinds. He was tall, broad-shouldered, spreading and loosening to flesh. He was dressed in a white shirt and black trousers, holding the newspaper in his right hand, his left sleeve empty and carefully fastened across the breast of his shirt by a conspicuous diamond pin. A heavy Breton beret sat flat on his large head. Look at him from the east and he had the bronzed, sternly lined face, the steady eye of a man who has climbed in great winds to the high snows. Look at him from the west and the lines were curved and smiling, the skin ruddy, the eye that of a man who'd split you for twopence. The doctor watched him, now from the east, now from the west, going and coming beyond the foot of the bed. It was like watching two men: twins, a hero and a rogue.

'Waiting for you to wake up, I was reading the morning paper.'

'It was considerate of you not to disturb me.'

'This was what I was reading.' His back to the window, breaking with his body the bars of yellow light, he read: 'Twenty people were drowned when a bus, jammed with passengers, plunged into a canal near the town yesterday. The bus was carrying forty-eight people. The accident occurred at a bridge when the bus skidded and toppled over before falling into the water.'

'Add that to your collection of clippings.'

'I might. There's another bit further down that says —' Very cleverly he managed the paper with his one hand. 'It says . . . oh, here we are: Three people were killed today when a car crashed through a level-crossing barrier at Belfield-Westhouse and collided with the Strasbourg-Mulhouse express, says Reuter.'

'Very nice of Reuter.'

'Further down here there's some fascinating material.' He looked up, a quick, cunning, squinty glance, over the edge of the newspaper. Seeing his full face, the doctor searched it sharply for the line of division where the flesh of the man who dared mountains had been grafted on to the flesh of the cheap rogue. 'Simply fascinating. Some figures here about acute anterior poliomyelitis; some hard facts, solid information about rubella, erysipelas, infective mononucleosis, and infective hepatitis. Not to mention our old friend tuberculosis. But I'm afraid I bore you.'

'Not at all.'

'It's just that I take a certain interest in these things. Now, down here, there's a most interesting case about —' The paper wriggled free from the one hand, dropped to the floor. Diamond pin, white shirt, black Breton beret vanished, a setting sun, for a moment, below the rim of the foot of the bed, then straightened back into view again, face a little flushed with stooping. '— an unfortunate young mother who for some reason or other allowed her six-month-old child to starve out of existence. They sent her to jail too. I wouldn't have been so harsh. And here . . . something about an eighteen-year-old girl, sweet and pretty, I suppose, whose ball-dress caught fire at a dance. She died from burns. And right underneath that, five lines to say that the King and Queen of England have sent congratulations to an aged lady, no longer pretty for certain, on her one-hundred-and-first birthday. Think of that.'

'Quite a coincidence.'

'And here a labouring man was pinned and crushed under a stonebreaker in a muddy quarry. The papers make interesting reading.'

'So interesting.'

'I really am boring you. You're thinking all the time about that bus in the canal.'

'Not all the time.'

'You were a wise man to leave it when you did.'

'I suppose so.'

'What a hurry you left in, too. You're getting into the hurrying habit. The way you left that hotel in the border town. You almost took me unawares.'

'Almost?'

'Well, you see, inside information. What's the point in

running away, anyway? A man roaring along in a racing car is often only rushing to meet me. He thinks he's really living, speed and the wind whistling past, and then, smack, he's in my hands and generally in embarrassing shape too. I'm not so awful that people should want to run away from me. Look, I could read you a passage, a piece from the letter of one author to another, a very understanding fellow who had heaps of bad health, spent years spitting blood and getting to know me intimately —' From the floor beyond the foot of the bed the black bag was dragged into sight, opened, searched for a book. 'It's understanding fellows like this who reconcile me to my contacts with men. Listen to this: Death is no bad friend; a few aches and gasps, and we are done; like the truant child, I am beginning to grow weary and timid in this big, jostling city, and could run to my nurse, even although she should have to whip me before putting me to bed.'

'It's a point of view.'

'It's all that. Later on he writes: I keep returning, and now hand-over-fist, from the realms of Hades. I saw that gentleman between the eyes, and fear him less after each visit. Only Charon and his rough boatmanship I somewhat fear.'

'Are you also Charon?'

'Ah, now! These classical allusions. I like the sound of them myself. But they don't mean a thing. There isn't any river. Transport's much better nowadays, more rationalized.'

'Is that an invitation?'

'Look — I wish you wouldn't be so suspicious. You sit there in the bed. Eyes bloodshot. No razor. No shave. Staring me straight in these eyes.' The one hand free of book and bag brushed across the odd, contrasting eyes as if, living two lives and masking death, they burned and hurt. 'You make me feel a heel. I'm not, you know. I've a damned awkward job and I try to do it as well as I can, to be nice to everybody.'

'Is this the end? Are you trying to break it to me in an easy, gentlemanly way?'

'No, look, I just came along to reason with you. To say to you: what's the point in running away. I like you. You're a man in a rather special position and, on the whole, you've used your power with tact.'

He had walked back to the chair beside the bed, sat down

again, displaying the profile of a noble mountaineer, Roland wounded to the heart by the unexpectedly base action of another hero. 'What did you do with the duffle coat?'

'It served its purpose. It was a clumsy garment. Too hot for this climate. The poor poet only wore it as a gesture. It made him look as odd as he felt.'

'You found a new coat.'

'Oh, this! Not bad. Between friends, I'll tell you how I came by it.'

On the other side of the bed the doctor lowered his feet to the floor, began rapidly to dress. 'You'll find I'm well known in this town. People'll salute me on the streets, occasionally ask my opinion about this or that: the devalued franc or the weather. Even pilgrims will remember me since they last came here to pray, and to wash in the water at the grotto.'

Moving briskly across the room, the doctor ran water, hot and cold by turns, into the basin; washed and towelled. His razor was left with his luggage in the border town by the bridge. It might be in Paris before him — if he ever reached Paris.

'The joke is, that while they're talking to me they'll never suspect, never have a clue or a notion that the man they think they're talking to came my way in a hurry this morning. Tried to sit up in his bed when the first cock crowed at dawn. Gasped twice, coughed once, shouted once and nobody heard, and that was that. He lived alone, you see. Odd bird. War hero. Black marketeer. Bachelor with esoteric tastes. In a house a mile outside the town. They'll find him there tomorrow. The post mortem will shake the doctors, for at least seven people will swear they saw him abroad today; spoke to him, shook his hand, heard what he had to say about the danger of forest fires in the Landes. A burning topic at the moment, if you'll forgive me.' A deep mellow laugh. 'My life' — another laugh — 'has always these little ironic consolations.'

'Great fun,' said the doctor. Knotting his tie before the mirror, he wondered would this be his last time to knot a tie, to run a comb through his hair. How grey his hair was. And how black the beard sprouting on his long chin. Some holy man had said: 'Do everything you do as if you were doing it for the last time.' So he knotted his tie with special care, put a special twirl in the hand with which he held without a tremor the little pocket comb. The man in the mirror looked at him with unwinking understanding: no use running, no use being afraid.

'So for one day only I wear the body of a late hero. I can show you the town. All the sights. The hero was always showing visitors the sights. He took a great pride in the place. The grotto. The grey colour of the water in the river. The story of apparitions and miracles. The churches, one above the other, as if they were playing leapfrog. Thousands of pilgrims praying for life.' Pulling on his jacket, the doctor turned sharply from the mirror, from the man in the mirror — his own reconciled, encouraging twin — to stand staring at the double-faced man on the chair, to say casually as if he, too, were making queries about devaluation or the danger of fire in the dry undergrowth between the cupped, bleeding pines: 'When do you want your pound of flesh?'

'Oh that —'

'When —?'

'Please don't ask me for details. I'm in no hurry. My hands are full. When the time comes I'll give you five minutes' notice, if I can. Can a fellow do more?'

'So I don't even have the advantage of knowing when?'

'Would it be an advantage?'

'I want to know.'

'I'd tell you if I could. But orders are orders.' The forefinger of the solitary hand pointed up to the ceiling. 'Come out with me and see the town.'

'Is it worth seeing?'

'It is. Believe me, it is. Every town's worth seeing. The things that go on.' He rose from the chair, a little stiffly, turned towards the door. The bars of light sneaking between the slats of the blinds lighted the noble profile. 'What'd you like to do first?'

'Coffee and rasher and eggs. An island breakfast. Mushrooms for the man in the condemned cell. Then, if I'm still living, I'm going to the basilica to confess my sins.'

Be jocose with the demon, he thought. Dare the worst. He

opened the door, locked it carefully behind him. The one-armed man walked slowly down the stairs. The doctor followed, holding the key in his hand, rattling the attached ball and chain, saying: 'It's not that I think the things I did, bad or good, of any particular moment. But it's natural for a man facing the end of his days to look back to their beginning, to go back in spirit to that beginning.' Over his island breakfast, fortified by a bottle of mainland wine, he said: 'Every man at the end should return to the place he started in.'

'I'm not the argumentative sort. But suppose you began in hate and poverty and dirt. An unwanted, nameless child. Some people do, you know. Some people end there too; come to me that way. Buried in fear in the back garden. Keep the secret safe from the neighbours' tongues.'

'I'm talking now only for myself. I didn't begin that way. When I was a boy — snub nose, freckles, short pants, a gansy with a hole in it, mud on my boots, twisted stockings always bundled around my ankles — I went regularly, once a fortnight, to tell my sins, such as they were, to the priest in the curtained confessional in the church in an innocent town. When I say innocent I don't mean that human nature was different there from human nature in any other part of the world. But there wasn't much noise, there weren't many people in that town, and when odd things happened only a wise, experienced few even knew what names to give to them. You walked up the echoing side-aisle, generally a loose iron tip on the heel of a boot cutting echoes out of the angels carved on the rafters, to a confessional before a side-altar and beside a statue of Saint Anthony of Padua with the child Jesus standing on the pages of an open book. The other boys were queued and crowded there. You took your place in the queue, swapping chestnuts and marbles and boys' magazines. Then you lifted the curtain, stepped into the darkness, knelt down, waited at a grille until a sliding panel was pulled across, and began: Bless me, father, for I have sinned. How long, my child, since your last confession? A fortnight, father. In what way since then, my child, did you offend the good God? Father, I disobeyed my parents once, and I was late for school twice, and I copied my sums from another boy's exercise, and I broke my wee brother's toy horse, and that's all, father. Very well, my child, say three hail Marys for your penance, and now recite slowly the act of contrition. Be careful in future, my child, to obey your parents. Yes, father. Go in peace now and pray for me. And all the way home through the sleepy innocent town you'd run and jump and gallop like a horse, and make noises like a railway engine, and wonder why the grey-headed priest, seen dimly through the grille, needed the prayers of boys who played marbles and flew kites and robbed orchards when the season was in it.' The doctor drank deeply from the red bottle. 'That was innocence,' he said.

'I wouldn't know,' said the one-handed man with the quarrelling eyes. 'You want to find it again, here and now?'

'Before I die.'

'The word embarrasses me.'

'I want to return to innocence, to my moment of pure faith.'

'What a pity you haven't a fourth request.'

'For some fortunate men the moment goes on for years and years. They lie down on their last bed, look back, see through clear light, no shadows anywhere, all the way to the innocent beginning.'

'Far be it from me to argue. But I've seen such men ill at ease when they looked forward and doubted for the first time on their last bed. They see shadows crouching in the corners of rooms. They babble about the power of our old friend the dark horse. Some saints at the crucial moment have screamed more loudly than the greatest sinners.'

'We'll leave it so,' said the doctor. He wiped his lips with his napkin. He said: 'It's an abstruse topic.' He led the way across the dining-room. 'I didn't start the argument,' the man said. 'I never do.' At the desk in the entrance hall the doctor paid his bill. Counting out the floppy blue-green franc-notes, he said: 'I may not be back,' and the Jewess who gathered his money tenderly to her, said: '*Bon voyage*, monsieur,' and didn't even lift her eyes to watch the two men leave the hotel together, going out into the bright sunshine and across the crowded street. High on a pedestal a policeman waved his white baton above the lively traffic. Across the stretch of hot concrete before the basilica the pilgrims flowed in six or seven crisscrossing streams. Around the corner between the rock and the river other pilgrims sang a hymn. 'Wait for me if you like,' the doctor said, and finding a place in one of the streams, he moved slowly with it towards a quiet, shaded corner of the basilica, towards every second Friday of his boyhood.

III

By noon the crisscrossing streams of pilgrims had mingled and spread out to make one restless lake, coloured hats of women like blossoms drifting on the dark surface. The space between the rock and the river was packed with kneeling people, arms outstretched, not heeding the glare of the sun, praying aloud around the parallel lines of the sick, the twisted, the maimed, the suffering, on stretchers before the high rock. The candles in the grotto burned pale in the fierce light. By the edge of the river family parties sat on benches, ate bread, drank wine and ale and mineral waters. The mountains crouched around the town, dark animals lazy in the heat. All day long, under the rock, behind the altar, one slow procession moved, reverent hands touching, beseeching lips kissing, the dull stone until it shone. The sick went down with faith to the healing waters.

Darkness came suddenly. The doctor and the one-armed man walked up the steep curving road from one lighted church to the one directly above it. They looked down on the dark people, carrying red torchlights, assembling before the grotto.

'It hurts me,' said the one-armed man.

'What hurts you?'

'All these people, afraid of me, wanting to live. All the world's invalids who'd rather live on in illness than face me. All the world's lovers clutching at each other to keep the show going on.'

The singing rose up, one united sound, louder than the torrent.

'I heard you once belly-aching about suicide.'

'That's man for you. One extreme to the other. Nobody wants to meet me calmly.'

'Heroes facing firing squads? Martyrs standing on hot sand singing hymns to the leaping lions?'

'Did you ever see a calm hero or a cool martyr?'

'Never saw a hero or a martyr at all.' The voices of seven countries swept together, seven streams meeting to make one river, a strong line of Latin words: Ave, Ave, Ave Maria. The mother had always meant life for men. 'Why shouldn't they desire life?' said the doctor.

'All I said was that it hurt me. I'm a sensitive fellow. A poet once called me easeful. Like a vegetable laxative. Said he was half in love with me too. But the poor boy didn't mean it. Next minute he was wailing his fear that he'd fall into my clutches before he'd written all he wanted to write. That stung me. And me liking books the way I do. Nobody wants to be eased by me.'

High on a peak above the town somebody touched a switch, lighted two searchlights, swivelled them until they shone straight on the stone-and-glass face of the basilica. High on another peak somebody else touched another switch and a high cross of light stood up in the dark sky.

All day the doctor and the one-armed man had been together, walking, talking, drinking, eating. Townspeople often, and pilgrims now and then, saluted the white shirt, black beret, red face of the esoteric bachelor, asked him questions about the weather, the number of visitors to the town, the number of sick at the grotto, rumours of cures, fears of fire in distant forests, bullfights, the cost of living. He answered with knowledge and politeness. He was a good man to seek advice from, a lively man to argue with. 'Poor man,' the doctor said. 'You're not such a bad fellow. But so few people have the pleasure of knowing you well while they're still able to talk about your charm.'

Some days later, sitting in the Paris train in Dax station, watching vacantly while three young railway workers, chests and shoulders stripped to the sun, sluiced coal-dust off themselves under a spouting pump, he remembered with sour irony the moment above the grotto when he was reconciled to Death. A decent chap. A stout companion. An entertaining talker. Sergeant Death with the cold, friendly arms. A fellow with whom a young consumptive poet was once, listening in the dusk to the nightingale, half in love. The pilgrims waving torchlights came up the curving causeway, went down again along a similar causeway on the other side of the church, went far away under trees, torches jigging like erratic fireflies. Death, said a cunning Irish poet, was a bold rogue, a bad rogue, a rogue of high degree. At Dax the doctor remembered that that line might have warned him to watch out, to beware as they walked the streets through crowds of dispersing pilgrims, or sat in a lighted café, a wide room with latticed walls high above the river. A dance band played and couples danced. A singer opened and closed his mouth, but because of the river and the band and the shuffling couples, made no impression on the air. Then a comedian leaped to the stage beside the leader of the band, aimed cumbrous blunder-busses at the dancers and drinkers, pulled monstrous triggers, shot streamers of coloured paper around the room and over the balcony to trail down almost to the swift river. Life was fun and Death was friendly. The doctor laughed at the comedian; the dancers laughed; the man with the one arm laughed so loudly that he attracted attention, caused still more laughter.

At Dax the forests began: miles and miles of pines, cupped for resin; dry sand between the trees; an occasional lonely house; then miles of dark scorched earth where forest fires had destroyed the trees. He closed the window of his compartment against the smell of burned dead earth. He closed his mind against the memory of young living men scrubbing coal-dust off their bare torsos on the platform at Dax. Would it have been better to spend the thirteen hours of the journey to Paris in that windowless compartment farther down the train, his eyes fixed on a sealed coffin holding an embalmed body, his mind bitterly brooding on Death's adventurous ways? Adventurous? Greedy, cunning, treacherous, were better words. Did Death want to eat the world, green forests and young bodies? The one-armed man had sung with the singing people in the crypt at midnight, had stood among young priests drunk with the life of the liturgy, and among chaste, white-faced girls dressed in long, blue cloaks. He sang as if he belonged with those people. Or did he mean by his mellow singing that they belonged to him?

They said good-bye on a stony path by the edge of the

river, a castle high above them on a rock. In a shadowy corner at the root of the rock a courting couple huddled, a cigarette glowed, loving, living voices murmured. Fifty yards upstream the lights of the café dropped a frayed red reflection to the water.

'*A bientôt*.'

'Are you really going?'

'I'll be around. You know me. But now I must return my overcoat so they can find in the morning what's left of the poor fellow.'

The doctor, about to shake hands, took thought and didn't: the hand of a lonely man who in the morning would be found dead in his bed. Then, to comfort himself, he said: 'I'm not afraid of you any more.'

'I'm glad of that.' Was there a little edge of mockery in the voice?

'Those sick people praying with faith. Those blue-cloaked girls singing to God out of pure hearts. Even the people sipping pernod in the café and the comic man with his bullets of coloured paper. They mayn't all have forgotten you. But they can be happy while you're in the world.'

'Mostly they forget me. But sometimes when they stop to think they think about me.'

'I do, too.'

'But when next you stop to think don't be afraid, don't be bitter. I'm not so awful, am I? You're in my debt, but I don't keep reminding you of it, do I? I've an awkward job. I do my best for all concerned.'

All day the doctor, out of friendliness, had carried the black bag for his companion. Now he returned it, stood watching while the other went away, stepping carefully along the stony, unlighted path. 'One thing,' shouted the doctor.

'What's it?'

'The first day I met you. The little, cute man. The cap. The waistcoat. Then a poet with an unlawful passion. Then a one-armed hero, interested in the black market, proud of his own town.' His voice grew louder, for the white shirt, black beret, and trousers kept moving away into the darkness. 'Where's the connection? Or is there any?' The laugh that came back in answer could have been the cry of something from the water, a spirit swept down from the mountain. 'Let a man have his little secret. You have yours. The third request.' In the hollow under the rock the two lovers were gripping more tightly, thinking in fear and whispering: 'There are two shouting madmen on the path by the river.' The doctor thought: if the one-armed hero is in the morning found dead in his bed, the people, perhaps even those two whispering lovers, will say that all yesterday he paraded the town with a foreign man. Suppose in the morning the hero lies with his throat cut or with poison in his guts? The police will say, brown men with drooping eyelids and a huge imperturbability before evil will say: where is that foreign man?

Far away now, the white shirt shrunk to a shiny white spot, winked, the white of a wicked eye, through the blackness. The roar of the river was the threat of a mob of good citizens who loved the man who'd fought for his country and loved his town. The whisper of the lovers under the rock was a conspiracy or the bent whispering of jurymen weighing a point of damning evidence: this man leaped out of a bus before it crashed into a canal; this man came in a disturbed state of mind out of a wood on the top of a mountain.

Had he all day long been twisting a noose for his own neck?

He turned and ran away from the winking, vanishing white shirt. He came to a bridge and a lighted street that led towards the grotto.

IV

But when he came to the gate of the grotto he thought: I know already that running will do no good. He couldn't run the whole way home. The seas and hundreds of miles of dark land intervened. It must be too late now to go battering at the door of the hotel he'd left that morning, but in this town there were streets with solid blocks of big hotels, just as there were other streets with solid blocks of trinket-selling shops: souvenirs, models of the grotto, statues that chimed like clocks and clocks that looked like statues. Somewhere in those blocks of high hotels there must still be an open door, a lighted entrance hall, a porter who for a consideration would find him a room, rouse him for the first northbound train before the body of the one-armed bachelor was found dead in his bed.

So he stopped to study a plan of the town, fixed to the high spearheaded iron railings, tracing with his finger the path he should follow. The trees beyond the railings stirred slightly in a wind the face couldn't feel. There was no sign of life around the grotto or the basilica. At the nearest street-crossing two men passed staggering, arm-in-arm, singing.

He had satisfied himself that he knew well the plan of the part of the town he was going to, when a hand touched him lightly on the shoulder and a voice said: 'Pardon, if you please.'

It wasn't a policeman, or a man with one arm who should be dead in bed, or a poet in a duffle coat, or a contact man with a cunning eye. It was a tall, grave, grey-headed priest with aristocratic features who looked sharply at the doctor's startled face and said: 'I have studied you for some time before I had the courage to address you.'

The doctor said: 'Yes.' The monosyllable came out with difficulty. His nerves were getting into a bad way. He needed a rest; and for a dazzled instant the priest, the town of miracles, praying pilgrims, hotels, souvenir shops, vanished, and he saw a triangular village by a lake in the Irish midlands, geese on the soft green, crones on the half-doors, an old cross worn shapeless with persistent rain, ancient whitewashed walls, a pub with a low ceiling and the lamp-light shining on shelves of black bottles. He was sick for peace.

The priest said: 'You study the map. Perhaps you are trying to find your way back to your hotel.'

'Yes.' It was the easiest thing to say.

'I wondered and said to myself, it is the doctor from Ireland. Then again I thought, certainly it is not the doctor from Ireland. You see, we met only once.'

'We have met?'

'Yes, certainly. Do you not remember? Perhaps it is the lamp-light. Or the strange place. Or the late hour of the night.'

He looked to the right and the left, showing his profile, a

regular, classical, unquarrelling profile whether you looked at it from the east or the west. The doctor remembered. He thought: the château. He saw the three turrets, the high-windowed walls, strong stone soaked with sun, the steep slope down to the grey torrent, the patches of vines on the slope, the slow, yoked oxen, in the valley the maize plants denuded and drooping, poplars lined like graceful green giantesses along the river, in the distance cloven peaks in the clear air. He saw Pierre and the father and mother of Pierre and his own son and the Jesuit uncle from Lyons. He said: 'My apologies, father. I really didn't recognize you. Stupidity on my part.'

'Oh, no, no. How could you be expected to recognize me? Meeting here was a great surprise.'

'It certainly was. A pleasure too.'

'It is providential. For the last twenty-four hours my brother and his wife have been frantically trying to find you.'

They were pacing slowly along the pavement away from the grotto.

'Is that so?' He felt cold and weak.

'You haven't heard from them?'

'No. They didn't know where I'd be.'

'Of course, that is true. You left no forwarding address.'

'No. I wasn't sure myself where I'd be. I went south to Spain.' The cross still shone on the mountain.

'That was what my brother said. He sent a message all the way to Ireland, but they could tell him nothing of your whereabouts.' They paced across the bridge. The water was dark, streaked here and there with a ghastly white.

'I have a car here. Tonight, now, we can drive there.'

'Has anything gone wrong?'

'It is so difficult, so bitter to be the person who brings such news. But you are a strong man.'

'What has happened?'

'Your son. We must be brave. It is the will of the good God.'

'Tell me exactly.'

'Your son is dead. It tears my heart to tell you. God took him to Himself. You must think of that.'

'I'm thinking of it.'

The car belonged to Pierre's father. It didn't look like much, but it could touch high speeds and the holy father from Lyons was a skilful driver. So they drove for two hours and came in the early dawn to the place where Death had claimed the doctor's son.

Two hours later the people in the town of the pilgrims found the one-armed man dead in his bed. He hadn't been strangled. His heart had just stopped beating. The doctor read a few lines about it in the newspaper on the morning he set out for Paris. The heading said: 'Distinguished Patriot Dead.' It didn't say a word about the black market or the foreign man.

V

The brown railway workers at Dax laughed, joked, jack-acted as they washed at the spouting pump, and they were no older than his dead son.

He'd swung in the air on the *téléferique*, defying Death, and miles away Death had crushed his son, a part of his life.

The wheels beat out of charred forest and green forest, into endless farmland tufted with red-and-brown farm-houses. The slow Loire spread lax limbs across the flat country. Beyond the water little hills rose like dark hairy blisters, came to a head in white châteaux.

Death's a deceptive bastard, a bully flexing his muscles, extending chest and arms, showing his power.

Poitiers sprawled for ever, grey and uneven, along the rising and falling of a ridge. Chimneys and spires came up soaring out of the flat land. The sky darkened. Sunshine flowed away towards the south. Paris was an agony of nego-tiations, endless explanations, documents and documents and documents. Then, his precious, dreadful burden ready for the next stage of the journey, he had a few hours to himself. The sky darkened until it burst in thunder and bright lightning. Paris shrunk to a tiny café at the toes of a great cathedral, a striped blue-and-white canvas awning whipped and whipped and raped by the wind that came roaring when the sky burst, sheets of rain scouring and polishing the street and the square in front of the cathedral, gargoyles spouting water, thunder reverberating between the great square towers. Retreating before the invading rain, he sat in a corner of the café. Outside, the gargoyles spat and spouted with increased energy, tossing their thundery sputum to the middle of the narrow street. A woman dressed in a light summer frock, carrying balanced on her left shoulder a white plank, walked, not heeding the rain, along the flooded pavement.

The sorrow he was bringing back to his home went over him like a cold salty wave. People were moving again outside, splashing along the pavement, crisscrossing the square. He paid the *garçon* and hurried away to be with the moving people. Across the glittering river still pock-marked with the weakening rain, a watery evening sun shone out, gilding old windows, glancing under washed green leaves.

Then Paris was a hotel bedroom, too strange for sleep.

Tossing in his bed, he heard the thunder galloping again over the roofs. He'd searched all the little bars snuggled in side-streets off the upper reaches of the city's greatest avenue, hunting Irish whisky or, failing that, Scotch; finding only Canadian rye. In the dark, on the bedside table, he groped for the bottle, drank greedily, resigning himself to a morning of splitting headache as the payment for warmth, sleep, and forgetfulness. Sleep came at last, but not forgetfulness. Or was it even sleep? He couldn't be sure about that. Thunder pranced on the roof until the building shook. Bright lightning came and went. The downpour and the wind wrestled in the street. The red curtains came bellying into the room and ill-fastened shutters swung crashing open. Was it sleep? Was it a dream: the figure crouched in the corner of the iron balcony outside the window? An ape? A bat? A cunning little man with a black bag? Darkness and bright lightning and again darkness, and fingers or claws tearing at his throat, his half-strangled voice crying out in agony: 'Isn't my sorrow sore enough? Aren't you satisfied? Let me return to my own island with the lifeless body of my boy. Give me time to settle my affairs and end peacefully among my own people.'

'You broke your bargain.'

'You knew that when we were in the town of the pilgrims.

Why didn't you take revenge on me then and leave my son alone?'

'I answer no question. You saved a life you shouldn't have saved. So you lose your own. That's the game.'

'I ask you for mercy.'

'Mercy isn't my business.' So at last, with a weakened nightmare mind he understood Death, as no man, clear in the head and powerful in the body, can ever understand. 'Men have always know that mercy isn't my line of country. I've a tough job to do. I must be resolute. I walk by every man and woman, in their own shapes, in their own shadows. I crouch by every cradle and blossom like a black flower in every heart. I led Adam and Eve out of the garden and dug beside Adam in the new earth. I hold the hour-glass by the queen's throne and gibber at the lunatic when he gibbers at me —'

'Mercy. For a few years.'

'You've broken in on my little speech. I could go on like that for hours.'

'I don't want speeches. I want mercy.'

'I haven't any to give you.'

'Then I call for mercy to the golden-haired priest that I met in a room with twelve mourning, dancing men. I ask mercy for seven years for the sake of my wife who loves me in her own way, for the sake of my two children still alive, for the sake of a strong dark woman who brought my youth with her to the grave, for the sake of lovers walking in flowery lanes and sick people praying before a French rock, and for the sake of everything in the world that cries out for life.' He sat up in his bed. He cried out: 'I defy Death.' The red curtains flapped gently. The storm grew quiet through the long streets. Somebody in the next room had been disturbed by his nightmare shout, had stepped out of bed, turned on a tap, rattled a tumbler out of its chromium rack, spoke in querulous tones to a sleepy bedfellow. In the street the gutters ran like mountain brooks. One faint flash of lightning, a distant roll of thunder away to the awakening east. But there was nobody in his room and the iron balcony outside the window was wet and empty.

In the grey day that followed the gambler sailed for the islands.

Fifth Interlude

The servants carried the box of gold to the ship for the gambler, but Death came after them on the road and gripped the gambler by the throat.

'O friend, for the sweet sake of Christ,' says the gambler, 'I implore you to allow me to return to Ireland to give the gold to my family and to make my will between them the way they will not be quarrelling on that account.'

'You can have what you implore,' says Death. 'But it won't be long until I'm with you again.'

The gambler sailed for Ireland with his portion of gold.

SIX

I

'Please yourself, dear,' she said. 'It isn't as if we needed money any more.'

'No. I've made money in the last ten or eleven years.'

'Mother's will helped too.'

'It certainly did.'

'My only worry, darling, is that if you put this idea into practice you'll kill yourself with overwork.'

'I'm still fit for hard work.'

'You're not as young as you were.'

'None of us is.'

'I suppose not.' She looked at herself in the long bedroom mirror. Grief at the death of her son and later at the death of her mother had given to her face lines of dignity it had not possessed in the days of her plump, pretty youth. Nowadays when he looked at her he saw nobility, and realized more insufferably the guilt of his memories and thoughts.

'Your practice has been so comfortable. To go down now to work in some hole in the slums will be a terrible strain.' Carefully she guided her arms into the sleeves of the silver fox he held for her. 'We'll be late, darling. The curtain rises at seven-thirty.'

When they sat together in the car going towards the city, she said: 'I know you're acting with the purest intentions. I believe in you and I approve. It's so fortunate, too, that you can afford to be eccentric nowadays. Years ago, when your peculiarities left us lacking in money, an idea like this would have been madness.'

'My peculiarities?'

'You are an odd fish, dear. You might as well admit it. But you're wealthy enough to be odd in comfort. The newspapers will praise you to the clouds. Prominent physician founds guild for relief of sick poor.'

She was obviously delighted at the prospect of the favourable publicity destined for her husband's eccentricity, and although there was no satisfactory reason why, he still found her delight a little trying.

The young man in the theatre bar said during the first interval: 'What, Doctor, is the exact purpose of the new guild?' The play was *The Doctor's Dilemma*. The young man was a newspaper reporter thinking that if he got his information now he could save himself the trouble of going to a boring meeting with minutes, inane arguments, and interminable speeches.

'The exact purpose is to help poor mothers before, during, and after the birth of their children.'

'A valuable purpose,' the young man said, hoping that the doctor wouldn't leave the bar immediately the warning bell rang for the second act.

'Very necessary,' the doctor said. 'As you know, the infant mortality rate is very high in the poorer quarters of the city. The homes that the mothers must bring their children back to are, in nine cases out of ten, dirty and unhealthy.'

'Yes,' said the reporter. He'd once covered a story in which the roof of a tenement had fallen in on top of two poor families.

'We aim to give immediate treatment at our centre in the heart of the slums. Then, for holidays and for prolonged treatment, we have the new building in a seaside village.'

'A very good idea.' The warning bell rang. The doctor had his wife with him and would naturally go back for the second act. The reporter would have to find some way of unobtrusively attaching himself to some of the more habitual frequenters of the theatre bar.

'About State grants?' he said, swallowing his drink as quickly as the doctor swallowed his, looking at his watch as if he was leaping with anxiety to get back to Mrs. Dubedat and George Bernard Shaw. The cool nerve of the old root to write the way he did about the illiteracy of newspaper men. 'Eventually,' said the doctor, 'although this is off the record, the State must back us up.' Moving slowly on the fringe of the doctor's party, men and women in evening dress, jewels and pearls and bare middle-aged shoulders, the reporter waited for the proper moment to cut in on the conversation, to say he must speak to the two men still drinking in peace and comfort at one corner of the bar. 'We have a pamphlet ready for publication,' said the doctor. 'I could show you the page proofs.'

'Thank you very much. I'll call and collect it some day, if that's convenient.' Calling at a rich man's house, with ever and always yellow whisky in the sideboard, was a better game than going to a cold meeting.

'Certainly,' said the rich doctor.

'Thank you,' said the reporter. Then, to his great relief, the doctor's wife, flanked by another gabbling woman, wheeled around to say something to the doctor about the sincerity of the young actress who was playing Mrs. Dubedat, and a man with a squeaky voice said, 'Not at all, no sincerity whatsoever,' and in the ensuing confusion the reporter was able to back out unnoticed and sidle over to his drinking friends.

How could I, thought the doctor, as he sat in the darkness listening to Shaw's words and watching the movements of the mummers, how could I tell that poor young fellow the truth? He'd never believe me if I did. He'd never be able to write it for his newspaper, even if he was mad enough to believe me. Or how could I give my wife the slightest hint of the abominable lunatic nature of what she calls my eccentricity?

Let me speak, then, for myself, and to myself here in cushioned, comfortable darkness.

Strange things have happened to me that have not, as far as I know, happened to men I meet and talk with, who shake my hand and introduce me to their wives. Nobody could call me a mystic, but once, when I stopped in the course of a drunken day and thought of God, something dressed in the shape of a man spoke to me, intervened in my life. Afterwards things were different. No man could call me more than usually morbid, but once, when I sat in a dark room thinking of Death, something, also in the shape of a man, walked into the room, a knowing smile on its face, a black bag in its right hand. It isn't easy to tell people about those happenings or the things that followed. I went on a Spanish journey and visited a white house high on a rock. That house was really there, even if I'm always afraid that if I were to return I'd find no village, no rock, no house, no red-headed woman. Anyhow, I never will go back there; never again leave this island where a man may still listen to whispers from wet grass, to old melodious voices in warm corners by country hearths, to the sea singing around lonely rocks, and forget the world and hope to find his own secret. I'm not afraid now. I'm a rich man and I know the secret of Death: that men are afraid to turn away and go with Death because of things unfinished and tangles unresolved rather than for terror of the waiting darkness. A householder halfway up the stairs to his peaceful bed comes warily down again to see are the windows latched and the doors bolted against burglars. In the worrying mind nothing is ever completed. No story is ever told to the end, and Death's hateful because he interrupts us when we're adding up numbers, chiselling stone, cooking a dinner, dancing a dance, kissing or cursing, or putting money on horses.

A man should have the courage to strip himself of all he possesses and to begin life again. There's an echo of something in that, he thought, as he vacantly watched Dubedat, the doctor, and the dilemma. Then when Death comes along he breaks in on no established, valued routine. I'll anticipate Death by stripping myself gradually of the present. Then I'll have the laugh on the man with the black bag, for even as things are I've lived my life, had my love. My story is told as far as it can be told this side of the shadows, and I live only in remorseful memory. Long years ago, on a day of poverty and crisis, I looked for an instant at three means of escape. They were the rope, the river, and the road. To hang myself or drown myself would solve nothing, as I now see the world, my people, my place here, God and Death. But a tramping man on the road should surely have resolved all tangles so that he fears no interruption from skies falling or floods rising or the heart faltering and refusing to beat. Gradually I'll move towards that freedom, away from all the complications of consulting-rooms in a Georgian square and a large suburban house complete with wife and family. I'll go down into the deep slums to be with people who must fear only a little because they've so little to lose. I'll find, among the diseased and suffering, people who see the face of Death as the face of a friend. It's true, of course, that where life begins with all the cards stacked against it, I'll be there fighting on the side of life. But my real joy will be in being helped by people who take Death's power from him by meeting him with a smile. Poor coughing children. Old bent men. Rheumatic women with skin like yellow, wrinkled parchment. And the joke is that all the time they'll think I'm helping them.

The doctor sat at the play between his own wife and another man's wife. He was enjoying the mild form of ecstasy that comes from good clothes, food, drink, and intentions. He was pleased with his discovery about Death.

II

With sharp grey granite and frosted glass, the new centre for the care of expectant poor mothers was as distinctive as a jewel catching the light on the dull back of a dung-heap. Across the road and guarded by high railings, reinforced against robbers by vicious coils of barbed wire, was a church built of corrugated iron. The paint had peeled off the railings. Behind them at night, when the one gate was padlocked and the church windows securely shuttered, God was on the defensive. A tabernacle had once been rifled and the sacred vessels pawned and melted down, the white bread desecrated. The wooden box, slowly filling with pennies given by the poor to the poor, had twice been prised open and the pennies stolen. Above the church and above the new building jagged tenement houses stood up high as the sky.

In the depths of those crumbling-walled canyons he walked almost as in a dream. His life now was the moment of suspended breathing between one normal breath and the next. He was a man in a blitzed city, instinctively closing his eyes and hunching his shoulders and waiting for the roof to fall, not caring a curse whether it fell in a minute or a million years. At the end of the day's work he was always the last to say good night to the caretaker. Then he walked slowly the half-mile of swarming streets to the patch of black, grassless earth where the city authorities had set up a car park. As a medical student and as a young doctor in a small city, he'd grown accustomed to the sights and sounds of those decayed places. Old women, when the weather was warm, sat on the steps outside dark stenchy doorways. Boy children without trousers, girl children in tatters played around and around the aged people. Two girls as gaudy as peacocks sat on the steps outside a bakery and wondered, now that their bodies were proud in finery, would anything happen, anything exciting and new. A shouting, supplicating barman urged singing bruisers out to the pavement and closed the door on bottles and black barrels; Bacchus also on the defensive for a night among the poor. The jukebox in the chip shop at the corner by the car park sang to gallant adolescents about far-away places. It was all as familiar to him as the wallpaper in his bedroom or the pattern grained on his hall door, and only an occasional incident had the power to burst in on his dream before Death and leave a red, bleeding mark in his memory.

Once, walking by the corner of a lane, he was shaken out of his thoughts by the savage gesture of a ragged gutty throwing one pointed leg of a broken scissors at the door of a closed shop. His right arm flashed in an arc, as if in that shabby street a hero had brandished a sword. His companions applauded the force and accuracy of the throw. For the remainder of the walk to the car park the doctor's blood was livelier in his veins.

Once, looking out of the window of his room in the new building, he saw a drunken girl, gaudily dressed in a way that told the world what she was, stagger along the street, shadowy in the moment that comes between the end of daylight and the beginning of lamp-light. Outside the guarded church she stopped and shook her fist, then advanced, grasped the railings, tugged as if she'd tear them out of the ground. She wore a short fur jacket, unfastened in front, triangle-cut above her buttocks, and while she tugged the jacket flapped like hair-grown wings. The railing horned with barbed wire resisted. So she shook her fist again and staggered away. As she went the lamps came to life, gold sentinels rejoicing in the air over her degraded, defeated head. Was it hell in her heart that tried to shake and uproot the railings? Or an agonized desire for God in a heart conscious of the loss of God, conscious of the cramped pain of a body and soul twisted out of shape by the usage of the world? Or was it a heart hot with love resenting the stone — the railings, the wire, the locked door — rolled over to close in that stinking slum garden the tomb where man had put God?

In a way that at first he found difficult to understand, these and a thousand other images telescoped or melted into the impassivity of the big man who played cards with himself (beggar-my-neighbour, right hand against left, continuing for hours) in a corner of the chip shop, the noisy corner between the cooker steaming and sizzling and the yellow juke-box.

III

In the beginning he walked on the other side of the street past that raucous fish and chip saloon. Then, after two weeks, curiosity made him cross the street, move more slowly in the zone of sound and warm odours, look curiously as he passed at the bright interior. Seven days later he entered it for the first time, not without nervousness. Three weeks later he had developed a habit of visiting the place every evening before reclaiming his car from the patch of arid black earth. He may have been thinking of, or at least acting according to, a Frenchman whose words he had once read and learned by heart: 'Every day I change; my tastes of yesterday are no longer my tastes of today; my friendships themselves wither up and are renewed; before the final death of the mobile being who bears my name, how many men have already died within me?'

Perhaps he was simply tired from walking by evil-smelling doorways along crowded, unyielding pavements. He was no longer young, his hair white, his shoulders not square and erect as they once had been. His legs after much walking could often have been the legs of a man to whom a soothing, gesturing hypnotist had said: 'From the waist down you are now dead asleep, dead asleep, dead asleep.' It wasn't hunger that drove him into the saloon to sit on a stiff chair at a greasy, narrow table. The walls were enamelled a hideously bright blue, made brighter and more hideous by scarcely bearable fluorescent lighting. Although he always ordered the single dish the place provided, he made only one attempt, on his first visit, to eat it. Afterwards, to avoid offending the rough-skinned Italian girl who carried the steaming plates to the tables, he secretly passed on his portion to any adjacent tatterdemalion who looked hungry enough to accept charity.

The juke-box sang of those dear hearts and gentle people who live and love in my hometown. The tatterdemalions, and the joxers with swelling scarves and slick hair sang and shouted through clouds of pungent steam, stamped their feet, were suspiciously conscious of the man in the dark clothes who obviously didn't belong there. They were conscious also of the big man who sat card-playing by himself, not speaking, not eating, the suggestion of a smile on his huge face, in the corner between the sizzling cooker and the juke-box. The steam in that corner was more dense than anywhere else in the room, and there were times when the man and his gambling competing hands were cut off and curtained away from the doctor, the joxers, and the tatterdemalions. Only the Latin girl, coming and going with full plates and empty plates, seemed to have free entry to that cloud.

The real reason for my visiting this place so often is (as far as I know) a desire to get back to the days when my unpainted house, my unkempt garden, my unpaid account with a talkative grocer were topics to whisper about on a respectable suburban road. Those dear hearts and gentle people. It amuses me to think what all the people who come to my wife's parties would say if they could see me sitting here. When I'm here, too, I care no longer that I'm forfeit to Death, for, as far as my normal life's concerned, I'm dead already; and I feel or hope that if I stay here long enough that strong, dark woman may live again, walk in at the door, into din and steam, and say: 'Your green car's waiting. I'll drive you home.' If that happened, I think the big man would rise up from his chair, toss the circling cards away from him, stalk like a giant out of his shrouded corner, and tell me his name.

One night he walked into the saloon, escaping from cold, mizzling rain. The tops of the surrounding tenement houses were shrouded in damp mist that held and echoed the noises of the streets, cries of ragged children in the rain, disputing voices from rotten hallways, the beat of hard heels on the pavement. Moisture gathered on and dripped from the arms of lamp-posts.

Inside the saloon the din was louder than ever, the steam more dense. A white cloud of vapour cut off completely the corner in which the big man sat. Every chair in the place was occupied. A noisy jostling crowd of men and women, faces red from drink, stood two-deep along the counter. The doctor halted a few feet from the door, looking vainly for somewhere to sit, blinded by the shrieking light, deafened momentarily by the babble of voices, the blare of the juke-box. Conscious more acutely than ever of his own oddity, he would have retreated, but the thought of the drizzling misery of the streets outside, of the wheels of his car skidding over slippery surfaces towards his home, drove him forwards to pick his way between the crowded tables, to follow the Italian girl into the misty corner. No one rose to offer him a seat; not one of the hungry he had so frequently fed. Their eyes, cold with hostility, followed him as he walked. Their minds had absorbed enough of the gutter to be suspicious of an ageing rich man offering food to poor boys. They'd take the food, but suspect and feel morally superior to the strange person who offered it. In that instant he understood the folly of his search for a place where men had loosened the knots that tied them to life, where men could fool Death by forestalling him with ironic resignation. Feeling outcast and abandoned among the dregs of the life of the city, he stepped into the cloud, saw an empty chair, sat down quickly, saw on the table in front of him a carefully stacked pack of cards. Then he looked up into the face of the big man.

'Cut,' said the big man, and the gambler pulled off his gloves, flexed his fingers, and cut. The card was the seven of hearts.

The big man reshuffled the pack. His hands were monstrously large but exceedingly agile. He dropped his right hand over the resting pack, turned up his broad palm to show that the card he'd cut was the nine of hearts.

'What'll you eat, sir?' the Italian girl said to the doctor. She always said that, pretending to herself, perhaps, that there was more than one dish on the menu. The gambler didn't answer. He was staring straight at the big man. The face was so large and so close to him that it was hard to study more than one feature at a time. So he rested his glance on the broad forehead, an old, wise forehead, but completely free of the wrinkles that marked age or the bumps that indicated wisdom. It was as smooth as the cheek of an infant, and yet he felt it was old and wise. He looked lower down, then, at the eyes like dark blue bottle-bottoms wedged in between cavernous brows and strong, prominent jaw-bones. It was impossible to see beyond the bright glassy surface of those eyes. In a bright place they might have reflected the world. Here, in a corner dense with pungent steam, they reflected nothing.

'Have we met before?' asked the doctor.

'We have.'

'I can't remember where.'

The curtain of steam thickened and cut them off completely from the rest of the room.

'We seem to be oddities here.'

'Cut the cards again.'

The gambler cut, his hand doing a preliminary hover over the pack, a hawk over a thicket looking for the richest, tastiest bird. The card he turned up was the seven of spades.

'The streets are wet tonight,' the big man said. He reshuffled the cards and turned up the nine of spades.

'I know you now,' said the gambler. The great eyes, completely without expression, looked down at the card marked with nine black spearheads, at the split pack, the greasy surface of the table. Garish light filtering through steam gave a silky gloss to his circular jaws. The shape of his head was as round as a schoolroom globe of the world. 'Once upon a time,' said the gambler, 'I stepped out of a train at a station in a distant part of the country. I had to wait to catch another train, so I went into a small, warm buffet that was like a stranded ark in the middle of a draughty platform. A big man came in accompanied by two soldiers. He bought drinks for the soldiers, for myself, for everybody in the buffet, including the girl behind the beer machine. He was a generous man, and all the time he looked at me hard as if he knew me. But he said nothing and I said nothing. That man was yourself.'

'Cut again,' said the big man. Hawk over a thicket, lark over a nest, aeroplane over a concrete runway, golden angel over a poor man's cottage, considering hand over fifty-three pieces of pasteboard. The card the gambler turned up was the seven of diamonds.

'Later I remembered I'd known that man in my boyhood. He was a rich cattle dealer, master of herds, a remnant of the chieftains who swagger like emperors through ancient Gaelic stories. That day in the buffet he was coming from a fair in the south of the country where he'd bought seven wagon-loads of cattle. His pockets, every one of them, and his two wallets and the lining of his hat were stuffed with bank-notes.' The gambler, as he spoke, kept his eyes on the two great hands deftly shuffling cards, then hovering over the tidied pack. This time it was the left hand that swooped. The card it turned up was the nine of diamonds.

Behind and around them the curtain of steam thinned. In the bowels of the juke-box a record came to an end and the only sound from its bloated body was a restless repetitive scratching like the scratching and gnawing of a rat behind a skirting-board. The saloon was unusually silent. Were the joxers and ragamuffins and the drunken people at the counter waiting for another record to begin? Looking quickly over his shoulder, he saw that all the eyes in the place were turned on that corner, puckered eyes peering through the thinning steam. Imagination? With an effort he turned again towards the table, the cards, and the big man. What had he, any more, to fear from staring eyes or Death or even from a mysterious power that could overturn his mastery in gambling? Another record began, brave pipes playing a Scottish march, and feet were thumping on the floor. The steam grew dense again. The babble of voices recommenced.

'Amn't I lucky at the cut?' said the big man.

The doctor thought automatically: The devil's luck, and, toying with the cards, turning cold at the meaning of his own thought. Were these cards fixed? But, then, since the day when his luck turned he'd played against gamblers notorious for crookedness and won in spite of their wiles. Controlling his panic, he remembered and continued his story: 'When I was a boy my father's house was beside a semicircular holm by a curving river where this man used to graze his cattle. I spent many evenings walking by that river and listening to his friendly talk, trying to equal his long stride. From his words I first understood grass growing, the beauty of flat land, the meaning of wide rivers and cattle grazing. You were that man.'

'Try another cut.'

The gambler turned up the seven of clubs. He told himself he had nothing to fear from Death or the dark horse. He said: 'Later in my life I was a young doctor in a village in the Kerry mountains. I was too poor to afford a car of my own, so a man from the village used to drive me to the houses of the sick people in outlying parts. We became great friends.' The cards were reshuffled and ready; the big right hand descended to choose and cut. The gambler didn't look to see what the upturned card was. Instinctively knowing he was beaten again, he talked to hear his own voice, to keep the tips of his fingers touching reality, to protest against the sound of coarse food sizzling on hot wire, against the bellowing juke-box, against the babble of hostile voices. 'That man and myself covered together every inch of road in those brown, sombre mountains. I owe him a lot, because in his company I first understood mountains, lonely lakes, the words written in rocky places.' The uncovered card still lay exposed on the table. Against his will he looked. It was the nine of clubs. 'That man who drove a car in the Kerry mountains was yourself,' he said, and the big man said:

'I never lose a gamble. Will you try again?'

'I will not.'

'Why not?'

'This is a poor place for gambling.'

'All places are alike to me.'

'I don't like the noise.'

'Then come to a quiet place.'

'The light hurts my eyes.'

'I'll show you a darker place.'

'I don't like the steam all around us — choking the nostrils.'

'I'll bring you to my room. No steam there. But you'll be pleasantly warmed by a good fire.'

'Why should I go to your room?'

'Are you afraid?'

'Why should I gamble with you?'

'Haven't you gambled with and beaten all the men in the world?'

'So you do know who I am?'

'Aren't you a very famous man?'

The doctor stood up. He said: 'Is your room far away?'

'Around a few corners and along a few streets.' The big hand rhythmically shuffled the cards, then quickly snapped a rubber band around the smooth pack. They stepped out through the surrounding steam. The juke-box was silent; and the people were silent while the big man, moving slowly as if at every step his feet gripped the floor like roots of trees gripping earth, forced his way through the narrow spaces between the tables. The gambler, first out to the street, waited until the other had overtaken him. The rain had ceased. Mist rose from damp asphalt. They walked side by side along the chipped, sticky pavement, then across the dead, dark patch of earth where seven cars, one of them the gambler's car, were parked.

'We could drive there.'

'It wouldn't be worthwhile. Along a few streets.' Away from the cacophony of the saloon the big man's voice was loud, harsh, metallic. 'Around a few corners.'

So they walked around a few corners and along a few streets. The streets widened and were less repulsive. Around the last corner they entered a quiet square, a green island surviving in spite of neighbouring warehouses, factories, tall houses festered to slums. Bushes grew tangled and unkempt inside high railings. The surrounding houses were solid with good grey stone. Lamp-light showed them a church without spires, faint light glimmering in an oriel window. 'Here we are,' said the big man as, exactly opposite the church, he forced open, against clinging brambles and resisting bushes, a creaking gate in the high railings.

IV

'The strange thing about my house,' the big man said, 'is that you could go through every street in the city and find it or not find it — according to your luck.'

The gambler repeated: 'Luck.' In the darkness the one sharp word was like a prayer to the unseen. He tried to suppress in his voice, as one should always suppress in a prayer, the note of doubt and mockery. He could see nothing; not a sign of a house. Under his feet he felt only the dead surface of a pathway long overgrown by weeds and rebellious creepers. Keeping his eyes fixed on the bulk of the big man, a vague shape, blacker than the blackness, he shuffled forwards slowly. Long, damp brambles and branches touched his face. Within the railings the air had no odour of stone or the city's dust. Instead, he smelled the smell of green things sinking into the earth and rotting, the smell of deep sunless forests or of the gas bubbling up from the stirred edges of stagnant pools. No light from the square outside pierced through the tangle of branches. But still slowly shuffling forwards behind the big man, his eyes became accustomed to the darkness. He saw a short bridge, the ornamented parapet defaced and broken, that perhaps a century previously had spanned a tiny artificial stream. Where the stream had once flowed, giving sparkle and movement and delight to a city square, there was now only a shapeless wound, smelling of refuse, in the earth. He peered down as he passed into that dark malodorous pit. 'My ashbin,' the big man said. 'I live among ruins.'

'You might perhaps manage to cut away some of the brambles from your avenue.'

'If I did that my seclusion would be gone. Every person in the city could then walk into my house as easily as they walk along the pavements.'

'You're not sociable.'

'I am. Very sociable. But if approach was made too easy people would never turn aside to look at me. When I live in the centre of an overgrown, decayed square, when I lock the gate in the railings and reinforce the barbed wire twisted along their pointed tops, then people go to the most extraordinary extremes to get a look at me.' Once across the bridge the big man halted. The gambler couldn't see, but he could feel the great eyes turned on him in the darkness. 'Principally the children. They break through all obstacles.' The harsh voice softened with pride in the enterprise of the children. 'You must admit that a place like this is paradise for adventurous boys.'

'By day, perhaps.'

'The children aren't frightened away by my reputation for peculiarity. They climb the railings. They come creeping through the undergrowth. They peer in at the windows of my house to see me playing cards with myself. If they only knew, they could see as much in public in the bright light in the fish and chip saloon. But they love mystery. I like the feeling that when I sit alone in my house they're there whispering outside the window, rubbing clear circles in the dusty panes, trying to see me better.'

'In your place I'd feel I was being spied on.'

'I do. I like the feeling. I've nothing to hide.' The doctor glanced nervously over his shoulder. The lights of the street were so utterly gone, the occasional hammer of passing footsteps so dangerously, helplessly distant.

'Not afraid, are you?'

'Why should I be afraid?'

'I'm twice your size. This is a dark place. A man could be killed and robbed here. The people who live in the square mightn't know for days.'

'I've two pounds in my pocket and nothing to fear from Death.'

'That's a big boast.'

'Every man could say the same if he thought about it for five minutes. There's nothing in the world I wish to finish. There's no living person I want to see once again.'

'For a successful man you sound despondent.'

'I wouldn't call it despondency.' His eyes had sharpened, so that he could distinguish tree from tree, see and forestall the threat of drooping branches. Twenty yards beyond the broken bridge they escaped from the trees into the lesser darkness of a clearing. The low, rough shape of a house gathered substance out of the surrounding night.

'Is that your house?'

'It's small but it's cosy.' They went up three steps and stood in the shelter of a narrow porch. The walls, like the walls of the houses in the square, were made of good grey stone. 'The great thing is the seclusion.' At the first endeavour the big man found the keyhole, snapped the door quickly open, and stooping his shoulders, stepped into the house. The doctor hesitated on the porch. The way those shoulders stooped under the low doorway reminded him of something. He waited in the porch until he heard the snap of a match, saw the flame touched to a gas-lamp poised on an antiquated metal bracket above a wide ash-strewn fireplace. 'Come in out of the night,' the big man said, smiling openly for the first time — a curious tremor of flesh, a flash of white teeth that seemed too big and too plentiful. It was a disconcerting smile.

'Once I knew a man who lived alone in a house like this,' the doctor said. 'A house that looked as if it had been deserted, unlived in, for years. Ashes deep on the hearth. But the ashes were always so cold and dead that you couldn't help thinking there hadn't been a fire in the place for fifty winters.'

'I've had fires more recently.'

The room in which they stood seemed to occupy the greater part of the house. 'I'm not reflecting on your charming dwelling. But, as one stranger to another, it's a queer place to invite a man to.' The ceiling, high in the centre, sloped down at the sides to meet the walls in a dust-caked line of plaster plants and flowers. A high table filled one corner, blocked the way to a door opening, probably, into a bedroom. Two chairs stood before the fireplace. A third lay tumbled on the floor. Bent over the fireplace, the big man snapped sticks and piled coals with capable hands.

He said: 'I heard a lot about you as a gambler. I heard you never refused a challenge.'

'This man I knew who lived alone. He was about your height. He stooped through a low doorway the way you do. Under his left oxter he carried always a bundle of manuscript. He told the world he was writing the story of his life, but no eye ever read what he had written. He was a very happy man and quite mad, and I'm sure that the secret of happiness, like a chemical formula, was written down somewhere on that manuscript.' The sticks crackled. The flames leaped up. 'The lonely house he lived in was burned down one night. He was smothered. The story of his life was left in black ashes. Yet from the life of that man I suspected for the first time that it could be pleasant to be mad.' The big man straightened up from his bending position. 'You were that happy lunatic,' the doctor said.

'You're a great man for guessing.'

'Isn't that the truth?'

'We'll play cards first.'

'With my pack of cards.' In a carved case of thin ivory in his pocket, he carried the cards gathered on a memorable morning from the green table and the brown carpet in the club-house. They pulled the two standing chairs back from the fire to the table in the corner and sat down.

'No food? No drink?' asked the doctor.

'No distractions,' said the big man. Dust lay thickly on the surface of the table. With a red silk handkerchief the doctor cleaned a place for his precious cards.

'My favourite game,' said the big man, 'is Beggar-my-Neighbour.'

'Where I was reared,' said the gambler, 'we called it Strip Jack Naked.'

'It's a good game. It goes in a circle.'

'It's hardly a game of skill.'

'The great thing in a gamble is the chance of the cards.'

'It's hardly a game for two gamblers trying their strength in a dusty room.'

'Are you afraid to play it?'

'Poker's my game.'

'We'll cut to decide.'

'We will not.'

'Are you afraid to cut?'

'I'm afraid of nothing. Not any more.'

'Let me cut, so,' said the big man. He split the pack and turned up the seven of hearts. The gambler shuffled the cards, split the pack, looked down at the five of hearts. 'Who are you?' he said.

'I thought you knew.'

'I was guessing.'

'Guess again, so. Beggar-my-Neighbour's our game.'

'I could guess my father, who was a tall man too. From him I learned that life never ends.'

'May I deal?' asked the big man.

'You may not,' said the gambler, pulling the pack swiftly towards him, reshuffling and dealing the cards out evenly and slowly. How well he knew the feel of those cards, a little worn and dirty now and rounded at the corners; but for him they would always be the best cards in the world.

'I could guess a great athlete I admired when I was young, when I wanted to be a great athlete myself. Watching him, I knew a man's body could be glorious.'

'We'll play for a high stake.'

'Name it.'

'If I finish up with the full pack in my hand, then you lose your power over illness, your victory in healing.'

The gambler held his cards, blind sides upwards, in his left hand. That dusty room in that overgrown, neglected square was a stage where the events of a play pressed inwards and upwards to climax. But not by one movement, a starting hand, a startled rolling eye, or a twitch of a face muscle, did he show that his heart beat faster. 'Your lead,' he said, and the big man tossed to the table a red, lecherous queen of hearts. A thin, evil, red-lipped face smiled as if it lived. Used as he was to strangeness, the gambler could not conceal surprise. Never before had he seen that face pictured on the cards he had stolen from the club-house. On the table beside the red, evil queen he laid down methodically two unimportant cards.

The big man said, his harsh voice resonant with triumph: 'First blood to the challenger.' He gathered the three cards into his hand.

'I could guess —' began the gambler, then stopped in consternation, for the big man with a twist of his wrist, agile in spite of hairy, big-boned thickness, had exposed on the table a king of diamonds: a face that was all acute angles, diamond-shaped eyes smouldering with hostile greed. Never in all his days of card-playing had the gambler seen such a king of diamonds. Looking down at those sharp, red angles was like looking into a rusted pit at all the evil things ever done for the sake of land, jewels, money, or rank in the world. Slowly, very slowly, scrutinizing each card as he handled it, he counted out on the table three worthless cards, cannon fodder for the greedy king. If he hadn't himself dealt he'd have suspected crookedness.

'I've great luck,' the big man said, gathering his spoils, flicking a new card to the table. The gambler looked at it and waited, not playing, thinking once again — the luck of the dark horse, knowing by a chill, sick twinge in his stomach that he was not yet beyond fear. From the cleared space in the middle of the dusty table a monstrous black king, thick, brutal lips, eyes that in green jungles had gloated over the flogging of screaming slaves, stared him in the face.

He said: 'You seem to have all the coloured cards in the pack.'

He didn't look up at the broad, smooth-skinned face of the big man or at the surfaces of the eyes of dark blue glass. 'I've powerful luck,' the big man said.

'You're a powerful man.'

Two huge hands rested on the table. The cards lay neatly between them. The gambler, reaching quickly across the table, snatched the cards, joined the two sundered portions of the pack. He said: 'We needn't go on with this game.' The hands made no move to prevent him.

'In spite of the favour that was once shown you. In spite of the granting of your first request.'

'You're too powerful for me.'

'I'm the most powerful man you'll ever meet.'

'Then at last,' said the gambler, 'I can guess who you are.' He slipped his cards back into the ivory case. The odour of dust and dry rot was beginning to trouble his nostrils. He wanted to escape swiftly from this house abandoned in a tangled garden in a decayed square.

'Guess.'

'Once upon a time I walked up a coloured, steep stairway into a lounge bar where twelve men in mourning clothes were dancing in a circle.' The great hands lay on the table as if they had died. 'There was a thirteenth man in that room, a golden-haired priest with a voice like music.'

The hands closed and clenched into rigid, straining fists, and then there were three fists instead of two on the table, all clenched and straining; and seeing them more with revulsion than fear, the gambler felt that the whole great body was rigid with some searing pain. 'I sat down beside the thirteenth man. I drank the drink he paid for. He was generous. I believed him when he told me he was paying for the whole dancing, mourning party. Were you that priest?' He spoke slowly and carefully, nerving himself to look up at the big man's face, but, when he did look, he saw not the smooth face of a giant boy, but the rusted angular face of the greedy king balanced incongruously, a mask, on the thick neck. Diamond-shaped eyes burned and threatened and the gambler stepped backwards, away from the table, as the big man with the evil king's face stood up. The third hand had vanished. He said: 'For a long time I talked to that golden-haired priest. He told me things about myself that I thought nobody knew. Then I asked him his name.' He backed step by step towards the door. The big man moved one step in slow, inexorable pursuit. His face had changed again. It was black and thick-lipped — the face of the brutal king of bleeding slaves.

Then, more afraid of what he might see than of anything that could happen to him, the gambler shouted at the top of his voice: 'The golden-haired priest said his name was God.'

The face of the black king was gone. The big man, jaws working like the jaws of a man in a stroke, froth on his lips, his skin dry and wrinkled, was bending down, clutching the table, coughing in agony. When he fell heavily to the floor the gambler had the door open. When the big limbs stiffened and straightened in a paroxysm the gambler was going, as quickly as with safety he could, over the broken bridge towards the gate in the high railings. He found a spot where adventurous climbing children had twisted away the barbed wire from the spear-headed iron tops. He was proud that age had left him the agility to climb, to drop lightly to the pavement, to run from that square through wet slum streets as if he was running from hell.

V

The doctor and his wife slept in separate rooms. That night he lay in the cold, sleepless darkness regretting the cuddling life and warmth of young love. Sitting somewhere invisible, his companion Death spoke to him and said: 'Look. I'm your friend. I don't want to hurry you. But your time's coming near. You know that as well as I do.'

Death had no outline, no vague shape. He had the same size as the night, and the same colour. His voice was made up of the night noises of a suburb by the sea: the exhaust of the last bus, the banging and bolting of a garage door as a neighbour put his car under cover for the night, the giggling of a domestic servant and her lover in the shelter of a gateway, a jaded piece of music — singing and a piano — from some house notorious for parties, the hard footsteps of a late man going home, and far away in a mist the hollow roll of the sea on the suburban shore.

'Let me go free until I'm ready to face you. Until I've moved so far away from the treadmill of my days that there's nothing I want to finish. Until I've died so completely in all hearts that I can go with you without human regrets, and no one will notice that my place is empty.'

'Vanity and foolishness. Life's a strait-jacket. Life's a mesh made of strong ropes. No man ever disentangles himself. I have always to come and cut the knots at one stroke. No man's ever forgotten at the moment he dies, or for years after that. Not even the loneliest, most friendless man. Somewhere you'll be remembered, no matter how hard you try to be forgotten. A soldier with a scar on his face will think well of you. A child you once cured in the slums and who didn't afterwards find life a blessing will curse your name.'

'Life's a candle. Let me burn it down to the last guttering inch.'

'The end comes when the wind blows out the flame of the candle. Life's a weary journey. You should be glad of a rest.'

'There are parts of the journey I'd gladly cover again.'

'Haven't you all eternity?'

'I don't understand.'

'You will.'

'I want to save my soul by working for the poor.'

'You probably don't mean that. Not that it's a bad idea. Get the poor cleaned up a bit before they come my way. And the rich too.'

Then the night was silent for a long time. In the suburb there was no sound. When Death spoke again his voice was the distant voice of the hollow water.

'You want to live for a while?'

'I do.'

'I was never one to bustle my friends into a decision, but —'

'I want to live.'

'Live, then, until I come again.'

'When?'

'Seven minutes or seven years. Who knows? I don't myself. I obey orders. Expect me when you see me.'

'I can't see you now.'

'I'm here though. Even when I go away I'm still here with you. You carry me with you from morning to night, through every day onwards from the first moment of your first day.'

A long silence. The darkness muffling the sound of the sea.

'There I go. Making speeches again.'

The wind changed, blowing the noise of the waves away from the shore.

The doctor and his wife slept in separate rooms. He lay thinking of Death, regretting sun and sea wind and the glitter of a stream in a green, young place. She slept well. Her mother dying had left her a determination more valuable than her money, and every night, triumphing over the chagrins of the day, she willed to sleep well.

The children — now a young man and a budding girl — slept in their own rooms the restless, warm sleep of youth.

The boy who died in France was, like the strong dark-haired woman, part of the wet Irish clay.

VI

Next morning the doctor dressed with unusually scrupulous

care, choosing a sober, dark grey suit. The quiet, strong cloth expressed his acceptance of age, although frequently he flattered himself with the thought that his suit should be tailored from cloth the colour of a deep sky in suggestive summer dusk and scrawled with extravagant symbols — comets, dragons, fishes with stinging tails. But did many an old or ageing man not hide his wild adventures of the soul behind neatness and a good, dark suit?

At breakfast with his wife and family he was abnormally quiet. She remembered that afterwards; and she remembered also in exact detail the colour of his suit, his shirt, his tie, the way his hair was brushed; that he had on the back of his right hand a slight, fresh scar like the scar from a cut made by a bramble or a trailing wire.

He drove his black car towards the sea down the suburban road, turned along the flat sea-front towards the city. The mist and rain of the previous night had cleared away. The sun shone brightly. The water, turbulent behind the sea-wall, had the sheen of a salmon's belly. He waved to two men he knew who stood chatting outside the local public house. He waved to a young wife, an early shopper, who went proudly wheeling her pram along the pavement. Then, approaching a corner, he looked up at the mirror and saw the face reflected there, looked into the blue glassy eyes; and a heavy hand touched his shoulder. There was no mistaking that face or the dead pressure of that hand. He said: 'You're here again,' and with one turn of the wheel he swept round in a semicircle, faced away from the city towards the northern country. A neighbour driving to his office narrowly avoided a crash and, when he was afterwards interrogated, remembered that sudden, semicircling turn, but said that as far as he could see there was no other person in the car.

The doctor repeated: 'You're here again.'

The harsh voice said: 'It all depends on who you think I am.'

'Do I have to guess again?'

The suburb dropped away from them like a gaudy, flimsy coat. They were on a wide concrete road, the sheen of the tossing sea to the right and to the left a long wall overhung by trees.

'With an old friend you don't have to guess.'

'Last night I had to guess.'

'Last night you weren't with a friend.'

The doctor slowed up, turned around in the driving seat, had a good, long look. No doubt about it. The big man sat like a giant in the back of the car. 'You looked damned like a man I played cards with last night. Not a twin, are you?'

'You'll never learn. No matter how well you know me, you'll never learn. But people are like that. The better they know me the more I surprise them.'

'Go ahead and explain. I'm willing to learn.'

A settlement of white-walled, flat-roofed houses clustered around a cross-roads. He swung to the left, away from the sea, bumped over a level-crossing, passed a dairy farm with its high cooling-tower. Then they were out among deep fields. He didn't know where he was going or what he was going to do, but he watched the road and the quivering, mounting needle, and recklessly he craved finality.

'Last night you had an unfortunate experience.'

'You should know.'

'That poor man —'

'What poor man?'

'You asked me to explain.' They threaded their way through a maze of by-roads. For all he knew he might be driving around in circles.

'You played cards last night with a man who had the ill fate some time ago to fall into the hands of the dark horse.'

'The hands of a horse?'

'It's easy to joke. I'm trying to tell you the risk you ran.'

'I risked nothing. I've nothing to lose.'

'Do you think so? Every man has something to lose.'

'Until he loses it.'

'The man you played with last night had lost control of his soul. When you were lucky enough to mention a certain name he was killed by the fury of the dark horse.'

'Looked like a stroke to me. I saw him frothing at the mouth. I saw him fall.'

'You saw him coming my way. Getting accommodation for him was a complicated job.'

'So you borrowed his big body. Compensation?'

'And here I am again.'

'Last night I dreamt I was talking to you.'

'Was it a dream? Some dreams are true.'

'Why did you come again so soon?'

'Orders are orders.'

'Is my time up?'

'Very nearly.'

'How nearly?'

'That I can't say.'

'Why did you come this morning?'

'For a friendly chat. I've a liking for you.'

He drove out from the maze of narrow, crooked roads, turned northwards again along a shining highway. The land tilted gently upwards. Perched on the green horizon were the white buildings of an airport. 'Time for a drink,' the gambler said, and he drove at a steadily increasing speed up the road towards the white buildings. A two-engined passenger plane roared past over their heads, reflected the sun as it banked and glittered for a moment like a fish swimming in a pool, then dropped to touch on a concrete runway. In that moment, as he watched the glitter of the plane's body, the malicious idea danced like a grimacing hunchback into the gambler's mind. 'You'll have a drink with me?' he said.

'That'll be difficult. You see, our late lamented friend was a teetotaller.'

'I'm sure he had a mineral.'

'Could be. Anyhow, I'll step in with you and watch you drink.'

Will you, thought the gambler, will you? A second plane roared from the ground, went along another runway, soared steeply against the wind. He drove the car between high pillars, between lawns and bright flower-beds to the main door of the airport buildings. The high pillars of clean, radiant granite supported gates of ornate metal shaped in a semi-circle. On one side of the carriage-way the flowers were white, on the other, red. Cars came and went continuously. Uniformed officials walked smartly along concrete paths or darted like rabbits in and out of swinging glass doors. From somewhere unseen came the reverberation of an engine like the beating of a cyclopean heart. Intent on his impish purpose, he saw the scene with sharpened awareness. He thought: I'll remember this place for ever. Here I'll test the friendliness of Death, the efficacy of the powers given to me in my third request. Cutting off the engine, he leaped out quickly and said: 'Come on.'

For two or three minutes he waited, his heart convulsed with malicious delight. He said: 'What's keeping you?'

'This,' said the voice of the big man from the back of the car, 'hasn't happened to me for ages. Last time it was an apple-tree — or no, it was a phaeton, some time somewhere in the eighteenth century.'

'Do you distinguish between centuries?' The gambler laughed ostentatiously, for a passing official had given a curious glance at the big man struggling in vain to move from the back of the black car.

'I knew when you didn't want me to hear your third request that you'd something up your sleeve.'

'You never guessed what it was.'

'I'm not omniscient. I'm a paid employee. And I can't listen in on anything told confidentially to a certain very important person.'

'It works too.' Another official passed, looked sideways, and the gambler laughed aloud as if he'd just heard the joke that was the essence of all jokes. In the back of the car the big man also was laughing, dry bursts of hard laughter, regular as the beat of a slow-set metronome.

'It's scarcely friendship,' he said. 'Still, I suppose the joke's on me and I'll take a joke as well as anybody.' They laughed at each other through the screwed-down window, then stopped laughing abruptly and turned to watch a great plane, four engines roaring, rise over the roofs of the white buildings, over the tall flagstaff with the flapping tricolour. 'Go in and drink your drink. I'll be here when you come back.'

'You will for sure.' The gambler walked, whistling and sprightly as a boy, through the smoothly swinging glass doors. Pretty girls in brown uniforms smiled from glass boxes or went, flashing nylon calves and certain-footed as chamois, on high heels across slippery floors. He wanted to say to their smiling faces: I've your worries locked in a box, in a black car, in a Pandora chest; don't fear wrinkles any more or the loss of beauty or corruption in the clay.

From the main hall he turned to the left along a corridor that led to the oval-shaped, carpeted lounge. A few customers, waiting for a plane, perched on high stools. He carried his drink to a low table by the curving, unseamed window that made up more than half of the oval. Looking through the window and down the green slope, he studied the pattern of white runways, white snood on a green chignon. A plane came down from the sky. Another plane rose and roared farewell over the roof. The customers on the stools hunched their shoulders as if the roaring plane was going to pounce on them. Every sip of warm, yellow drink was rich oil on the flame of his self-gratulation. I have him now where I want him. The contact man. The spitting greybeard. The vicious soldier. The Spaniard in the duffle coat. The Frenchman with two profiles. The devil-possessed giant. I have him where he can't budge his big backside. What next? Make my own terms? For myself only or for men and women who want life more than I do: warm girls, enterprising young men.

After his second drink he felt like Faustus saluting Helen or listening to Homer, sitting in the bar of an airport, as Jove sat high in the clouds, learning the number of spheres, the number of heavens, the secrets of the seven planets, of the firmament and the blue empyrean. When he went out again through the glass doors and saw the big man still sitting like a statue he stood and laughed loudly, infectiously, so that two brown-uniformed girls laughed with him and one scurrying official paused to smile. They remembered that afterwards. They didn't know though — how could they? — that while they shared his laughter his mind was possessed by images of wry peasant faces looking up into green leaves and red fruit to see Death or the black devil tied in knots in an octopus of an apple-tree.

'Were you lonely?' he said.

'Too busy thinking.'

'I've given you something to think about.'

'Indeed you have.'

Between the white pillars the car was held up for two minutes while a uniformed official directed towards the airfield two green buses loaded with passengers for the planes.

'I never expected it of you,' the big man said. 'I played fair with you. All open and above board.'

'You talked to me because you wanted company. Even you feel the pinch of loneliness.'

'Have it your own way.'

'Be serious. How could a man be friendly with you?'

There was a long silence. The gambler drove the car easily westwards. Flat, green land for quiet miles, then the earth crumpled and rolled and undulated, remaining still green, showing yet no grey for rocks, no brown for heather.

'I try hard enough. I've tried for centuries. But I suppose my job's against me. I make no friends.'

'Like a bailiff. A process-server.'

Then grey rocks flashed out from the sides of the hills and the green fields ran up to scrubby, uneven moorland.

'You know the consequences of what you're trying to do.'

'Trying? I'm doing it. I don't give a damn about the consequences.' They flashed past a cross-roads, frightened a farm-house, set hens squawking and flappingly trying to fly, dogs barking. The road narrowed and climbed, heather-dressed hills sloping up steeply on both sides; and turning a sharp corner they almost crashed into a line of parked cars, saw one spur of the hills black with watching people. 'What is this?' the gambler said. His brakes squealed and he pulled into the side, because until the road cleared there was nothing else to do.

The big man said: 'What do you intend to do with me?'

'Take you for a ride.'

'Where to?'

'I haven't made up my mind. But it's a small country.'

'When you get there where you're going, what then?'

'We could talk about an agreement.'

Seven motor-cyclists, goggled and helmeted, numbers on their backs, leather jackets and breeches spattered with mountain mud, steered cannily past parked cars and crowding spectators, twisted down a sandy track towards the mountain spur black with people. Then a man waved a flag, a pistol cracked, and one by one the motor-cyclists faced the trackless slope, struggled upwards, went out of sight one by one over the top. The crowd shouted encouragement.

'I imagine,' the gambler said, 'that having you helpless there, I can make my own terms.' Two more motor-cyclists set off to show their skill and the hill-climbing power of their machines.

'If I refuse to accept your terms?'

'Then you'll have a long wait where you're sitting now.' One of the two motor-cyclists struggled over the skyline, and, the crowd applauding, was gone. The second wasn't so fortunate. A skid sent him crashing sideways down the slope, the crowd scattering frantically out of his way. From the over-strained engine of his cycle flame flashed yellow and wicked. Somebody screamed. The crowd closed in again and there was a chill silence. Looking at nothing and apparently with reference to nothing in particular, the big man said: 'The show must go on.' They sat, not speaking, while the injured motor-cyclist was carried down the slope, placed in an ambulance, driven hurriedly away, the ambulance bell ringing.

'Was that a demonstration?'

'No,' the big man said. 'It happened that way. But now that it has happened it reminds me that I must correct a few wrong ideas you have about the way I do my work.'

'Go on.'

'It's only natural, of course, that you shouldn't understand. You take a one-sided view. Then you've been reading books and watching plays and pictures, lapping up the ideas of people who, like yourself, take a one-sided view.'

'Go on.'

'If I don't agree to your terms you plan to keep me here a prisoner.'

'Exactly.'

'What'll you do with the car?'

'Need I do anything?'

'Ah, look now. Let's be reasonable. What do you think would happen to all the people I normally cater for if I'm locked up a prisoner in the back of your car?'

'They'd go on living.'

The big man's loud, dry laughter rocked the car: 'So you still think I kill people. What do you think happened to that hill-climber? I sat here. He was killed up there —'

'You know he's dead.'

'The fall and the flame.'

'I don't know what to think.' The scene, the valley, the hills crowded with people, the road jammed with parked cars, the climbing motor-cyclists were idiotically unreal. 'But I know I have you where I want you.' The crowd on the mountain spur had forgotten already the flame, the fall, the young man silent in the ambulance. They didn't yet know he was dead. They waited eagerly while three more brave men dared the steep slope.

'You keep on thinking me your enemy, the enemy of those daring boys on the machines, of the soft girls walking on the slippery airport floor.'

The gambler gripped the steering-wheel tightly, but he didn't in any other way show surprise. He said, quietly accepting strange things that he should have accepted long ago: 'You know a lot.'

'I've been a long time learning.' The voice was as sad as harshness would allow. 'A long, friendless, misunderstood time. I was foolish enough after all I knew to think you might be something different. Now, like many another fool, you want to make me a prisoner, stay my hand, cashier me —'

'Like many another —?'

'Oh, it's been tried before. Apple-trees. Phaetons. Spanish galleons. Chinese junks. Roman chariots. Never once has it been a success.'

'Never once?'

'No, never. If it ever had been a success, do you know what would have happened? People would have gone on dying. I don't kill them. I'm not your enemy. I wouldn't for the world kill a beautiful girl or a brave boy on a motor-bicycle. But if you could lock me up here —'

'If I could?'

'People would die and their relatives would help them as far as a hole in the ground and no farther.'

'That could be far enough.'

'Then they wouldn't know where to go. No advance-booking agent. The world walking with homeless ghosts.'

'Why should I worry? I'll know what's wrong.'

'You've no idea how vicious a ghost can be when it has

nowhere to go. It mayn't matter to you. But be social. Think of all the people who are afraid of ghosts. You're not an inhuman man.'

'Who told you?'

Another climbing cyclist fell, rose again, went grimly again at the steep ascent. The crowd bravely cheered the brave man. Why, thought the gambler, should I worry whether or not all those shouting people, those fools on roaring motor-cycles, have anywhere to go when they die? Why should I worry if those who live are crowded out of their beds by homeless ghosts? Right or wrong, wise or foolish, I want finality, and I know what I'm going to do.

He opened the door of the car, swivelled around his long legs, touched his feet to the ground. 'Come what may, you stay here. The car stays too. I don't ever want to see it again or to see you again.'

'You'll see me again.'

The car would stay parked there until darkness came. The motor-cyclists and their cheering supporters would think it belonged to somebody gone walking over the moors, and in a way they would be right. With luck it could stay in that lonely place undisturbed for days, long enough to set the world in turmoil, long enough to give the gambler time to reach the place that was for him, glowing in his mind, the only remaining reality. The big man said: 'I've done my best to warn you. This will do you no good, here or anywhere else.'

'To hell with warnings.'

'Your powers aren't exactly what you think they are.'

'Go to hell.'

'If I were you I wouldn't mention that place too often. You're doing something today that may be remembered against you.'

'By you?'

'By somebody with more influence. Come in and sit down at your ease and I'll give you documentary proof.' From the floor of the car the great hands had raised into sight the black briefcase.

'Let it be remembered, then,' said the gambler. 'I can't wait for a reading lesson.'

'Never say I didn't do my best.'

'Let it be remembered here and hereafter. I want no warnings. I've met you too often. I've been bothered with you too long.'

Three times he swung the door backwards and forwards, then slammed it heavily and locked the handle. In the back seat the big man sat, his elbows on the black briefcase, his head sunk on his hands as if the decisive slamming of the door had shocked him into a stupor. He didn't look up once. He didn't make a sign or try to speak. The gambler turned his back on the car, walked thirty or forty yards along the crowded road, turned down a narrow, sanded path, then directly up the spur of the mountain, catching at clumps of heather to steady himself when his smooth leather soles went slipping on polished wiry grass.

VII

On the top of the first ridge two girls stood, holding in their hands plates filled with pieces of oranges, giving a piece to each cyclist as he came strained and breathless from the effort of climbing. The girls wore leather jackets and tweed skirts. Their hair blew straggly in the wind. Every second man in the crowd watching the climbers wore a leather jacket, a black beret, had his trousers splashed with mud. In his good, dark suit the doctor felt odd; a stranger from another planet, from another age, intruding on some ritual of flame and iron and climbing in high places towards the sun.

He walked away from the crowd, past the two orange-giving girls. One of them laughingly handed him a sliver of orange. He accepted it seriously, mechanically, held it in his hand until a bump in the moorland concealed him from their sight, then pitched it, shining yellow, into deep heather. Years of hill-climbing trials, and before that the feet of goats and sheep and shepherds, had marked a track across that wilderness. Now and again, when he heard behind him the sound of an engine, he leaped off the track, waited knee-deep in heather while a competitor passed, carefully increasing speed, rising in the saddle to counteract bumps, steering zigzag up the slope to disappear again over the rim of the moor.

Why should I care about souls who have nowhere to go? Here in this visible place most of them have nowhere to go, nothing to do, motor-bicycles driven along moorland tracks, making circles in lonely hills, always arriving back bewildered and mud-splashed at the point they started from.

He didn't give a damn what was or was not found in the car when the door was finally opened.

Beyond the second ridge the track, become rough and stony, dropped steeply, went narrowly between two deep, black lakes with precipitous sides. He picked his steps meticulously. The shoes he wore had not been cobbled for walking in uneven places. Halfway down he heard the approaching engine, leaped aside as a motor-cyclist went past shouting with anger, watched quite callously as on the track between the lakes something went seriously wrong. The machine leaped sideways like a timorsome horse. The deep water swallowed the man and the machine; and when the gambler reached the place there wasn't a ripple on the surface; not a sign to show what had happened, except one deep, twisted wheelmark pointing from the track towards the lake. No watcher, no course-steward, no girl with skinned oranges was there to see and to scream for help. The gambler passed the place with no more than one long look sideways. In the black lake searchers would sometime find the drowned cyclist as in the black car they would find the big man. In his mind the images of lake and car turned and changed places like dancers on a floor and, absorbed in his delirium, he walked for another mile without noticing that the track had twisted to the left, was descending gradually towards a sleepy village. Houses lined evenly along a quiet street. The whole village was exactly bisected by a river and a round bridge.

Except for five lazy dogs, a few running children, some gossiping old women and chewing old men, the street was empty and as quiet as a grave. The young people were up in the heather watching the climbing trials. In the narrow, oblong dining-room off the bar of the village hotel he sat for hours eating and drinking. The walls of the room were painted a pale blue. The floor was covered with cold linoleum. From the kitchen behind the bar came the voices of the proprietress and her children and servants. In a glass case on the sideboard a stuffed brown trout, meditative among fake weeds and stones in a fake river, told him that the hotel was a busy place only when strong men in tweeds and rubber waders came to fish in the gravelly mountain water, or stronger men with guns came to walk the moors. Every ten minutes a motor-cyclist, his climbing trial ended, raced up the street. Once or twice noisy, thirsty strangers came into the bar, but none of them penetrated as far as the dining-room, and, secure in his cold comfort, the gambler felt like a fugitive hiding in a cave or in a hollow under an overhanging river-bank and listening breathlessly to the hounds running, baying the scent lost, escape certain. Dusk came. His car was probably still parked undisturbed on the road in the valley, the big man sitting motionless in the back seat. Let him sit. Down in the deep, cold lake a brave young man lay entangled with his motor-cycle. Let him lie. He felt equally and joyfully responsible for the immobility of the big man in the car and the brave young man in the lake.

He said to himself, aloud in the cold, unlistening room, aloud to the skin of a trout for ever immobile in a motionless river: My time isn't far away. Let it come, then. Let my spirit be homeless with all those other homeless spirits; with the spirit of a young man who proudly rode a machine up a mountain-side and then sank like a stone into deep water; with the devil-possessed spirit of a big man who one night was an overcoat for the dark horse and the next morning an overcoat for my old acquaintance, my contact man, my spitting ancient, my murderous soldier, my dear dark woman, my Spanish poet, my French black-market man. . . . Then, although he couldn't hear it or could see nobody, he knew there was laughter in the room — the deep laughter of Death at the futility of the third request, at apple-trees, phaetons, Spanish galleons, Roman chariots, Chinese junks; at all the places where a spirit could not be imprisoned, where Death could drape his borrowed coat and slip away laughing, unseen.

The narrow, cold room was now as hostile, as hideous as a coffin to a creature buried alive. He wasn't afraid when in the darkness he stepped smartly away from the village towards the railway station. But he walked like a brave hunted man in enemy country, eyes cutting the night for the first sign of ambush, the jut of a hunched shoulder, the flash of a knife, ears straining to hear the shuffle of a foot or the tiny click of a released safety-catch.

The station was quiet, because most of the watchers came to the trials by car. Standing at the window of the ticket office, offering money, mentioning the name of his destination, accepting the slip of stiff pasteboard, was a challenge, a final ritual, a last sacrament. He knew where he was going, and why. He had once known peace in that place. Walking up and down, waiting for the train, he kept to the middle of the platform under the line of three dim oil-lamps, away from shadowy doorways, from all corners where something might shelter. Invisible in darkness the river babbled over gravel. He repeated again and again as he walked: Every man should return in the end for forgiveness, for peace, to the place where he began.

VIII

Shortly before midnight he reached his destination. An evening newspaper purchased at the junction where he changed trains told the story as it appeared to police, newspaper reporters, motor-cyclists, and others. It said: *'Tragedy dogs motor-bike trials.'* It added: *'Three deaths: one by drowning.'* It added further: *'Well-known doctor wanted for questioning.'*

'Triple tragedy,' the reporter had written, 'dogged the annual meeting of the motor-cycle hill-climbing club which is once a year the Mecca for motor-cycling enthusiasts. One well-known rider, as the result of a mishap on the first ascent, died of shock and burns on the way to hospital. Another, as far as can be known, skidded off the track and crashed into a lake which is near the course. Unable to extricate himself, he was drowned. The tragedy was discovered by some people returning from the trials to a neighbouring village, who observed wheelmarks leading to the edge of the lake, which at that place is, according to local tradition, bottomless. The body was later recovered. An hour afterwards the police, acting on a report from the secretary of the club, investigated the circumstances surrounding a car left parked on the side of the road at the point where the first ascent commences. The car was locked and a man was apparently asleep in the back seat. On investigation it was found that the man, a well-known recluse, was dead. A well-known city doctor is wanted by the police for questioning. The authorities, however, do not suspect foul play.'

Then further down, and in smaller print, the story was repeated in greater detail. He skimmed those details. Death had gone his own way and the police had found his overcoat. The granting of the third request had been a dirty mockery. By now his wife and children knew that something had gone wrong. They might be worried; they might even be grieved. One of the small printed details leaped out at him, ironically, from the page: 'The doctor's wife stated to our representative that her husband's conduct had for some time been verging on eccentricity.' Not one of the details dealt with a black bag stuffed with bones and books and newspaper clippings.

Quite callously he had ceased to concern himself about the worries or the griefs of other people. He had worked for the poor in the slums mainly in the hope that they would help him to cast his own life easily from him, a snake casting its slough, a grinning tramp swapping clothes with a scarecrow. For so many years now he had lived oppressed by a burdensome knowledge of God and Death, given to him without his asking, when on one bright day he walked in, and enjoyed, his deepest despair, when he had violated his most precious memory. No one had offered to share the heaviness of his secret. No one had known that he had a secret; but now at least the world knew that there had been something eccentric about him, and the solemn police wanted to question him, even if they didn't suspect him of what the newspaper called foul play. Over the corpse of the big man the police doctors had assuredly said: 'Death from natural causes' — as if that solved everything. Inspecting the vast, still flesh, they would not understand why a well-known doctor had for twenty-four hours kept a corpse in the back seat of his car, and they'd search the country for him to question him and set their little perplexities at ease. As if answers given to the police solved everything. As if a murderer's confession ever indicated what mysterious powers stood near when the fatal blow was struck.

He tore the newspaper into pieces, treating it as he'd have treated an ill-written, threatening, anonymous letter. A hunted murderer reading a newspaper and finding that the police are in possession of new clues may feel as if the voice of doom has spoken. But in the columns he had just read, the doctor could see nothing more than a futile footnote to a finality he had accepted. He tossed the torn fragments into a waste-paper basket on the platform and walked briefly out of the station, wanted for questioning but not suspected of foul play. They wouldn't look for him in this place for a long time. It wasn't one of his usual haunts. It was merely a sleepy, innocent town in which he had been a boy. So many years ago he had left it, and never except in memory at moments of weakening nostalgia had he returned. But one old woman here would not have forgotten him; would be too old to be surprised when he sheltered for a few days in her house, protecting him as years, long years ago, she had protected and nursed, for an ailing mother, a puny, complaining child. Once a month he had written to her, sending her money that paid her rent and bought food and fuel, feeling every time he wrote her name and address on an envelope that he had reached back and touched innocence. A few times she had answered his letters, thanking him for his kindness in remembering his old nurse, asking him to come some day and visit her so that she could see how the child she once cared for had grown into a famed, successful man. Yet he never had visited her, and accepting his absence as a condition of his remembering assistance, she had ceased to invite him; ceased to write, grew older and fantastically older; opened his letter every month as she would have opened a letter posted in the heaven in which she hoped to spend eternity.

Not for some time would they think of searching for him here. By that time he would, in all likelihood and in his own hope, be beyond the reach of questioning policemen or shocked friends or indignant relations. For, walking from the station through poorly lighted streets, he knew he was approaching the end and the end was not far away. Things changed and did not change. His eyes searched the darkness for remembered marks and outlines: lights from the thin windows in the red-brick house where the station-master lived; the shape of a hoarding placed so as to catch the attention of travellers coming from the station. But the hill behind the hoarding had lost its round regular outline and now showed jagged with a huddle of roofs and patterned with lighted windows. The yew-trees still stood solemnly around the single-story gospel hall. Were they, after all these years, the same trees; and what was the length of the life of a yew-tree? A late group gossiping at a lighted doorway paid no attention to the stranger passing, no more than if he were invisible or had walked along soft-footed on the other side of a high wall. The sound of their voices was alien and strange, and although he glanced quickly, piercingly at their faces, he saw nothing that reminded him of boyhood. The years between had been too many. Perhaps it was a mistake to come back here, to attempt to complete the circle of his days, as once on Saturday afternoons, walking the country roads with school companions, he had chosen always to leave the town by one road and return by another, so that, standing tired on his father's doorstep, he could say: I've made a circle on the surface of the world.

From the town's main street he turned to the left along a narrow lane that widened gradually as it went on and climbed towards two churches, one with a stumpy steeple, the other with two soaring spires. The house in which she had lived for all these long years was crushed against the wall of one of the churches, an absurdly slender house, three stories high and only one room wide, yet it was dwarfed by the spires. As he put his hand to the polished knocker the street lamps were switched out and the night dropped on the town like a snuffer on a candle.

She slept lightly. She was so old. Without fear she opened the door to a strange man in the darkness. She said: 'No, I don't know you. But there's something familiar in your voice, son.' She was so old she called all men son. She was tall and thin like the house she lived in, and the lighted candle held high in her left hand showed a triangular face, yellow and wrinkled, bright eyes hiding in deep hollows, the bridge of her nose scarcely covered by worn, wax-like skin.

'You must remember me,' he said.

'Your voice, yes. Your voice.'

'My father's voice,' and he told her who his father had been. The pain inside him was for his son who was dead, for his son and daughter still alive, for the woman who, giving him her body, had given them life. Why was he standing here? Why had he left his wife and children to explain to the world as well as they could the madness of the man who had deserted them? 'I left them wealthy,' he muttered. He might have startled the old woman by the crack of self-discovering horror in his voice if she hadn't been too old to notice such things; if she hadn't already flung the door wide open to welcome him into her house.

Wealth, he knew, mattered a great deal to them, but did not matter so much as normality, the transparent skeletonless cupboard, nothing to hide, nothing to set the neighbours talking. Abnormality was in his bones.

He followed the old woman along a narrow passage and down three worn steps to the kitchen. Startled from her dry, light sleep, she had pulled on an antique overcoat to cover her trailing nightdress. While she rekindled the fire in an old-fashioned barred grate he explained that he would stay, secret in her house, for some time; listening to the bells in the blessed church, saying his prayers. She was so old, so utterly old, that she accepted what he said without a question. Watching her as she prepared his food, he knew he had come to the right place.

None should outlive his power. . . . Who kills
Himself subdues the conqueror of kings.

Well, better than that poet who gave his body to the sea, he, the gambler, conqueror of men, the doctor, healer of men, knew that all men and not only suicides killed themselves, or were killed by other men. The conqueror of kings was no better than the workers who on the crooked streets of this town swept and shovelled refuse, carted it away to a smoking pile between the railway and the houses of the poor.

Exempt from death is he who takes his life:
My time has come.

No; but exempt from the agony of dying were the men who had ceased to value solid, enjoyable things. Laudanum-soaked poets, dyspeptic millionaires, saints, crazy men. Here he was, knowing his end wasn't far away, in the one spot in the world as, outside lunatic asylums, he knew it; where nothing was solid, where normality was a handful of straw.

IX

The grocer, now retired from business and living in a new house so that he wouldn't have too far to walk to the church, telephoned the factory owner — also retired and being cared for in an expensive flat by a young lady, described as his niece, who had once been a cutter in the part of his factory that made overcoats. The grocer said: 'Have you read the paper? Did you see the news?' The retired factory-owner said: 'You were always right about that fellow, something queer there'; and later he telephoned the professional golfer, who now owned and managed a small hotel, and said: 'I always knew there was something queer about that fellow.' The ex-professional telephoned the bookie, who now managed a stadium, and said: 'What in Jesus came over that man? Is it a woman or what?' The draper, now at the head of his trade, was visiting in the magnificent office used by the stadium manager when the ex-professional rang, and the two men together decided to ring the professor and put a few discreet leading questions. The professor, who was no longer young, had been made genuinely unhappy by the news in the paper. He said he hadn't an idea, he couldn't guess, but he was sure it would all come right in the end; that, odd as things seemed, there must be some rational explanation; that there was, in fact, a rational explanation for everything; and he hoped that nothing had happened to the doctor who had, to his knowledge, been doing wonderful work for the poor in that new health centre. Leaving down the telephone, the professor thought that if anything had happened to the doctor the whole community, and not only his own personal friends, would feel the loss severely, so to set his mind at ease he telephoned the doctor's wife to offer his sincere sympathy, to ask if he could be of any help, and was there any news later than the newspapers. The doctor's wife, startled by an event that pitched her back to fears and forebodings that in wealth and respectability she had almost forgotten, exasperated by idiotic inquiries to which she had only one monotonous answer, dropped the phone with an angry crash when in one uncivil breath she had told the professor that no she had no news whatsoever that she hadn't the faintest idea what could have happened to her husband that by all appearances the newspapers who shouldn't in the first place have printed scandalous rumours knew more about it than she did much more indeed good-bye and thank you so much.

X

He slept in a small room off the kitchen. The white walls were blobbed with sacred pictures. Three times in the night he awoke and heard Death distinctly speak to him.

The First Awakening

Death said: 'Weren't you the fool to think I could be trapped for ever in the back seat of a motor-car?'

'Was the granting of my request, then, a mockery and a lie?'

'The granting of your request wasn't a lie, wasn't a mockery. But I'm not quite an ordinary man, you know. I've a thousand shapes —'

'Overcoats.'

'— you've seen a few. If you lasted long enough you'd see a few more.'

'Is this the end?'

'What do you think?'

'Here and now?'

'At the appointed time.'

But when he asked Death, who had the size and shape and colour of a small, unlighted room, what the appointed time might be, he heard only the steely chiming of the town clock and the wind around the high spires. Listening to the wind and to the receding echo of the chimes, he fell asleep again.

The Second Awakening

Death said: 'Let me read you something from today's newspaper.'

'I've read today's newspaper.'

'Only the bit about yourself, I'm sure. Let me read you something much more interesting to the general public. And to myself as a collector.'

'Oh, read away.'

'It's about an agricultural labourer in County Carlow, who is said to have spent fourteen days and nights in a cabin with the body of an old woman he's alleged to have murdered. Are you sure you didn't read it in the papers?'

'I may have.'

'His name is. . . . But I suppose his name doesn't matter.'

'Not in the least.'

'Apparently he hit the old lady on the head in the course of a row, then tucked her carefully into bed, and every night for fourteen nights he slept peacefully on his own bed in the next room. Only a thin partition and two thicknesses of wallpaper between them. Every night before he went to bed he looked in at her to see was she still asleep —'

'Which goes to prove?'

'Nothing in particular. It's a neat story.'

'A bedtime story. To brighten me up before the end.'

'To remind you that you're as good as alone here, hiding in a house with a queer old woman. She may collapse at any moment of the day or night. Suppose she ceased to be your old nurse and became one more of my shapes.'

Sitting up in his bed, reaching out into the darkness as if to grasp and crush something, the gambler knew suffocating panic. That yellow, triangular face, the body, gone arid, that should have years ago gone to Death. How was he to know, to remain certain from moment to moment, from day to day?

No chimes. Only the sound of the wind around the spires. Not real sleep, but a sort of stupor made uneasy with cold wondering about that old woman. Was she at this moment stretched in her room gasping for breath? If he could shake off the chill stupor he would go bare-footed out of his room, up the narrow stairs to see was the old woman living or dead. But he might have been tied with wet shrunken ropes to his bed until

The Third Awakening

Sitting suddenly erect, no longer cold or paralysed, spots of fearful heat tingling and pricking his body. Death said: 'To coin a phrase, have you anything to say before the court passes sentence?'

'Nothing.'

'No request? No last wish?'

'Let me say one sincere prayer.'

'Would you know how?'

'Give me time to try.'

'Must I hold up arrangements for ever while you go hunting sincerity?'

'Is it so hard to find?'

'A prayer free of yourself, of tiredness, disbelief, mockery, selfishness, fear?'

'Let me try.'

'Oh, very well, very very well. I never rushed a friend into anything.'

'That means my time isn't now.'

No answer. Steely chimes. The window blind turning grey. A cold dawn flowing, as quarrelling, porter-brown streams flowed, down from heathery upland, then warming and spreading out over the river valley, over the good green land, over the gambler hid in an old woman's house, over hundreds of men and women hiding from or facing and fearing Death in the corners of their dreams.

In the room above him the old woman was stirring. He

lay awake until he heard her raking the kitchen fire. Then he fell asleep and when he awoke again day was in it and Death wasn't to be heard.

XI

'What age are you now, Jane?'

'More than ninety. I was thirty years of age and with two children of my own the first night your mother ever trod the floor at a dance. She was a lovely girl.'

Back all the way to the garden and the first kiss, the first conspiring of man and woman against God, generations overlapped, old women and old men remembered and babbled about loveliness, sorrow, tragedy, red battles; all lives and all stories were plaited together, fibre for an endless rope.

'Your children,' he said. 'I never knew.'

'Gone long since, dear.' She was the other woman in his life who repeatedly called him dear. 'One to America and one went to England. They wrote for a while and sent me things, and then they ceased writing. It could well be that they're gone on before me.'

Later, after a silence long and deep as the unpierced sweep of a wave in the middle ocean, she said: 'You're the only child ever remembered me or came back to see me.'

Days of silence unbroken except for the bells above or the town clock striking. The murmur of life in the streets never filtered down as deep as that narrow kitchen. Nobody ever visited the house. Men knocked, left bread on the spotless doorstep, poured milk into the waiting jug, knocked again and went whistling back to the world. Every second morning Jane walked out, tall, bonneted at an angle, a tottering, dry tree-trunk, almost branchless, swathed in dull black cloth. She visited God in the church with the two spires, shunned what she called the cold walls of the church with the single steeple, then visited the grocer and the newsagent, carried back with her a straw basket stuffed with groceries and the folded newspapers of the day and the previous day. She could, she said, no longer read, and he remembered that she never could read, not even the prayer books large-printed for lisping children, so he read aloud to her snippets about some of the things men and women were doing to each other on their way to meet Death. Quietly to himself he read the account of the way some men, and at least one woman, were pursuing himself; felt obscure gratification as the length of the paragraphs dwindled and the fact that he was missing gradually lost all importance. It was like watching his own last illness.

Once the police had 'greatly feared that the missing doctor might have met with foul play'. Later it seemed, and it didn't say for what reason, that 'police fears on the question of foul play had been allayed'. Since no one had ever known about his regular letters to aged Jane, it was unlikely that they could ever trace him to this place; and when after nine days his name no longer appeared in the paper he felt he could count on peace, sitting in silence or occasionally talking to Jane — a man who had abandoned life, had been forgotten by the living, who no longer had anything to fear or to lose.

On the tenth night, when darkness capped the town securely, he walked out on the badly lighted streets, his collar turned up, his hat brim twisted down to hide his eyes. On the eleventh night he turned down his collar, and on the twelfth night he went hatless. The weather was exceptionally mild. The skies were low and dull and dripping with mizzling rain falling softly, undisturbed by any wind. On the thirteenth night he sat in a cinema and watched a film about murder in New Orleans, and didn't know whether he was farther away from the story of the film or from all the breathless members of the audience. Many of them must have been young when he was young and in the same innocent, dull place. On the thirteenth night he paid his way into a dance-hall, watched the dancers for a while, but didn't dance. The town was still so innocent that a strange elderly man, paying good money so that he could watch young boys and girls twirling to coloured music, wasn't regarded as suspicious. No heavy-browed men with pock-marked faces and cauliflower ears were instructed to keep an eye on him.

On the fourteenth night he stood in a public house, elbows on the high counter, listening to the talk of drinking men. The fifteenth night was a Sunday night, so he knelt in the church at evening devotions, his face in his cupped hands, his body partially hidden behind a pillar. Afterwards he walked the streets for the last time, thinking the threatened moment is nearer now at every step, feeling that fifteen days of seclusion in that town had been a purifying in the desert, a plunge in icy water, a wallow naked in nettles. He could happily, recklessly leave tomorrow to walk once more in a green place by the sea.

At the door of a cheap restaurant three urchins quarrelled, two jeering, one — the smallest — sobbing and pitifully knuckling his eyes, sniffling an unwiped nose. The gambler stopped and bent down and said: 'What's the trouble?' Should he do this, since he had stopped for ever interfering in life? The face of the crying urchin was unpleasantly marked with a sore. 'What's the trouble?' he asked again, and then, to end a fidgety, foot-shuffling silence: 'I won't murder or arrest you. What's the trouble?'

The larger of the two jeering urchins said: 'He doesn't know his prayers.' The crying boy cried with increased bitterness. 'And the size of him,' the third boy said.

'He's not so big,' said the gambler.

'He's wee for his age, mister.'

'Has he nobody to teach him his prayers?'

'His ma's dead and his da's in England and he's always mitching school.' The sobbing changed gear, became a series of choking gulps.

'Come with me,' the gambler said. 'We'll eat a meal and I'll teach him his prayers.'

So on the fifteenth night he sat in a cheap restaurant with three ragged boys. He bought them food and watched them eat. When the meal was ended he recited slowly the words of a prayer that in his childhood he had learned in this town. He walked with the ragged creatures to the place where they lived. In those naïve streets, where weaknesses were not named as they're named in the rotten streets of big cities, no one suspected him of anything worse than charity. Seated with the three urchins at the top of a dark, stinking stairway, he repeated the words of the prayer until they knew it by heart. It was an old prayer, prayed by peasant women in time of famine, a spell, an incantation against hunger and shaking fever:

When Our Saviour carried his cross
He trembled with an ague. . . .

They chanted with him, voices of children in a game for children, sincerely saying words they did not understand.

I am the Son of God
He who says these words in memory of me
Shall never take the fever or the ague.

When the ragged children had gone, innocent money jingling in their pockets, to sleep in poor rooms, he sat for an hour on the bare stairs, the house around him like a clinging, uncomfortable cloak.

When Our Saviour carried his cross. . . .

Shuffling of feet, creaking of hard beds, a mother's voice soothing a crying child, and then a silence as if the world had died all around him and he was the last place where blood pulsed, the last spot of heat in a choked yellow fire.

He who says these words in memory of me. . . .

In all the world there could be nothing less than this place where for the benefit of a child with a sore on its face, *I am the Son of God*, he had prayed, sincerely as an old woman prays, against famine, fever, the shaken body, the overwrought mind. Descending the stairway he slipped on dirt and wearily fell, crashing and grabbing for support against a rotting unstable banister. With momentary terror he gripped the yielding, decaying wood. But he didn't scream or shout for help. Death was the depth and shape of a dark hallway. Death, after all the talking, welcomed him in silence. He went down to meet Death as simply as a stone drops into a pool.

XII

The doctor's wife heard the news two hours later. She fainted, recovered, cried, and, when she was able, rang the grocer to see could he do anything about controlling the newspapers. 'I can't tell you how sorry I am,' said the grocer, 'that tragedy has visited your house,' and telephoning the retired industrialist, he said: 'Clever as he was, he's gone before us,' and, 'I always felt he'd have a sticky finish.' The retired industrialist no longer had any influence in newspaper offices because too many people knew about his housekeeping niece, so he rang the ex-professional, whose influence was only with the sporting staffs. As this was not a sporting matter, he rang the bookie, who rang the draper, who rang the professor, who, because of his learning, was respected by editors. Later the professor was able to tell the doctor's wife that everything had been arranged, that nothing would be printed except the most respectable obituary paragraphs mentioning:

. . . the deprivation that the sudden death (manner and place unspecified) of this distinguished man was to the country at large;

. . . the dead man's academic status from primary school and diocesan college onwards;

. . . the sociable disposition that made him beloved among a wide circle of friends and acquaintances;

. . . protected by round brackets and inverted commas, the name by which he was known to his intimates;

. . . the golf club to which he belonged and his handicap;

. . . his generosity and eighteenth-century contempt for money;

. . . his wit;

. . . the titles of the papers he read to medical societies;

. . . the work for the poor to which he devoted his later years;

. . . the fact that the centre for the care of expectant mothers would be an enduring monument to his greatness;

. . . the fact that various important people had sent telegrams of sympathy to the bereaved widow and her children;

. . . the fact that the interment would take place in such a cemetery at such a time.

This, the doctor's wife thought, was a great deal better than headlines saying:

MISSING MAN FOUND
or
FAMOUS DOCTOR DEAD IN SLUM
or
TRAGIC EVENT IN COUNTRY TOWN

One paper didn't print the obituary notice because space had to be found for an exceptionally lengthy editorial on unofficial strikes. Another paper mis-spelt the doctor's name. Another said he was survived by his widow and three children. It was so hard for strangers to know accurately who was living and who dead.

Sixth Interlude

The gambler sailed for Ireland with his portion of gold. The night he returned home he was talking and chatting about his adventures until the candle burned down to the last inch. Then he carried the inch of candle to the bedside and he lay down. When he was stretched on the bed Death gripped him by the throat.

'O friend, for the sweet sake of Christ,' says the gambler, 'I haven't yet made my will. I ask you for a space of time until the inch of candle is burnt.'

'You may have it,' says Death.

The gambler puffed at the candle and quenched the flame. 'That inch won't be burned for seven years,' says he.

'You tricked me,' says Death. 'But let it be so for seven years.'

Death didn't come back to the gambler until the seven years were spent. But no matter how long the day is, night comes at the end. A night at the end of the seven years when the gambler was lying on his bed Death gripped him again by the throat.

'You must come with me now, gambler,' says he.

'O friend, for the sweet sake of Christ,' says the gambler, 'the thought sets me mad with thirst. If you would pull an apple in my orchard and give it to me before you take me with you, perhaps it would ease that devouring thirst.'

Death went out to the apple-tree, but when he put his

hand on an apple he stuck fast to it and the apple stuck fast to the tree. The gambler leaped out of his bed.

'You'll be there until I feel like releasing you,' says he.

'So that,' says Death, 'is the third request you got from God and kept a secret from me. Let me go now and I won't come near you until the end of another seven years.'

The gambler freed the hand of Death and didn't see him again for seven years. At the end of that time Death came, gripped his claw of a hand on the gambler's throat, and gave him a good choking.

'O friend, for the sweet sake of Christ,' says the gambler, 'you're too hard on me. I ask only one other favour from you, and it isn't for life I'm asking. Allow me to say the Lord's Prayer — a thing I didn't say ever since I commenced the gambling.'

'You may have that favour,' says Death.

'Then I'll never say the prayer,' says the gambler.

'I see,' says Death, 'that you want to be alive after me and after the world.'

Death went away and seven years went round and the gambler was getting richer every day. He was one day walking out for pleasure when he saw a young boy sitting crying on the margin of the main road.

'What's wrong with you?' says the gambler.

'They won't let me go to Communion,' says he, 'because I don't know my prayers.'

'Why doesn't your father or mother teach you your prayers?'

'My father and my mother are dead and I am an orphan,' says the boy.

The gambler pitied him. 'I'll teach you your prayers,' says he.

He began on the Lord's Prayer and the boy recited it after him. When the prayer was said Death stood up out of the shape of the boy and gripped the gambler by the throat.

'You'll trick me no longer,' says he — and he choked him dry.

The gambler took with him to hell his pack of cards.

SEVEN

I

The dark horse is a hypnotist invited by unsuspecting people to a party in a suburban house. Look carefully at the point of this nail-file and at the dark glistening pupil of my right eye. Is the light hurting your eyes? Do you see my aura all around my head? Think now that you're falling forward, forward, forward, backward, backward, forward, backward, forward, backward, forward, gently forward, down, down, down, until my strong right arm supports you. God is a light. God is a bright day, but the dark horse gallops in the night through dreams that counterpoint the day. In the bright day the boy, displaying his bravery, walked, no hands holding, along the bevelled parapet of a railway bridge. In a boy's magazine he had read about Blondin. His six friends cheered him as he walked balancing, but only one had the courage to imitate him. Then, dreaming that night he went falling, falling, spinning in the air, a chestnut, a pine cone, a winged seed from a beech-tree, a fragment of twig from the beak of a nest-building bird, down, down to smash on stones and sleepers and iron tracks, while six phantom companions screamed and a devil-black express train, a dark iron horse, minced his mangled body. Sit down and clasp your hands and think they are glued together and that you cannot separate them, you cannot separate them, tightly together, tightly together. *An meiner Wand hangt ein japanisches Holzwerk.* Clasp your hands tightly together and think you are falling asleep, falling, falling asleep, fast asleep, sleepy sleep. On my wall hangs a Japanese wood-carving and, painted gold, it is the mask of an evil demon, and with pity I see the swollen veins of his forehead telling how hard it is to be evil. Sleep, sleepy sleep, says the hypnotist with the golden face; why should you worry if the souls of all men are homeless? Climb up the great gazebo in the deserted demesne, a young man and a young girl climbing hand in hand up the dark, dusty stairway, smelling the dead, stale air. Kiss her lips warmly and make love, crouching on the top of the tower, and climb down again and find yourself climbing down alone; no hand in yours, no laughter musically touching your ears; no vivid flesh beside you; down and down and down into the darkness, down and down and utterly alone; finding no outlet, the spiral stairway becomes eternal, the hypnotist's oily hands smoothing your forehead, the tips of his fingers like the padded feet of small animals running down your cheeks; down and still down over your shoulders and arms; down to your hands relaxed on your wooden knees.

You can now hear nothing but my voice.

In the smothering darkness the gambler knew he was awake even if he was hypnotized, and that he had ceased falling. But he could see nothing, not even one faint glimmer of light. Far away the voice of the invisible hypnotist told him: 'You cannot raise your right hand because it is as heavy as lead, and your body is as rigid as a bar of steel.' Then, after a long pause: 'You are now quite calm, quite peaceful, quite happy.' But he didn't believe the hypnotist. He existed in darkness, neither lying nor standing nor walking nor sitting, waiting for revelation and the meaning, waiting for words that would be awakening and rousing, the words of the thirteenth man spoken either in mercy or condemnation. But he heard only the lulling, dangerously soporific words of the invisible, golden-faced hypnotist. He tried to speak and choked and couldn't speak, yet the intensity of his thought in the darkness was as penetrating as words. The hypnotist answered: 'You are already condemned. The doom has been spoken.'

'I heard nothing.'

'You can now hear nothing but my voice.'

'Why didn't I hear my own condemnation?'

'It was spoken by yourself.'

'When?'

'When you would have condemned the souls of all men to homelessness.'

'Was that my sin?'

'Your greatest sin.'

'Why didn't I hear again the strong musical voice of the thirteenth man?'

'Neither to see nor to hear. Utter deprivation. Be content with my voice.'

'It's a soothing voice.'

'It is.'

'It's a false voice.'

'Then my powers have failed to persuade you completely. Clasp your hands again tightly together. Think you are relaxed and falling down, down, down, falling down, down.'

The boy fell whirling towards the wooden sleepers and the iron tracks. The abandoned lover wept and stumbled for ever down the spiral staircase.

'Why can't I see you?'

'Do you wish to see me?'

'Not particularly.'

'I'm very beautiful. Didn't you once look into the pupil of my right eye?'

'I saw nothing there.'

'You are now falling asleep.'

'So I'm in hell.'

'Sweetly asleep, sleepy sleep, sleep, sleep.'

'I know two poems about hell. One is a poem about a linnet lost in hell and perched singing on a blackened bough.'

'Sleep, sleepy sleep.'

'The other answers the question: what is hell? I suppose I'll know soon enough.'

'Sleepy sleep, sleep.'

'The answer is that hell is oneself, the other damned people merely projections. There is nothing, said the poet, to escape from and nothing to escape to, and one is always alone. It sounds dull. The old ideas were better. Flame and sulphur and brimstone and red demons. Livelier.'

'Sleep, sleep.'

'I suppose mass-observation man would find relief rather than torment in coloured demons prodding with tridents. Every age dreams its own hell. Dullness is the worst thing we can think of. We see too much of it. Even our wars, except for the brief and exceptional moments, are more ennui than adventure. Ask any infantryman. In dry, hot deserts prophets threatened evil-doers with eternal flames.'

'Sleep, sleepy sleep.'

'I do wish you'd stop the lullaby. If you are Satan, then you should try to sound less like my old nurse.'

'Sleep, sleep, sleep.'

'You may be using the best methods. But I can't see you, not even the pupil of your right eye. I'm more awake and less hypnotized than I was in the beginning.'

A silence for a moment perhaps, or perhaps for a million years. Then in the darkness the gambler felt the other mind beating like a pulse: 'You're a difficult subject.'

'I'm condemned. Let me know my sentence. I'm a doctor. I was a doctor. So tell me the worst and no beating about the bush.'

'Your time on earth was exceptional. You had privileges.'

'Please don't remind me of them. They turned out a sad disappointment.'

'Having those privileges meant that to a certain extent you sacrificed your will. You couldn't lose at cards. Under certain conditions a patient couldn't die under your treatment.'

'In a castle in Spain I used my will. Or did I?'

'Where you are now you'll never hear such questions answered.'

'Tell me my sentence.'

'Sacrificing some of your will in life means that your will is stronger than the wills of those who normally come under my care. It has more stored-up energy. I cannot control you completely and, being where you are, the loss is yours. You can still look back and desire the past. Being where you are, that power will intensify your pain.'

'I don't follow.'

'You will.'

'I can't see. There's no light.'

'Your memories will bring their own light with them.'

'Tell me my sentence.'

'To remember and desire and have no further power. To be a homeless soul.'

'I can't see your face.'

'That isn't necessary.'

'I want light. I want light.'

Not standing or sitting or running, walking or lying down, but simply being in pungent darkness, he desired light, cried loudly for light. The darkness vibrated with jeering laughter. The more he called the more the darkness increased, until it threatened to suffocate him. Then, despairing of light, of the vision of the bright day, hoping no longer even to see the dark horse galloping in the shadows he remembered and remembered, green light from grass, blue light from sky and sea, light stained by the colours of tiny flowers, the sound of light from a small chattering stream.

Ready, steady.

The tips of the toes of their left feet were poised on the short, dry grass, their right knees an inch from the ground; their bodies leaning forward eagerly were supported by the tips of their fingers. Ready, steady. By the green light, the blue light, and the light from the small flowers, he could see them distinctly. The boy wore corduroys and a woollen gansy, the girl a white dress; and although he could see and hear them, although unseen he stood beside them, hidden in darkness, he could not, desire as he would, feel as they felt; ready for the race, the leap, the splash, the subsequent laughter. Ready, steady, go, and they ran, and only the boy leaped, landed safely, turned, waved his arm, called laughingly, challengingly to the white, laughing girl. He could remember but not feel the boy's pride in that leap, the sweetness of the rushing air, the water sparkling, green ground rising up again to catch him, his first consciousness of manhood, the knowledge that only a narrow stream separated him from something warmly desirable. She walked back lightly, crouched again, ran again, and this time leaped. Invisible in the darkness he waited for the splash, for pleasant laughter and the wringing of silver water from soft, drenched cloth, for the half-understood, momentary glimpse of white skin. His spirit in the darkness tried to move, struggling towards the waiting boy to be again one with him, to wait and feel and laugh and touch soft, wet cloth, to breathe not pungent darkness but the lively air, to shelter his homeless soul. Then her white fluttering leap, the splash, but no following laughter.

Instead, a hideous racked scream. The boy was laughing, but his face was contorted with a demoniacal joy. The girl, screaming, was sinking into stagnant, rust-coloured water, one with all the world's drowned children destroyed by the sea, tumbling into dead canals or head-first into narrow, cold, cylindrical wells or from rocking, rickety boats into bottomless lakes.

To the darkness he shouted, not hearing his own voice, hearing only the fiendish laughter of the boy, the last scream of the girl before the stinking water closed over her head. 'That didn't happen. I was never that boy.'

'Was that laughter not hidden somewhere in your heart?'

'No. No. No.'

'Think now. Be honest with yourself.'

'Who are you to talk of honesty?'

Without moving, he fled from that memory, the green light, the blue light quenched. In that laughing boy there was no home for his spirit.

The darkness divided into shapes: a road by a grey sea, gaunt trees strained by a furious tempest, a high wall, a gateway, high pillars, two dogs — one perched on either pillar — talking to each other. This, he thought, is the gate of hell. Or were they dark dogs talking, or bats or monkeys, or just black shapes crouching; or damned lovers separated from each other for ever by the width of a scorching gateway?

'Within these walls,' said the shape on the left-hand pillar, 'there's a dark, weed-choked lake smelling always of dead, decaying fish.'

'Who are you?' asked the shape on the right-hand pillar.

Somewhere, some time the gambler had heard that voice, and he was ready to answer when the shape on the left-hand pillar said: 'You know who I am. I control everything that goes on inside here. You've spoken to me before now.'

'I can't remember.'

They didn't see him. Their chat from pillar to pillar was not meant to include him. Cold with hopelessness, he remembered where he had heard that voice before — once in a darkened room when his own deep voice had been played back to him off a wire recording machine.

'Above the lake,' said the shape on the left-hand pillar, 'there's a steep slippery bank of hot blue clay. To step on that bank is to slip down into the dead water, and to touch that water is to startle blue, stinking flames, and to hear voices singing unlovely songs.'

'These are pathetically medieval horrors.'

'Step in through the gate and see for yourself.' With a straining effort the gambler ceased to see them or to hear them: his own voice and the voice of the unnamed dark shape who knew and had power over the horrors of hell. He accepted the darkness unbroken by any light of memory. It was so much easier to be hopeless, to leave in abeyance the gritty remnants of his own will, to cease to desire a home, a rounded container, for his dark, condemned soul. But, even as he had known when alive, once the thrill is over, damnation is tedious; and at intervals in the darkness, not measurable by days or months or years or centuries, the will to remember became too powerful to be controlled by that other gritty fragment: the will to forget. Then light would come breaking through, coloured by air, earth and water, and green things that grow, and the warm flesh of men and women all beautiful because they were alive in brightness. He was with them and alive. He was also apart from them and from his living shadow, hidden and damned in darkness, not knowing whether what he saw and wanted to feel or what he felt was reality. He was shut out and prevented from speaking to himself, from breaking like a burglar back into his own life.

Seven men played cards in a club-house. He could hear the sweet whisper as the rectangles of pasteboard kissed the green baize. He could hear the breathing of the men. But all his efforts of fragmentary will to make them turn and look at him only managed to hide them from him in a cloud of cards coloured white and black and red, flickering like leaves falling in autumn woods, blinding his eyes again into descending darkness.

Two wise children made fairyland homes on the concrete floor of a suburban garage; and the fairyland homes closed around them like prisons shutting them into the horror of life. He was powerless to warn or to help.

A plump, pretty mother smiled down at her new-born child and never for a moment suspected that a demon stood at her bedside. When he tried to speak to her, through the man bending down to touch perfunctorily with his dry lips her warm, moist lips, the darkness closed around him like a suffocating smoke.

A dark, strong woman cooked breakfast for a man who was proud and mystified because he had thought intensely of God and Death and his luck had turned at gambling. He wanted to inhabit that man, to speak to the woman and warn her, to say: keep away from me, I am more than man now and dangerous to walk with. But, losing sight of her, he saw only dark clay dug from a pit under a boor-tree bush to make room for the body of a dead dog, or a poor room in a dark slum, and a sick child and a spitting old man. Outside in the sour lane rain fell steadily, and the blinking street lamps were drowned one by one, and he was alone, so unhappily alone in the darkness.

Perched yet on the pillars to right and left of the open gate, the two shapes chatted — dogs or crouching apes or stunted, twisted men. The shape that spoke with the gambler's voice said: 'Suppose one passed the lake safely and didn't slip on the hot blue clay. What then?'

'No one has ever passed the lake safely. No one has ever failed to slip on the blue clay.'

'In the waters of the lake, what happens?'

'The waters of the lake are blue fire.'

'What happens, then, in the blue fire?'

'The blue fire is a funnel pointing downwards.' The gambler wanted to shout at them, tried to shout until the effort of his will brightened the place around the pillars, showed him dirty stone crisscrossed with the burning track of slimy things, and beyond the gateway a rutted, muddy track of steaming clay. On the tops of the pillars the black shapes swayed backwards and forwards, shaking bundles caught as in a high wind in the force of his will. Then the effort became too much for him, and he dropped as quickly back into night as if a cold, unseen giant hand had pushed him from the edge of a precipice.

Although he had fallen interminably down and down for millions of homeless years, he found himself, when the darkness again dissolved, high in the air above a road, a broad river, over green morning fields. He wanted to speak to the man in the green motor-car, to take his place at the wheel; to speak to the dark-headed woman; to warn them of red danger approaching down a steep side-road. He could see it all so clearly. So clearly, indeed, that he even realized that the man at the wheel knew in some secret part of his mind of the approaching danger and went deliberately to meet it, because on the previous night joy had stepped out on a high windy peak high above the incoherence and disjointedness of the world. Every turn of the wheels of the green car was a descent from that peak. Anything was preferable — to be smothered and crushed under an avalanche, to pitch shrieking off the edge of a cliff — than to find oneself again netted alive in the valley by the necessity of speaking words, thinking, working out problems.

'I wasn't that man. I didn't want her to die.' He was in darkness again. His protest went unanswered. He was the shape on the right-hand pillar trying to see across the steaming width of the gateway the outline of the shape on the left-hand pillar. He was tugged this way and that way by the force of some opposing will, yet he kept his place on the slimy stone. Then a friendly, familiar voice said: 'Don't try any more to go through the gates. You're bad news here. You wouldn't be a peaceable subject of his majesty the dark horse.'

Brown steam fountained upwards from the base of the pillar and the darkness thickened. Try as he would, he couldn't see the top of the other pillar, but he saw once, when the wind slackened, a dark room opening off a cobbled laneway, a port-holed cabin of a room, a stout, short man with red face, yellow waistcoat, bright tweeds, pudgy beringed fingers. He could never forget that voice. He said: 'What are you doing here?'

'I was your friend before the fall. I couldn't desert you after the fall. Even though twice you tried to play shabby tricks on me.'

'Were they such shabby tricks? You had your desire.'

'The desire of a fallen poet.'

'Your desire too. Don't deny it.'

'No, not mine. For I knew beforehand what would happen to the red-headed Spanish woman when she gave herself into the poet's arms.'

'What was that?'

'In all the times that I ever spoke to you, did I ever touch you?'

'No. Not that I remember.'

'Except when you dropped down a stairway into darkness.'

'What do you mean?'

'It's not my fault, you know. It's my nature. But when I touch a person they're never the same again.' The brown steam was more dense. The shrieking wind of that other hostile will grew louder and more shrill in its effort to whirl him away from the unwelcoming gates. He cried: 'What do you mean? Tell me exactly what you mean.'

'I left that Spanish house so hurriedly to warn you and to save the poor poet's body from further mutilation.'

'What do you mean?'

'Her husband was angry when he found her dead in another man's bed.' The wind stilled for a moment, then attacked again with such intensity that he went sideways from the slimy pillar to the muddy, steaming ground. 'So I saved one life in order to destroy another more valuable life, and to break my own bargain.'

'That's about it.'

'Were the answers to my requests, then, nothing more than tricks?'

'No. No. The answers were as they should be if life was a straight line. But it isn't. It circles and twists and turns corners and goes off on long curves. It boomerangs back on itself. It's a knave and a rogue. It's all the things I'm blamed for being.' The clinging mud was the deepest darkness.

On the morning of his operation they gave him a red pill and a pointy injection. He desired hell, because hell might be a home with warm flames and the shrieking company of the damned. In muddy darkness triumphant wind blew the water away from the shore, exposing hideous shining slime and colourless crawling monsters. So bravely he bounced out of bed and found, after pill and injection, that he was reeling drunk around his nursing-home room, staggering forwards to clutch at the glossy reality of the objects on his dressing-table; to clutch the cushioned back of an arm-chair, seeing himself in the wardrobe mirror with sweating brow and popping eyes and pyjamas disarranged, body ignominiously shaved. He could hear no longer the dark shape that spoke with the voice of Death, the contact man. A soft, stout nurse held his dragon-patterned dressing-gown while he slipped his arms into the silken sleeves and wobbled a bit and laughed, leaning against the nurse, and said: 'Nurse, I've drunk enough to die happily.' Out of the clinging mud came classical images of hell: wailing companionable souls calling to a ferryman by a desolate river, the iron gates of Dis, living grimacing faces of bad Christians (in pious pictures) who had for ever lost God, great Dantean rocks crashing together, great Vergilian wheels turning, iron-bellied serpents harrowing into ecstasy the bodies of the lost. On the trolley at the door of the theatre he laughed very merrily and a white-robed nun said: 'What's the joke, Doctor?' He said: 'Not a doctor, Sister, a gambler, and ready to stake my life on another man's skill.' God was the masked surgeon and God's Son the redeeming knife, and sweet ether was the soothing spirit of God, and between them they had power over life and death. Under the mask, round and enclosing as a purple sky, he laughed and the world laughed with him: nine thousand white nuns, masked doctors, and anaesthetists all laughing at his search for a home for his soul.

In narrowing, ascending circles he whirled into darkness searching for his lost soul. His soul was the common centre of those circles, a point of light in the grooved darkness. If he could touch and sink into that point of light he would find and know God and would split exactly into two pieces the process of time. Then the point of light was the penetrating point of the knife that was the Son of God touching his drugged, wounded body, and he was screaming aloud the one word telling the truth about heaven and hell and the earth and man's life on it, and about the wind defending the evil gates against the approaches of unwelcome souls, and the sea shrieking away before the wind from a slimy reptile-writhing coast.

'That,' said the shape on the left-hand pillar, 'is exactly why you wouldn't be welcome inside these gates.'

He waited for more words. Able to see nothing, he could still hear the long scream of the sea, and on the other side of the sea was the confused murmur of life. 'That shout,' the shape said. 'That's the worst of carrying with you to the gates of hell the broken fragments of a gambler's will. Within these gates the damned are happy, having no will, in damnation. Nobody can remember. Not one of them can or wants to shout. They don't know or won't realize that they're in hell. Between friends now — imagine the effect of your shout on a population like that. You'd wake them up. They'd remember. They'd get out of control. While I haven't much love for his dark majesty, you must admit that in your case he has sound reasons for keeping you out in the cold.'

'What am I to do, then? Where can I go?'

'Give me time now. I'm thinking hard. It's my job to do something for you.'

'What are your instructions?'

'Private and confidential between the boss and myself.' The darkness was only around and above the pillars like branches and foliage above the trunks of trees. He asked: 'Where is the boss?' When he looked through the gateway he saw not a steaming, muddy track, but a wide, white concrete road. 'If you listen,' said the shape hidden in the darkness above the left-hand pillar, 'you may hear him, but from this place you cannot see him.' He listened carefully and heard above the scream of the sea that strong, confused murmur. 'Amn't I lost, then, and condemned?'

'You've been so for a long time.'

'How long?'

'Long enough to teach you the darkness of a soul when it has nowhere to go.'

'Was that my purgatory?'

'Look through the gates now and see your hell.'

'See my hell. I see a clean white road.'

'Hell can be met on a clean white road as horribly as in mud or ice or darkness or in hot flames. Hell has many shapes. Your hell, I'm sure, would be shaped like a respectable suburb. But the torment is always the same.'

'Am I not condemned, then, to my hell — whatever its shape may be?'

'Apparently not. Nobody wants you in hell.'

'For what reasons am I not condemned?'

'That I can't tell you. You'll find out in due time.'

'Condemned without trial.'

'You mean pardoned without trial. Final condemnation is within these gates.'

'What is within these gates?'

'For you I don't know. Except that you tell me that now, with the darkness clearing, you see a clean white road. You shape some part of your own hell.'

So he sat in grey light and waited for more words, and waited for the voice of adventurous Death, the contact man, to tell him what to do and where to go. Hell within these gates would probably be for me a most respectable neighbourhood; no slums, no working-class houses, three golf clubs, a yacht club, a fair scattering of wealthy, ignorant, pious people. They'd have no vices. They'd be careful about the sort of books they read. They'd know from whispered gossip that certain nasty things went on in eternity, but they'd have no wish to discuss such things aloud or to read about them except in the evening newspapers. They'd all hate each other. They'd read only stories of murder in which life, God's image, the murmur from the far shore of the sea, would be destroyed, and in which law would punish without mercy. A story of love in which life, God's image, was created or preserved would be suspect unless told in general terms and spancelled by regulations as cutting and unyielding as thongs. But over a killing these nice people would in secret lick their lips, lovingly syllabling the names of the poisons, the nature of the knife, the details of the punishment of the scapegoat killer.

They'd never know, or never acknowledge, the truth that they were drowned in hell.

In that respected neighbourhood those irreproachable people would live in faultless houses and sit in circles congratulating one another. If once in a while a solid business man or a virtuous matron, knocking an elbow against a wall, drew foul fumes from the plaster, nobody would pretend to see. Still less would they ever admit that all their French windows were blind with dull, faulty glass and unopenable because the locks were broken, and that by pressing the eyes closely to the glass one could see, not green lawns or flower-beds or even kitchen gardens, but darkness bloodshot with flame; or that at the corner of every road was a broken-down bus, and that as you walked past you could feel the malevolent glance of the driver following you from the dark, cramped cab in which he was locked for all eternity; or that the shores were always stopped and stinking and the traffic lights always red; or the trees always leafless.

Would I meet there all the people I had ever known and find them — like myself — demon or part-demon: wife and children and fellow-gamblers, patients I cured and patients I couldn't cure, a boy from a château near Pau, a Jesuit from Lyons, a beloved dark woman, a boy who carried an umbrella and listened to my advice in a green place by the sea, a young girl with a tendency to pimples, a soldier with a gashed face and the soldier who did the gashing, a brown girl I followed like a satyr, a Spanish woman whose husband I healed to give him the pleasure of finding her dead in the wrong bed, a contact man in a Dublin pub, a poet in a duffle coat, a Frenchman with one arm and two profiles — a handsome cleric on a windy mountain, in a salty baptistry, in a lounge bar, at a circular table in an expensive restaurant, in a garden where children played and old men dreamed in the evening? He told me his name, but how do I know that he told the truth or that I have yet seen his face?

If I should shout and waken them, would the devil whom I have met, talked to, played cards with but never seen, lead me back again to this grey gate, and where would I go then? He might say: All the people in these sedate houses are stirring and, because of the cry of your intruding, unnecessary will, realizing where and what they are; once they know they're in hell I'll have the devil's own job controlling them. It hurts me more to lose you than it hurts you to go, but for all our sakes . . . well, here's the gate and take your cards, and farewell.

Farewell is all very well, but where am I to fare to? Back in the muddled world I was always foolish enough to think that, on this side of man's drop into darkness, matters were better arranged, more — in fact — like a well-run office.

From the shadow over the left-hand pillar the friendly voice advised: 'Go north.'

'Which is the north?'

'Between the sea and the walls of hell.'

'And what then?'

'Find out as you go.'

No longer in darkness but in grey light, he possessed a body he could not see. On one side grey water screamed; on the other the wall of hell stood up like a cliff. Sleeping and waking, moving and resting, he passed from grey light to green light, away from the sea and the tortured trees and the towering wall.

Seventh Interlude

The gambler took with him to hell his pack of cards. Himself and the devils were gambling until he didn't leave a square inch of hell in their possession. Then they banded together against him and banished him and his pack of cards.

The gambler went off until he came to the gates of heaven. But the gates were closed against him and he wouldn't be allowed to enter.

EIGHT

I

At the closed gates of the airport the two uniformed guards said: 'You can't come in here.' Their uniforms were made of a dark, shining blue metal. One had a black face and one had a white face, but their profiles, features, peaked caps, wrinkles, and birth-marks were identical. It was a place of strange green light; but he had seen the airport buildings before, white as bleached linen, and the shapes of the flower-beds were familiar, although the colours of the blossoms were different. In the bed to the right of the main drive the blossoms were a burning gold, in the bed to the left they were coloured a regal purple. He supposed it was a different season of the year.

No brown-uniformed figures darted in and out of swinging doors or went hard-heeled along concrete paths. The paths looked more like solidified snow than like concrete. The doors weren't swinging and they looked less like glass than like rough, glittering quartz. No planes ascended or descended. No motor-cars, buses, or station-wagons came and went. No engines reverberated from the whale-bellies of hangars. There was no flag on the slim, white flagstaff. The whole place was without noise and without movement; nobody to be seen except the two guards. No matter how hard he tried, the gambler couldn't see himself.

'Who sent you?' asked the guard with the black face.

'A friendly voice from a cloud on the top of a pillar.'

'That fellow again,' said the guard with the white face.

'Your credentials,' said the guard with the black face. Carefully from his pocket the gambler took the carved case of thin ivory in which he carried his cards. Reaching them towards the guard with the white face, he could see the case clearly, but he couldn't see a sign of his own right hand. The white-faced guard opened the case, took out the cards, looked at them earnestly, asked: 'What are these?'

'The fragments of my will. What else?'

'What do you aim to do with them on this side of the gate?'

'Join them together in unity and join the unity to the will of the man who made me a gambler.'

They tightened their lips and screwed up their eyes, except for the colour, identical lips and identical eyes, meditating on the merit of his answer, and, after meditation, seeming satisfied. The white-faced guard, retaining the ivory case, handed the cards to the black-faced guard, who cut them, thumbed them, shuffled them as if he was about to deal. Ignoring the gambler, he said: 'There's a lot against him here.'

'There's a lot in his favour, too.'

'We'll toss for it,' said the black-faced guard, and suddenly his right arm swung upwards straight from the shoulder, the arm of an automaton, and the cards went soaring into the air like birds and fluttering like ample-winged Asiatic butterflies, up and up until there wasn't a card to be seen. The two guards stood at attention, hands extended before them, palms up as if they waited to catch manna white and fresh from illimitable blue countries. The gambler looked uneasily at the silent buildings. His greatest sin had commenced in such a place.

One by one the birds dropped down again to roost and the bright butterflies fluttered to rest as if the extended hands were willing desirous flowers. The guards didn't speak or the gambler didn't speak until the fifty-third card, the pointy-chinned joker, had settled grinning on the left hand of the man with the white face. 'Now we'll count them,' said the guard with the black face, and each counted slowly his share of the cards, blowing at the edges to make sure no two cards were stuck together.

'Twenty-six,' said the guard with the black face, and the guard with the white face said: 'Twenty-seven.'

'A close thing,' the gambler said. He was now interested in the game. 'Which way does it go?' They said with one voice: 'In your favour,' and the black-faced man gave his twenty-six cards to the white-faced man, who added them to his twenty-seven, restored the fifty-three to the protecting case, and restored the case to the gambler, and said: 'You can step inside.'

'Thanks a lot.' He moved towards the shining buildings.

The white driveway crackled pleasantly under his feet. 'No details, I suppose,' he said. 'Which was the odd card?'

The guard with the black face said: 'To find that out we'd have to count all over again.' The other guard said: 'You're home safe. Why worry about details?'

'I suppose that's wisdom.' He was moving rapidly away from them, but he could still see them clearly, stiff and straight and shining, two pillars of blue metal. He called: 'We haven't been introduced,' and listened to them intoning together, voices of monks chanting under the cold, cloud-high arches of an abbey: 'In the dullest man there are at least two souls. We've known each other all our life.' He wanted indignantly to tell them he had never been the dullest man: but then he thought: What am I? What was I? A gambler. A doctor. An unfaithful husband. A morose and unkindly father. A limited suburban man. An emperor or a great poet or a murderer or a witch of a courtesan might have been confronted at the gate by regiments of guards with faces all the colours of the spectrum. So, accepting dullness on earth as the humiliating payment for happiness in heaven, he shouted: 'What names shall I remember you by?'

'If you must have names you can call me Dismas,' said the guard with the white face. 'And my friend may be called Gesmas. Names don't matter. You'll never see us again as you see us now.' Then he could no longer see them. Nor could he without halting and wheeling round, his back to the buildings, see the gate they guarded. But as clearly as he had ever seen it during life, he saw his own right hand clutching the white case of cards and he saw his own feet, naked and unshod, on the drive leading from the gate to the airport buildings. 'This,' he thought, 'is fun, and no mistake,' and he walked on, afraid to look at anything except the ten toes of his striding feet.

Naked as a root dug up, peeled by sharp spades, from protecting earth, he stood on the floor of the great central hall of the building. To his relief, his mind remembering Adam's shame, no high-heeled, handsome girls went flashing nylon calves from swinging door to swinging door. The hall, a place of brown and cream colours, was more quiet, more empty of life than the green place by the guarded gates. But, remembering also the make of the airport where he had commenced his greatest sin, he walked directly towards the glass box that should hold the chief booking-clerk; and, peering through the glass, he saw a wise, old, bearded, Eastern face, a scrawny neck, shoulders and arms covered in coarse, grey cloth, a twisted hand playing with a huge key. He had expected to see a brisk, clean-shaven man in neat uniform. The old, wise eyes looked at him steadily. He said: 'Well, here I am.'

'We were expecting you.'

'Since when?'

'Since the twelve men danced to celebrate a death.'

'Since the day of my damnation.'

'Salvation.'

'Nobody ever told me who was dead.'

'You were told many times. But you weren't paying heed.' The key was rattled down on the wooden ledge. 'Your credentials.' The gambler slipped the cards from the white ivory case and passed them through the slot in the glass. One by one the ancient clerk picked up the cards, gravely inspected them, holding them close to his eyes — a monk of a savant reading some minute inscription brought to daylight after thousands of years in the darkness of a pyramidal Egyptian tomb. Then one by one he tossed the cards out to the floor at the gambler's feet, where they formed a tricoloured pattern, pictures of places and people who for all eternity were portion of the gambler. Voices, some accusing, some defending, rose like vapours from the coloured pattern.

— He was my sworn husband and should have kept his heart and his body only for me. But he was an odd man, and perhaps it was too much to expect him to be ordinary; and in his own way he was kind.

— He was a foreign man who followed me through the streets of a Spanish town, but I was a young girl and being followed gave me more pleasure than panic.

— He was my lover and I loved him always, and I died because he wanted me to die, on a sunny morning when our love was perfect.

— He played cards with the six of us and risked everything on the flip of a chance. Some of us liked him. Some of us didn't. But, taken all in all, he was a good companion.

— He taught me prayers and was kind to me.

— He sewed up my face when it was gashed open.

— He came to a slum on a wet night and healed my child.

— He healed my husband and sent me to lie with Death.

— He walked with me when I was a boy and talked consolingly to me about the foolish ways of young girls.

— He did great work for the poor, for his own peculiar motives.

— He was our earthly father and we never understood him, nor did he bother to understand us.

Voice pursued voice, swiftly and more swiftly, until all the voices were one sound — a rush of wind, a rising fountain, a sound growing in volume as it went towards the high roof. In the glass box the old man, beating time soundlessly with the huge key, chanted: 'A mixed and patchy story. Did they gain or did they lose by meeting you? That's the only test.'

'Who am I to judge?'

'True enough. But you're here now, anyway, and you want to fly.'

His will was abandoned for ever on the floor at his feet. He asked: 'Is that what I'm supposed to do?'

'There's no other way of getting from here to where you're going.'

'Where am I going?'

'Ah, curiosity. Curiosity and impulse. I suffered from them also — once. You'll know in good time. You're flying, so you're going up. Isn't that enough to know?' The tri-coloured pattern on the floor shifted and varied as if a wind with delicate, thin, accurate fingers was moving the cards from place to place. Once he thought he heard the sound of the wind. Then it was the sound of a deep reverberating engine. 'Look yonder,' said the ancient clerk.

Sitting, half-sleeping, in a great red arm-chair in a far-away corner of the hall, and dressed like the pilot of a plane, was the biggest man the gambler had ever seen; bigger by far than the blue-eyed, baby-faced, devil-possessed man who had played patience in the smoke of a fish and chip saloon. He hadn't been there when the gambler entered, nor had the red chair, for it was hard to understand how eyes could miss seeing a man so large or a chair so red. 'That's your pilot,' said the clerk. The giant raised his head, shook sleep away from him with a movement of his shoulder, stood up then, and walked towards the gambler. Stepping carefully around the cards, the wind still playing games with the pattern, or was it the thirteenth man playing patience? — the gambler went to meet the pilot.

'I have never seen a man so big,' he said up to the long bearded face. 'Yet your features are familiar.'

'They should be. My photo is all over the place.'

'But I can't remember where —'

'Perhaps in Munich, in the Alte Pinakothek, in the left-hand panel of the triptych known as the Pearl of Brabant. The artist was Bouts the younger.'

'No. It wasn't there.'

'The clothes are different, of course. Bouts showed me with robes tucked up and my bare legs in a river in a gorge. A staff in my right hand. A mysterious land in the background. The tail of my cloak trails in the water and the child sits safe on my shoulders.'

'I've never been in Munich.'

'Perhaps you've read about me and seen my picture in the book. My story is interesting.' He had an accent that reminded the gambler of New Zealanders, heroes in Africa and Crete, tall, brisk, clean men from a new well-fed country.

In the glass box the ancient clerk chuckled: 'He's a great man for autobiography. The number of times I've heard that story. Born in Syria, martyred under the Emperor Decius a century or two after my own time, the son of a heathen king in Canaan —'

'Arabia,' said the pilot.

'It's a debatable point.'

'Who should know better than myself?'

'Very well — Arabia. Known first as Offerus, Offro, Adokinus, or Reprebus, and dedicated to the gods Machmet and Apollo. Said to have been twelve feet in height —'

'Twelve feet one and a half in stocking soles,' said the pilot.

'It's a lot of growing for one man,' said the gambler. 'I wonder was it glands,' thought the doctor.

'So proud of his strength,' said the clerk, an edge of good-humoured gibery on his tongue, 'that he vowed to serve only the mightiest on the earth.'

'We all have our idiosyncrasies,' said the pilot. 'There was a man once who swore too violently that he would never betray his master.'

'So he served a king,' said the clerk, speaking more slowly, the edge of gibery replaced by a note of melancholy. 'Then, because the king was afraid of the devil, he turned his coat and served the devil until he discovered that the devil was afraid of a better man, whom we all know and serve, so one more turn and there he is — a proficient pilot.'

'You like strong masters — dictators,' said the gambler to the pilot.

'A taste I advise you to cultivate,' said the clerk to the gambler. 'Especially since you've laid your cards on the floor.' The wind still worked with the coloured pattern of the forsaken cards.

'This is our way,' said the pilot, and he gripped the gambler by the arm and pointed to the door leading directly from the great hall to the wide airfield. 'You made a mess of my story.'

'I know. I know,' said the clerk. 'But I can't bore every passenger with the full details.'

'It's an interesting story.'

'It is indeed,' said the gambler.

'Very well, then, very well.' The clerk's words chased each other, trod on each other's heels. 'He was converted by a hermit, refused to do any fasting or praying —'

'I wouldn't blame him,' said the doctor. 'It takes a lot of food to keep such a man alive.'

'— but instead he offered to carry pilgrims across a broad, unbridged river —'

'And one grey day,' the pilot said gently, 'when I had realized how hard and cold was the penance I had chosen, the child came. Every step I took across the river the child on my shoulders became more and more heavy. When I fell in a heap on the far bank, he said to me that, with him, I had carried all the sins of the world.'

'On your way now,' the clerk said, 'unless you wish to

tell us how you planted your staff in the ground and found it next morning a fruit-bearing palm-tree.'

'That was different. That was completely different.'

'Or how one can read all about you in the *Legenda Aurea* of Jacobus de Voragine, first published at Nurnberg in 1478.'

'You're a cynical old man,' said the gambler.

'My job makes me that way. I open the gates for the strangest people.' He rested his bearded chin on his hands and watched the cards constantly changing pattern, dancers in dresses coloured white and black and red. 'I know you now,' the gambler said to the pilot. 'In my green car, and then in my black car, my wife, wherever she is, had fixed silver plaques showing you with the child on your back.' Beyond the open door was the vast green-and-white extent of the airfield. The clerk called: 'Happy landing,' and: 'Don't be offended at an old man's fun.' The pilot said dismally: 'Fan photographs, those silver plaques. You should have gone to Munich when you had the chance.'

The clerk watched them until they vanished into green light. Then he listened for the reverberation of engines like the high sound of a thousand organs or the beat of the wings of angels or the welcoming hymns of happy souls.

On the floor the cards were quiet. The pattern was fixed for ever. The wind at last had shaped it to its own will.

EPILOGUE

I

The gambler went off until he came to the gates of heaven. But the gates were closed against him and he wouldn't be allowed to enter. He sat outside on a rock and began to play patience. Peter of the Keys took pity on him.

In the end Peter opened the gate and asked him in because of the pity he had shown to the orphan when he thought he didn't know his prayers. The gambler with a glad heart threw his cards from him and he walked in at the gates of heaven.

The cards of the gambler are spread on a rock at the gates of heaven from that day to this, and they may be seen by any person who goes that road.

II

Where the gambler and the pilot went we cannot follow. For a mortal storyteller can with a glib conscience tell lies about hell, an everlasting lie, but not about heaven, an immortal truth.

But on the way across the wide airfield to the waiting sound of organs, angels' wings, and happily singing souls, the pilot may have hinted that in the place to which they were going the gambler might find and understand, probably for the first time, the people who had moved through the dream of his life. 'You'll understand why men dance at death, and the symbolism of twelve men and their master. For in heaven one learns a lot. The hell of hell is that the soul endures so much and finds out nothing.'

After the happy landing, assured by the parting wish of the clerk, the pilot, having his work to do, would leave the gambler to go on alone; to stab into the centre of the white light; to find out the exact differences between ending and beginning, sin and sacrifice, darkness and light, and why every man must at least once in his life say 'God' and then look around for angels, and must once say 'Death' and walk on, fearfully willing to look back, afraid to look back.

No storyteller with corruption in his tongue could follow the gambler into the place of wise white light. Arriving there, like the stab of a knife, he would, obviously, know so much more about his own gambling story than an old spitting man in the corner by the hearth could ever know or tell to the half-circle of listening people, their faces self-satisfied from the friendly heat, their hearts always uneasily conscious of the wind outside, and the sea, the rocks, the cold lakes, the mountains barren and dangerous with white shale.